Scoundrel IN Disguise

JOURNEYS OF THE HEART BOOK 2

Scoundrel
IN
Disguise

a historical romance by
SHAELA KAY

Other books in this series

The Sailor's Kiss
A Heart Made of Indigo
The Rodenburg Girl

Published by Blue Water Books
Richland, WA

Cover photo © Alexey Ivanov / iStock
Cover design © Blue Water Books

© 2016 Shaela Kay Odd
Visit the author at www.shaelakay.com

This book is a work of fiction. While great care has been taken to ensure historical accuracy of dates and locations, characters and events in this book are products of the author's imagination and are represented fictitiously. Any likeness to any person, living or dead, is purely coincidental.

For John,
who is the love of my life.

Thank you for giving me wings.

$\mathscr{P}$*rologue*

5 years earlier
Surrey, England

The horse's hooves beat a thundering cadence, spewing rocks and dirt behind him as his rider drove him ever faster. The pounding of the horse's gallop was nearly as loud in Rex's ears as the beating of his heart, and even though each hoofbeat brought him closer to his destination, every second seemed like an eternity. In another half mile he would turn down the drive, and the lights of the house would guide his way instead of the nearly full moon that had been his companion since London. He whipped his horse ever onward, determined to bridge the distance between him and his beloved Mary in as little time as possible.

He yanked on the reins, and the horse stumbled as he turned off the road and down the drive. As soon as they were clear of the large oak tree that marked the entrance to the estate, Rex spurred his horse faster, confused that he could not see the lights of the house shining through the trees. Surely the entire house would be ablaze, anticipating his arrival.

But no. As he crested a small hill and came clear of the copse, his heart sank. Only a solitary window glowed in the corner of the massive building, and Rex knew that could only mean one thing.

He was too late.

Nearing the house, he pulled up on the horse's reins, forcing the beast to skid to a stop. Rex swung his leg over the side and was running to the door before his mount even had a chance to get his footing. He burst into the house, turning down a corridor to the left and nearly running over the old butler in his haste. The servant's grim face said it all.

Mary.

The house was silent as the two men stared at one another. Rex's chest was heaving as he strove to catch his breath, fighting for air to ask the impossible question. Before he could form the words, the older gentleman shook his head.

"You are but two hours too late, sir. She is gone."

Rex heard the words as if from the end of a long tunnel. He knew what they meant, but his heart shied away from the pain in their meaning, refusing to accept what his mind understood. Mary was gone. She was dead. He would not see her smile, nor hear her laugh ever again in this life. He shook his head slowly, trying to stop himself from crashing into the wall of pain he felt himself spiraling towards.

"Dr. Jones has gone, but he said he will return tomorrow," his butler offered. Rex remained silent. "Come," the older man said gently, taking a step towards the stairs. "She has left you something."

Rex watched his old servant slowly climb the massive, curving staircase. The butler paused and looked back, until Rex mechanically put one foot in front of the other, following him to the second floor. They turned down a corridor and stopped at the very end, where the faint glow of candlelight could be seen issuing from underneath a heavily carved door. The butler opened it, standing to the side to let his master enter first.

Rex stepped inside, and the woman standing by the far window turned. Slowly she approached, holding out the small bundle in her arms as she reached his side. Rex held his arms out automatically, taking what she offered. A whisper of a cry sounded from the tangled blankets, and he looked down into the tiny face of a newborn child.

The minuscule human stretched its weak arms out, its tiny face twisted in soundless displeasure. Rex stared at the child, reeling at the weight he suddenly felt upon his shoulders. He looked up at the woman standing beside him.

"She left the child... for me?" he asked, his voice as unsteady as he felt.

The woman nodded. "Mary gave the babe a name before she died."

"And it is?"

"Her name is Caroline."

3

Chapter 1

August 1833
Leicestershire, England

It was a lovely wedding. Katherine wore a beautiful gown of ivory lace, with rosebuds woven in her hair and a train nearly five yards long. She and Charles were married in May, and Sarah smiled to herself as she remembered how happy she had been that day, seeing her only brother marry her dearest friend. The happy couple chose to spend their honeymoon at the estate in Leicestershire where Katherine had been raised—a decision which pleased not only Sarah, but the countess as well. Lady Rockwell knew that her granddaughter would be returning to India with her new husband at the end of the summer, and she was anxious to spend as much time with her as possible. Sarah, too, was glad for the three months to spend with the two people she loved most in the world before being separated from them indefinitely.

But August had come at last, and with it the ship that bore

the two young lovers away. A week had now passed since their tearful parting, and the depressed air that had lingered in the house following their departure had dissipated. Sarah's was not a melancholy disposition, and her natural cheerfulness soon lifted her spirits, as well as those of Lady Rockwell.

Sarah came down the stairs to breakfast one morning, humming to herself as she took the seat across from her hostess.

"You seem cheerful this morning," Lady Rockwell observed.

Sarah's smile faltered. "I am trying to be. I miss Katherine and Charles, but I have had *such* a headache from crying so much, that I am determined to be done with it. No amount of tears will bring them back, so what is the point in carrying on so?"

"It is natural to miss them. Your brother especially."

Sarah nodded. "And I am sure that your ladyship misses Katherine."

A lump rose in the old woman's throat, but she forced herself to smile. "Yes. *Meine Leibling.* I feel as if she only just returned with me to England. But now she is gone to India again." Her voice drifted off, her thoughts following her granddaughter on the long voyage around the tip of Africa to the hot, humid subcontinent. She shook her head, as if to dispel the melancholy that clung to her words.

"*Meine Leibling,*" Sarah repeated the unfamiliar words, and the countess smiled.

"*Sehr gut, Fräulein.* German suits your tongue quite nicely."

"Where did you grow up, Lady Rockwell? Katherine told me it was somewhere in Prussia."

"Strausberg."

"*Strausberg,*" Sarah repeated, trying to mimic the throaty

sounds. "Is your family still there? Are you never lonely?"

The countess smiled, her paper-thin skin folding into a dozen wrinkles around her mouth. "How could I be lonely when I have you for company?"

Sarah returned her smile. She had been overjoyed when Lady Rockwell extended an invitation to stay with her in England. Having spent her entire life in India, Sarah had yearned for the sights and sounds of a true English home, and had dreamed of spending a season in London ever since she was a girl. Now, at the tender age of eighteen, she was finally getting her wish. Her blue eyes sparkled with anticipation as the meal began.

A liveried footman stood behind each of their chairs, serving them from the vast array of dishes on the table. Lady Rockwell ate her food with calm elegance, and Sarah attempted to follow her example. When the servants cleared away the last of the china at the conclusion of the meal, Sarah breathed a sigh of relief.

"I am afraid I shall never grow accustomed to the formality of dining here," she said with a laugh.

Lady Rockwell raised her eyebrows as they made their way to the sitting room. "I hope you are not in earnest, Miss Mendenhall, for there are a great many more formalities with which you must accustom yourself, if you are to spend the Season in London."

"Is it really so very different from India?" Sarah asked doubtfully.

"Of course it is," Lady Rockwell replied, seating herself comfortably on the sofa. "You may have been raised in the home of an English gentleman, but you resided in a heathen nation. No matter how proper you felt your social customs were in Calcutta, I can assure you that there will be far more expected of you whilst you are here."

"Such as?"

Lady Rockwell ticked them off on her fingers. "You are never to walk out alone, except in the garden next to the house. You must always wear a hat and gloves when you go out, and carry a parasol if you are walking in the park. A lady must always have a chaperon when she is in the presence of a gentleman who is not her near kin. You are never to dance with a gentleman you do not know or to whom you have not been introduced, and never," she looked at Sarah sternly, "are you to ask someone to call you by your Christian name."

Sarah hid a smile. She had thoroughly shocked Lady Rockwell upon her arrival when she asked that her hostess call her Sarah instead of Miss Mendenhall, and the countess lost no time in lecturing Sarah on the impropriety of such a request. The older woman lifted her eyebrows, and Sarah sighed in resignation.

"Very well. I shall do my best not to embarrass you."

"*Gut.* I have high hopes for you, Miss Mendenhall. With my name and connections, there is a very good chance of your marrying well."

Sarah shifted uncomfortably in her seat. "Of course I wish to make an eligible match, Lady Rockwell. But I do not want to be married right away. After all, I am only eighteen, and this is my very first season in London! I want to thoroughly enjoy myself, without any thought of matrimony or matchmaking or eligible young men."

7

"Indeed! Though surprised to hear such a declaration, I confess that it eases my mind considerably. It will probably be to your advantage not to take thought of marriage just yet. Let London get under your skin first; you will be older and wiser next year and will have plenty of time for that sort of thing then."

Sarah nodded, but a knot was beginning to form in the pit of her stomach. Though she had accompanied Katherine and the countess to several dinner parties and private dances since her arrival, she had yet to attend a grand affair in London. She worried that when the time arrived she would not be fashionable enough, or that she would do something to embarrass herself or the countess.

Her fears were not unfounded. Sarah had been raised on a small indigo plantation outside of Calcutta, India, by her brother Charles, who was eight years her senior. They had been left alone in the world when their mother, father, and elder brother died in the cholera epidemic that swept through India in 1818. Without a mother to guide and direct her, Sarah had grown up to be sweet but rather impulsive, and she was by no stretch of the imagination an expert on the strict social customs of refined society.

Most of the well-to-do families in Calcutta sent their children to England for a formal education, but that particular privilege had not been Sarah's. Instead, she was educated at home by an elderly governess, whose own accomplishments were sadly lacking. Though Sarah had a firm grasp of grammar, arithmetic, history, geography, and other such mundane subjects as complete a well-rounded education, she had not been given any instruction in music or art, and very little in French and German. Free to pursue her own interests instead, Sarah had spent her spare time poring over the ladies magazines and newspapers that trickled in from London, hungry for the society that was hers by birth but not by means. As she matured, Sarah developed a keen eye for fashion and a natural style of elegance uniquely her own. But she knew that her début in London would not be a test of her appearance alone, but of her manners and accomplishments as well.

"Now, Miss Mendenhall," Lady Rockwell began, smoothing out the burgundy folds of her taffeta morning dress, "when I offered to let you stay with me, I knew that I was taking upon myself the responsibility of introducing you into the finest society. Your father was a gentleman, and as a gentleman's daughter, you are expected to conduct yourself with the utmost grace and decorum. Your manners are very pretty, but I find that your education has been sadly lacking. You will be expected to study and improve yourself while you are here."

"Yes, Lady Rockwell," Sarah said meekly.

Lady Rockwell laughed at her worried expression. "It will not be so hard as you think, *Fräulein*. Let us begin in the music room, and then we shall practice your French."

It was not the first time Lady Rockwell had made the effort to give Sarah music lessons. They had been attempting the pianoforte for several months, but her pupil was not making much progress, so Lady Rockwell decided to try the harp.

"Elbows up, Miss Mendenhall," she reminded, thirty minutes into their lesson.

Sarah bit back a retort. Her arms were tired and her fingers were sore, but she complied. The simple melody was indiscernible from the sheer number of incorrect strings Sarah plucked. She struggled through ten more minutes before dropping her hands to her sides.

"It is no use, Lady Rockwell—I shall never be able to play an instrument."

"Nonsense! You are doing quite well, I believe."

Sarah gently massaged her swollen fingertips, dismally staring at the music before her on the stand. The expression on the countess's face softened.

"Voudriez-vous essayer quelque chose de nouveau?" she asked.

"Oui, s'il vous plaît!" Sarah responded eagerly.

The countess laughed lightly. "Very good, my dear. Your French has improved."

Sarah flushed with pleasure, removing herself from her place at the harp. "What did you have in mind?"

"It is not something I can teach you, I am afraid," the countess replied.

Sarah's interest was piqued. What could she possibly learn that would require the skill of someone other than the countess?

Lady Rockwell ignored her curious glances, walking instead towards the doors leading to the library.

"I shall hire a tutor for you, but in the meantime, let us take some refreshment in the library. I have just received a copy of Frederic Shoberl's translation of *Notre-Dame de Paris*. Let us see what Monsieur Hugo has to say."

Chapter 2

April 1833
Surrey, England

Jameson Rex turned his horse down the long drive, passing the massive oak tree that had marked the lane for centuries. He had traveled down this road many times in his thirty years, and every time the impatience of being so near to home compelled him to hasten his pace.

Five years had now passed since that tragic night when his beloved Mary had died, and along with today's delight there was also a pang of sadness. There always was, when he came home to the last place where Mary had drawn breath. But he shook his head swiftly, determined not to let a cloud of sorrow overshadow the joyous homecoming he was sure to receive. He smiled in anticipation, urging his horse into a faster trot.

Sitting astride his steed, Rex cut a fine figure. He was roguishly handsome, with jet black hair and a long, straight nose. His mouth was a straight, uniform line, even when he smiled, and no dimples softened his angular cheeks. A strong jaw, dark brows, and neatly trimmed side whiskers gave him a somewhat stern appearance, but his blue-gray eyes danced with hidden merriment, and a hint of a smile often drew up one side of his mouth in a rakish grin. He was tall and lean, an expert horseman and a skilled hunter. The ladies were wild about him—a circumstance which he, surprisingly, did not appreciate. Unable to bear the self-serving women who threw themselves at his feet, he nearly always left London by May. This year he had chosen to spend the entire season in Bath, hoping to find the society in the resort town less tiresome. But Bath proved nearly as bad as London, and he was glad to escape for the country as soon as he could.

He drew up in front of the large stone house, memories of his childhood churning in his mind. The estate was in wonderful repair considering it had been in his family for five generations. As an only child, Rex grew up knowing that he would inherit Summerwood one day, but he had not anticipated calling it his own so soon. His mother had died in childbirth, and his father had passed away shortly after Rex returned from Oxford, which meant that his only living relative now was his Uncle Wallace, his father's brother.

No sooner had Rex dismounted than the front door burst open and a tiny personage with bouncing golden curls dashed out to meet him. He held his arms out, laughing as he embraced her.

"Papa, Papa!" her musical voice sang. She nuzzled her head to his chest, her tiny arms wrapping around his neck.

"My dear little Caroline, how I have missed you!"

"I missed you too, Papa. Did you bring me any presents?"

Rex laughed. "What do you think I have in my pocket?"

Caroline squealed, and began reaching her dainty hands into his many coat pockets. She finally unearthed a small parcel wrapped in brown paper and string.

"What is it? What is it?" she cried, her blue eyes dancing with excitement.

"Let us go inside and find out."

Caroline scampered off with her treasure, and Rex followed her into the house, waving off the servants who approached him. They made their way to the sitting room on the second floor and settled themselves comfortably on an overstuffed sofa, where Caroline made quick work of the paper and string.

"Ooh!" she said, her eyes and mouth round with delight.

Tucked inside the folds of paper was a scrap of emerald silk, and when Caroline carefully unfolded the fabric a small, gold locket fell into her hand. It sparkled and shone in the light, and Caroline picked it up reverently.

"Is it for me?"

"Of course it is," Rex chuckled. "Here, let me show you." He took the thin chain and fastened it around her neck. The golden oval rested against her chest and she held it out, examining it. Rex showed her how to open the tiny clasp, and he read aloud the inscription inside. " 'To my darling Caroline, with love from your Papa.' "

Caroline smiled and hugged him. "Thank you, Papa." He kissed her atop the head, then she wriggled out of his arms and ran off to play.

Rex watched her go with a smile, but when she was gone he sighed, making his way to a window at the far end of the room.

The last five years had been hard, and he was more concerned than ever about what to do with her. It had been too difficult to return to London the season after Mary died, so he had stayed in the country, drowning in grief. The only excursion he embarked upon was to visit his uncle in Hampshire, and that was only from a sense of duty. The next year was much the same. But he could not remain a recluse forever, and people had already begun to talk. The last thing he wanted was someone arriving uninvited in order to discover the reason for his self-imposed exile.

So the following spring he pushed aside the pain and the guilt of his past to face the task ahead: finding a wife. Caroline was being cared for by a doting nurse, but Rex knew she needed a mother. Nothing but his ardent desire to find a suitable lady would have driven him to the marriage mart the last two years, but his efforts seemed in vain. Perhaps he was too particular in his choice of lady, for although he was courted and wooed and "set up" with any number of eligible young ladies, the right combination of compassion, wealth, understanding, and beauty was proving difficult to find. His situation was complicated, and he needed a woman who was not afraid of marrying into it. *Not that she will know what she is getting into,* he thought ruefully.

Rex surveyed the view from the window, which overlooked the back of the manor. A fine English garden stood near to the house, its straight, graveled paths and symmetrical hedges skirted with multicolored flowers. Beyond the formal garden stretched the rolling lawns of the park, broken here and there by stands of tall trees. In the distance, a small rotunda sat atop a knoll overlooking a picturesque lake.

Though modest in size, the estate was very nice, with several tenant farmers who cultivated the land surrounding the park. The income they provided helped to cover the expense of maintaining the house and grounds, but not much more. When the property came into Rex's possession, heavy renovations were found to be necessary, and the expense was substantial. Thus his income, though quite large, was countered with considerable debt. Rex left nearly every meeting with his steward troubled over his financial affairs, and if it was not for the generous allowance provided by his Uncle Wallace, he would have been in dire straits indeed.

Uncle Wallace was a widower, and having no living children of his own had named his nephew his heir. He had a large estate in Hampshire, where he lived a quiet, complacent life, rarely venturing beyond the bounds of his own park. Though not an affectionate man, he had a strong sense of familial pride. Since Rex was his heir and it was important to keep up appearances, he allotted his nephew a generous sum each month in order to "live in style." Not being as frivolous as his uncle, Rex found the addition to his income sufficient for his needs, even considering his debts.

Aside from the allowance he paid to his nephew, Uncle Wallace's sense of duty did not extend past a single visit once per annum. Since his uncle did not like to leave Hampshire, and Rex did not wish for him to visit Summerwood, the two men met at Uncle Wallace's estate, much to the satisfaction of both parties. Rex usually traveled to Hampshire directly from town at the end of each spring, and spent the majority of the warmer months there. But this year he could not bear the thought of a long, tedious summer spent in his uncle's languid company. He left

Bath early, hoping to visit Summerwood and Caroline for a few glorious weeks before resigning himself to Hampshire for the remainder of the season.

Rex watched as Caroline danced around the manicured lawn and in between the hedges. He could not help but smile as his gaze rested upon her, but he knew that things could not continue in the way they had for much longer. Caroline needed a mother, and his mind needed rest from the burden he had born the last five years. Sighing, he turned away just as a knock sounded on the door.

His butler entered the room, bearing refreshments. "Welcome home, Master Rex," he said as he set the tray down.

"Hello, Bradshaw. I trust you are well?"

The old man nodded. "I am well enough, though not as young as I once was."

Rex smiled affectionately at him. "You have served our family well, old friend. I will hate to see you go."

Bradshaw straightened and looked stern. "I am not going anywhere, sir. There are still plenty of years of service left in me, I assure you."

Rex chuckled. "Of course there are. And since I have no intention of dismissing you at present, you may be certain there will be no more talk of that."

His butler smiled and poured some tea. Rex sipped it thoughtfully for a moment.

"How has Caroline been getting along? I trust she has been healthy and well?"

"Yes, sir. Mrs. Partridge takes excellent care of her, though she is quite a spirited girl."

Rex smiled. "Like her mother before her. I am sure it has not been easy, but it is a relief to know that she is under such good care in my absence. Thank you, Bradshaw."

The butler inclined his head. "Will you be needing anything else, sir?"

"No, thank you. I have business to conduct with my steward this afternoon, and shall retire to my study shortly. Please let me know when Mr. Arnold arrives."

The days blended pleasantly together, and soon a week had passed. The meeting with his steward left Rex unsettled, as usual, and one afternoon he sent Caroline out to play while he pored over the accounts in his study. Caroline skipped around the garden path, stopping now and then to examine a rose, or to follow a butterfly that fluttered in the warm spring air. The garden was small but well kept, and it was one of her favorite places to roam. A large square fountain sat in the middle of it, the pitted gray stone covered with lichens and moss. Caroline leaned over the edge of the pool, watching the colorful carp swim in the still waters. She peeked at her nursemaid, Mrs. Partridge, who was nodding off in the shade of a nearby tree, before dropping a handful of pebbles into the water. The fish bobbed and thrashed in the water below, thinking it was food that had been dropped into the pool. Caroline giggled.

She soon tired of watching the carp, however, and wandered towards the side of the great stone house. Crouching down, she followed a beetle as it marched across the grass, but the sound of a horse's hooves as they crunched on the gravel drive brought her head up. A rider was nearing the house, and she wondered who it could be. Sneaking a glance back at her dozing nursemaid, she scampered across the lawn to investigate.

The stranger was just getting off his horse when she came around the corner. He was a middle-aged gentleman with graying hair and a paunchy stomach. He looked at her with amazement as she walked up to him.

"Why, hello there, young lady. Who are you?"

"I am Caroline, sir."

"Indeed!" the stranger responded, clearly surprised.

"Are you here to see my Papa?"

The stranger shook his head. "I am not sure that I know your Papa."

"He gave this to me." She held out the locket, which was clasped around her neck. The gentleman nodded.

"You have a very nice Papa, I see."

"Yes, he is grand. I do not see him much, but he always brings me presents when he comes."

The stranger regarded her thoughtfully. She was a beautiful child, with honey-blonde hair that curled in soft little ringlets on her head. Large blue eyes looked up at him from a cherubic face, and two tiny dimples appeared in her cheeks when she smiled. She suddenly reminded him of his late wife, and the thought pained him. He turned briskly from her expectant face.

"Forgive me, young lady, but I must see to my business at present. Good day."

He tipped his hat and turned from her, striding up the steps and rapping at the door. A glance behind him revealed that

Caroline was watching him, but since the butler opened the door to admit him just then, he turned away and entered the house.

"Good day to you, sir. Can I be of assistance?" Bradshaw asked him, shutting the door behind them. His eyes were guarded and his manner cautious. Uncle Wallace looked at him incredulously.

"Assistance? Good heavens, Bradshaw! I know it has been several years since I was here last, but surely you will not stand upon ceremony with me. I wish to see my nephew," he finished gruffly.

The old butler hesitated, but since Uncle Wallace looked at him with an air of impatient annoyance, he nodded. Bradshaw led him down a corridor to the right, towards the study. He knocked at the door and opened it when bidden, announcing the arrival of Wallace Rex. Before Rex had a chance to register the news, his uncle stepped into the room.

"My dear nephew!" he cried joyously, crossing the room to embrace his host, who stood in mute astonishment behind his desk.

"Uncle Wallace?" Rex replied weakly, his face pale.

Uncle Wallace chuckled. "I know, I know—shocking, is it not? I know I am unexpected, but I heard from a colleague of mine that you left Bath earlier than expected, and since I knew you were not due to see me until June, I assumed you were coming here, and I decided to surprise you."

"Indeed," Rex murmured, still in shock.

"It has been many years since I have been to Summerwood," Uncle Wallace continued, sitting down in a chair. He looked solemnly around him. "Not since before your father died," he added. Rex stood in a daze, and did not respond. "It looks very well. You have kept it in good repair, I see. I should very much like to see over the house," he hinted.

This declaration brought Rex to his senses. "The house is very much the same as it ever was, Uncle. But let us see the grounds—they have been much improved, and I should very much like to discuss something with you," he said, making his way to the door with a forced smile on his lips. "There are plenty of horses in the stables, and we shall have no trouble finding you a fresh mount."

His uncle scoffed. "No, indeed. It was a pleasant enough ride from Hampshire, but I should think—"

The door to the study burst open and a shrieking, laughing mass of curls ran inside and buried itself in Rex's legs.

"Papa, do not let Partridge get me!"

"Come 'ere, you little terror! Master, forgive me; she slipped away an' I could not stop 'er." The red face of Mrs. Partridge appeared, reaching for Caroline.

For once, Rex did not join sides with the little girl. Instead, he reached down and gently pried her off his legs. Caroline giggled and screamed again, fighting against what she thought were her nursemaid's arms. But when she realized they were masculine hands that gripped her, she stopped writhing and looked up, surprised. Rex's face was pale and stern, and he handed Caroline gently to the nursemaid, who ushered her quickly from the room. When the door shut behind them, Rex slowly turned to face his uncle.

Uncle Wallace was on his feet. His mouth hung open and his face was pale, and Rex closed his eyes, preparing himself for what was coming.

"What... what can be the meaning of this?" Uncle Wallace asked.

Rex said nothing.

"I met the child outside. She was... charming, delightful. But I did not know... How can she... how can you..." His disbelief turned suddenly to anger. "What have you been playing at, Jameson? Tell me at once!"

Rex looked at his uncle with anguished eyes, measuring his words carefully. "Uncle, please—there is more to this than meets the eye. It is not what you think."

"Then what is it?" his uncle burst forth, taking a step towards his nephew. Rex was tall, but his uncle was considerably larger in girth, and in his anger he was quite imposing. Rex did not flinch as his uncle shouted at him again. "She called you 'Papa!' "

Pain and sorrow flashed across his face as Rex nodded. "Yes, Uncle. I am her Papa."

The horrified look his uncle gave him was a knife to his heart.

"You... you are her Papa?"

Rex nodded again, meeting his eyes. His uncle was fighting for control, trying to understand what his meaning could be.

"You have never spoken to me of her before. Surely she is not..." He paused. "Have you married a widow, then? Is this child yours through marriage?"

Rex turned, walking slowly around his uncle. He sat down behind the desk and dropped his face into his hands. After several moments of tortured silence, he lifted his head and addressed the man standing before him.

"No, Uncle. I have not married a widow. I am not married at all. I never have been."

Chapter 3

October 1833
Leicestershire, England

Sarah concentrated on the table before her, unaware that she was chewing on her bottom lip. The ivory vase held only a few pale pink blossoms, their vibrant shade faded from the unforgiving sun. It was the first week in October, but Lady Rockwell's gardener had managed to gather one last cluster of roses before the frosts claimed their lives for the year. With the winter fast approaching, Sarah knew that her botanical subjects would be scarce. She wanted this painting to be perfect—or, as perfect as a novice artist could reasonably expect.

Holding the brush loosely in her hand, she carefully dabbed the color onto the paper. A hazy resemblance to the flowers before her was slowly emerging from the page, though it lacked the precise details of a proper still life. Her brow furrowed.

"You are making progress, Miss Mendenhall."

Sarah sighed heavily, setting the brush and palette down. She glanced at Lady Rockwell before turning to stare dismally at her work once more.

"But in which direction?" she replied.

Lady Rockwell laughed quietly. "Your work shows improvement, Miss Mendenhall, not regression. You cannot expect perfection after so short a time."

"Yes, I know. But it is frustrating nonetheless."

"More frustrating than enjoyable?"

"Oh, no!" Sarah's face lit up as she looked at the countess. "I enjoy painting immensely. I am so glad you thought to hire Mr. Thornton to teach me."

Lady Rockwell smiled affectionately at her. Sarah was nearing nineteen now, and was a very pretty young lady. She had a heart-shaped face and large blue eyes rimmed in thick, dark lashes. Her pointed little nose turned up at the tip just enough to be endearing, and though Sarah had tried every method imaginable to erase the scattering of freckles across the bridge, they remained as evident as always. Her chestnut hair was piled in fashionable loops and curls atop her head, but a few careless locks had come loose from their pins, framing her face nicely. She had a fine, petite figure, though it was currently obscured by the artist's frock she wore to protect her gown. A faint smudge of gray pigment graced one cheek, and Lady Rockwell stepped forward to rub it off.

"I am glad to hear it," the countess said. "Though Mr. Thornton is an admirable teacher, you will get far better training when we go to London."

"And when is that to be?" Sarah asked, putting away her paints and brushes. The eagerness in her voice was unmistakable.

"I prefer to spend Christmas in the country, so we shall not leave until after the new year," Lady Rockwell said. "But we shall find you a tutor as soon as we arrive. Though the season will not begin in earnest until March, there will be people enough in town, and you shall not want for lack of a social life."

Nervous little flutters began in the pit of Sarah's stomach at these words, but she smiled in spite of them. "I shall be glad of the chance to gather my bearings before embarking on all that the Season has to offer."

"Quite sensible of you, my dear. Now, if you are finished in here, I believe there is a parcel waiting for you in your room."

All pretense of sensibility was swept away with those words. Squealing with delight, Sarah ran up the stairs to her room, followed more sedately by Lady Rockwell. "I do so hope it is the gowns," she fretted as her maid helped her remove the frock covering her dress. "I am positively wild to know how they have turned out!"

Lady Rockwell sat down on a chair, chuckling. "I have no doubt it is. Your gloves and hats arrived the week before Michaelmas, and Madame Julliot promised that she would have the gowns ready by now."

Sarah unwrapped the parcel and withdrew a morning dress of pale blue silk, with delicate lace at the collar and sleeves.

"Oh, how lovely!"

There were two more morning dresses, a pink afternoon dress and another of navy blue taffeta, and underneath them all were two shimmering evening gowns. Sarah withdrew one carefully.

"Oh, Lady Rockwell, is it not exquisite?" she asked

rapturously. She held the silky ivory dress up to her figure, fingering the ruffles and lace at the neckline. The bodice was pleated with delicate folds, and three tiers of ruffles hemmed the skirt. Sarah swung the dress back and forth like a bell. Carefully she set it down and reached for the other one. It did not have nearly as many gathers and frills, but the rich peacock blue gown was striking in its simplicity. Sarah's eyes were wide as she held it up.

"Ooh," she breathed, for once moved beyond words. Lady Rockwell smiled.

"I thought that shade of blue would look lovely with your coloring," she mused. Sarah turned to her with pleading eyes, and the old woman laughed. "Go on, then. Betsy, help her on with the dress."

Sarah took the gown into her dressing closet, followed by her abigail, Betsy. The satin flowed like water over Sarah's skin as Betsy slipped the dress over her head. Lacing it up the back, she helped her mistress smooth out the skirt. The flutters of excitement in Sarah's stomach grew in intensity as she looked down at herself. The gown was stunning. Sarah bounced on the balls of her feet, anxious to see how she looked in the glass.

She reentered her bedroom, looking to Lady Rockwell for approval. The older woman smiled. "My dear, you look beautiful," she said. Sarah's cheeks turned pink with pleasure and she dropped a small curtsy.

"Thank you, ma'am."

Turning, she walked to the large looking glass by the window, the fabric of her dress rustling quietly as she moved. She twisted around and looked in the mirror, delighted with her reflection. Lady Rockwell had been right. The deep blue gown set off her creamy pink skin beautifully, and it made her blue eyes sparkle like sapphires. Sarah sighed euphorically.

"Lady Rockwell, I could die tonight a happy woman," she said with contentment. The countess gasped, a look of consternation on her face.

"Do not speak so, Miss Mendenhall! Do you not know that vanity is a very great sin?" She frowned. "I think I shall send the gown back if you feel thus."

"Oh, I am not *really* vain," Sarah said matter-of-factly. "How could I be, with these abominable freckles? I know this gown would look much prettier on many other girls, but it *does* look so becoming on myself that—"

"Miss Mendenhall," Lady Rockwell said sternly, "Vanity is evidence of a weak mind and a deplorably susceptible character. I hope you will work to rid yourself of such a shortcoming."

"Yes, Lady Rockwell," Sarah murmured. She fingered the silky folds of the rich blue fabric, biting her lip.

"Come now, Miss Mendenhall, do not be cast down. I am sorry I spoke harshly." The countess sighed. "I was very fond of my fine gowns when I was your age, too. But I had to learn—as do you, *Fräulein*—that pretty manners are more important than pretty dresses. The rules of society may have changed since I was a girl, but the virtues of honesty, humility, and obedience will always be favored."

Sarah plopped down on the rug, her skirts billowing around her. "What was it like, Lady Rockwell? Growing up in Prussia?"

"It was so long ago, I can hardly remember."

"Were you happy there? When did you come to England?"

The countess shook her head dismissively. "That is a story for another day. Betsy, please help Miss Mendenhall out of her gown, and see that it is pressed."

Chapter 4

January 1834
Surrey, England

The wind howled eerily around the ancient stone building as Rex leaned against the mantle, staring into the fire. A massive gust rattled the windows and he looked up, his reverie broken. The blackness of the January night pressed in on him, and he sunk into a chair, exhausted from the weight of his burden. He had waited too long, had been too particular in his choice of lady, and now it was too late.

He was doomed. Caroline was doomed.

And he knew not what to do about it.

He stood again and paced to the window, white hot anger boiling up inside of him more suddenly than he anticipated. *Blast my uncle!* he thought viciously. His dark brows drew together until they were nearly indiscernible from one another, and his hand trembled as he drew the curtains, blocking out the starless night.

Uncle Wallace had taken the news badly, just as Rex had feared. He had been careful in his communications over the years, and did everything in his power to keep his uncle from visiting the estate where he and Rex's father had grown up. The latter had not been so very difficult, as Uncle Wallace was more fond of his own comfortable home in Hampshire than the painful memories attached to Summerwood, but Rex knew his uncle would have found out about Caroline eventually. Rex had hoped to be married by then; hoped to have shown his uncle that a kind, gentle lady of breeding had been able to overlook his past, and therefore pave the way for his uncle to do the same. But he had found no such lady in the last five years, and now it was too late.

Scowling, Rex walked slowly back to the fireplace, considering what had occurred that fateful day last spring. His uncle had refused to listen to reason. He had ranted and raved and sworn at Rex, lecturing his nephew about the disgrace Rex had brought upon the family with his actions. He would not think of Rex, nor the child for whom he was solely responsible. Declaring his resolution to cut his nephew off forevermore and never see him again, he rode away from the house without a backward glance.

Rex's anger intensified as he thought of his uncle's parting words, which condemned Caroline to a life of illegitimacy and poverty. "She will get what she deserves, and so will you," his uncle spat at him. Sweet, innocent Caroline! Perhaps Rex deserved his uncle's censure for the lies and falsehoods which covered his past, but all that Caroline deserved was a happy home, where she was loved and cared for by her doting Papa and his hoped-for bride. But Rex's hopes were vanishing as swiftly as smoke in the wind, and he did not know if the happy ending he wished for them both would ever come to pass.

A timid knock sounded at the door, and Rex called out to grant whomever was there admittance, grateful for the distraction. The door creaked open and an anxious little face peeked around the corner at him.

"Caroline?" he said in surprise.

The little girl inched her way into the room, her golden curls tousled from sleep, her shuffling steps hesitant. Rex smiled at her.

"Do not be frightened; I am not angry. Only tell me, what is the matter?"

Caroline broke into a run as Rex crouched down and opened his arms. She threw her arms around his neck and buried her head in his cravat, a sob escaping her throat.

"The wind—it frightens me!" she said.

"There, there. The wind cannot hurt you. You are safe here, with me."

As if to refute his comforting words, a mighty gust of wind suddenly slammed into the house, rattling the windows and shrieking around the eaves. Caroline tightened her grip, burrowing even deeper into Rex's neck. He chuckled.

"Let me tell you a story."

Rex picked her up and carried her trembling form to the chair nearest the fire. He sat down amid the cushions and settled her more comfortably in his arms. Tucking her nightdress down around her toes, he reached up and brushed the hair away from her face.

"Once upon a time there was a little boy named Jack," Rex began. "He lived in a little stone house at the top of a very big hill. The wind blew all day long up there. Sometimes gently, sometimes fiercely, but always steady.

"One day the little boy went outside to play. But there was no one to play with. He was lonely. He sat down in the grass and he cried, because there was no one else who lived on the hill with whom he could play."

Caroline turned her head so that one little blue eye peeked up at Rex.

"Suddenly, the boy heard a voice. It was a soft, quiet voice. It tickled his ears and lifted the hair brushing his cheek. It was the wind."

"What did the wind say?" Caroline asked, turning to look at Rex with both eyes.

"The wind asked the boy why he was crying. And the boy said, 'I am crying because I have no one with whom to play.' To which the wind replied, 'I will play with you.' "

"The wind cannot play," Caroline said with a frown. Rex smiled.

"Oh, but it can."

"How? What does it play?"

"What do you think? What is something that you can play with when the wind blows?"

Caroline was quiet for a moment. Her little pink lips twisted in a thoughtful grimace. Suddenly her face lit up.

"My kite! The one you bought for me last summer. The wind can play with that."

Rex smiled, twitching her nose, and she giggled. "It certainly can. And that is just what the little boy did. He made a kite out of paper and string and two straight sticks. He and the wind played with his kite all the day long. Up and down the hillside, the boy ran with his kite, while the wind chased the tail and mussed the boy's hair.

"And then, when the sun was beginning to set and the boy was tired and sleepy, do you know what happened?"

"What?" Caroline asked, breathless.

"The wind sang the boy a lullaby."

"A lullaby?"

"Yes, a lullaby. The wind whistled through the trees and danced around the house and squeezed through the cracks in the window."

Caroline sat up on Rex's knee, looking at him earnestly. "What did it sound like?"

"Much like it does tonight."

"It does not sound like a lullaby to me," she said, wriggling back into Rex's arms. He laughed softly.

"That is because tonight the wind is sad."

"Why is the wind sad, Papa?"

"Because the boy has grown up," he explained. "And now the wind has no one with whom to play."

Caroline was thoughtful. Outside, the gale continued to blow and the panes in the windows rattled again. "I still do not like it," she whispered, hiding her face.

Rex rested his cheek against the top of her head. "Shall *I* sing you a lullaby, then?"

She looked eagerly up at him. "Oh yes, Papa, please!"

He smiled, brushing his thumb down her cheek. Her clear blue eyes were wide with anticipation, and her slightly parted lips revealed an endearing little gap between her front teeth. Looking down into her round little face he was once again struck by how much she looked like her mother, Mary, and a pang of sadness and regret stole through him. He closed his eyes, shutting out the pain of the past, and began to sing.

His rich baritone voice filled the empty room, drowning out the sounds of the storm. Caroline burrowed into the crook of his arm, letting his voice wrap around her like a blanket. Rex stared into the fire, smoothing her tangled curls while he sang.

> *Sleep, my child—the day is waning,*
> *See the bright stars overhead,*
> *Ere long I shall hope to find thee*
> *Sleeping in thy little bed.*
>
> *Do not fear the silent shadows,*
> *Nor the whistle of the wind,*
> *I shall keep thee safe, my darling,*
> *'Til the daylight comes again.*

Caroline's breathing was quiet and even. The fire in the grate slowly burned down, and the wind outside began to calm. In the dimming light, Caroline's face was peaceful, her look content. No longer was her little brow furrowed in worry; no longer did her tiny limbs tremble with fear. Rex gazed at her fondly for a moment, but then he sighed.

"My dear little Caroline," he said, his voice catching as he murmured her name. "What is to become of us? What is to become of *you*?"

"Mr. Arnold for you, sir."

The butler bowed as a middle-aged man with fair hair and a medium build entered the room.

"Felix, thank you for coming on such short notice," Rex said as he rose to shake his steward's hand. The gentleman nodded, and Rex poured some refreshment for them both before sitting back down behind his desk. Mr. Arnold took the seat opposite, his straight back and attentive expression evidence of his desire to get on with business.

"I met with my barrister," Rex began, "and it is as I suspected: the vast majority of the estate is tied up in the entail, and cannot be divided."

Mr. Arnold nodded, unsurprised.

"However, there is a portion that my father purchased later in life that was not legally bound to the rest of his lands. Mr. Halifax assured me that it can be sold, if necessary."

"The northwest corner of the estate," Mr. Arnold replied, spreading out a large paper before him. "I remember when your father made the purchase."

Rex leaned over the desk to where his steward pointed out the location on a map.

"I have the accounts from all of your tenants for the last year," he continued, riffling through his leather satchel. He produced a sheaf of papers and donned a pair of spectacles before reading from them.

"It is a fairly small portion of the estate—only 60 acres—and it brings in roughly £350 per annum."

"And have you any idea what the land may sell for?"

"Hard to say. Three, maybe four thousand pounds. Provided the purchaser wants to retain the tenants."

Rex shook his head emphatically. "I will not sell it otherwise. The purchase agreement must stipulate that the families are not to be evicted."

His steward inclined his head as Rex turned his gaze towards the window. "Three or four thousand pounds," he murmured to himself. "Will it be enough?"

The wind from the prior evening had blown itself out, and a light snow was falling. Rex watched as dozens of tiny white flakes fell from the sky in haphazard succession. The snow barely covered the ground; a pristine, white mantle blanketing the earth. It was cold and bleak, much like his prospects.

"Have you had any word from your uncle?" his steward asked, breaking into his thoughts.

The harmless question made Rex flinch. "No, I have not," he said quietly. "He has not returned any of my letters, nor made any attempt to contact me. All hope of reconciliation is lost."

Mr. Arnold was silent, and Rex once again slipped into reverie. Every person he had ever loved had been torn from his life as violently as one plucks a flower from the ground. His father. His beloved Mary. And now his uncle. All that remained was Caroline. Would she be ripped from his life as well?

No, Rex thought emphatically. *I will* not *lose my little girl. No matter what it costs.*

"I shall ask Mr. Halifax to draw up the papers and list the property for sale," he said, turning back to his steward.

"Very good, sir. Would you like me to inform the tenants?"

Rex rubbed his hand across his brow. "Yes, please. Assure them that they shall not be evicted, but that once it sells I will no longer be their landlord."

Mr. Arnold nodded, collecting his papers. He removed his spectacles and placed everything back in his satchel. Standing, he extended his hand to Rex, who shook it firmly.

"Mr. Halifax and I will manage the affair. Shall I send word to you here? Or will you be going to town for the season?"

"I shall be in town, though I have not yet secured my rooms. I shall send you word when I am established there."

"Very good, sir. Good day to you, sir."

"Good day, Felix. Thank you."

Weighed down with worry, Rex left the comfort of his study to seek out Caroline. Her naturally bright personality always managed to lift his spirits, and he could use some cheering up. He found her in the kitchen, sitting at the worn worktable patting a lump of dough. A dusting of flour covered her head and face, and Rex laughed when he saw her.

"Here you are, you little imp! What mischief are you up to now?"

"I am making bread," she announced proudly, holding up the grayish mass in her hands.

"Are you indeed?"

"Yes. Cook is showing me how."

The stout little woman across the table smiled. "Aye, that I am. 'Ere now, 'ave you finished kneadin' it yet?"

Caroline nodded.

"Then put it 'ere," the cook continued, nodding at a tray of freshly formed dough. Caroline obediently placed her loaf on the tray, and the cook covered it with a cloth. She whisked it away to a warmer corner of the kitchen, wiping her hands on her apron as she returned.

"There. The dough needs to rise 'fore it can be baked. Run along wi' you now; I'll call for you when it's ready."

Caroline hopped down from the table, but before she could scamper off Rex caught her.

"Wait a moment, my sprite! You seem a bit dusty—here, come with me."

He took her hand and led her up the stairs to the nursery. "Mrs. Partridge?" he called upon entering. "Caroline is in need of some assistance."

"Merciful heavens!" the nursemaid cried. "Child, what have you been about?"

"I believe Cook was giving her a lesson in baking. If you could please clean her up and send her to me in the sitting room, I would be most obliged. I have something to discuss with her."

Twenty minutes later Mrs. Partridge ushered Caroline into the sitting room, where Rex was waiting for her.

"Come here, dearest," he said, patting the sofa next to him. Caroline climbed up next to him, snuggling against his arm until he wrapped it around her.

"Did you have a nice time in the kitchen?" he asked her.

"Oh, yes!" she said brightly. "Cook let me eat the extra raisins from the pudding, and I put the flour in the cake she made."

"And have you been a good girl for Partridge today?"

"Yes, Papa. But Partridge says I will need a gov'ness soon. What is a gov'ness, Papa?"

"A governess is a woman who teaches girls how to become ladies."

"Like my mama was?"

Rex's throat tightened. "Yes, Caroline. Like your mama." He shifted slightly in his seat. "I wish you could have known your mama, Caroline. She was a remarkable woman."

Caroline nodded. "Mrs. Jenkins says I look just like her."

Rex pulled her close. "Yes, you do. You are very much like your mama. Just as pretty, just as bright... and just as mischievous as well." Caroline giggled as Rex tickled her ear.

They sat on the sofa, enjoying the comfortable quiet of just being together. Soon Rex took Caroline's hand and looked into her large, blue eyes.

"It is time for me to go away again, my dear," he said softly.

Caroline frowned. "To London?"

"Yes."

"Why?"

"I must find a wife."

"Why must you?"

"Because," Rex said, a spark of bitterness in his voice, "if I do not..." He sighed, letting his anger melt away. Caroline looked up at him curiously.

He reached out a hand and gently stroked her curls. She was so sweet, so young! She could not know the truth. Not now.

"Because if I do not," he said again, this time more gently, "You will not have a new mother."

Caroline buried her face in his sleeve.

"I don't need a mother," came her muffled reply. "I have you. And Partridge. I don't want you to go away again."

Rex gathered her into his embrace, feeling her thin little arms wrap around his neck. He buried his face in her curls, breathing in the scent of her innocence.

"I know, darling," he murmured. "I wish I did not have to leave. But I must. I *must.*"

Caroline sniffed and drew back to look at him. "When will you be back?"

"As soon as I have found a lady to marry."

"How long will that take?"

"I am not sure," he said softly. "But this time I promise you: I *will* come home with a bride. You *will* have a new mama."

Caroline shifted uncomfortably, not meeting his eyes. "And if you don't?"

Her question echoed the fear in his heart, and he looked away.

He did not have an answer.

Chapter 5

February 1834
London, England

The week before Lady Rockwell and Sarah departed was a
whirlwind of packing, errands, visits, and shopping—not only for
the ladies, but also for the household. It was the first time in many
years that the mistress of the house would be going to town for
the Season, and the staff was busy covering furniture and shutting
up rooms for the countess's long absence. A few servants would
be staying behind to look after things at the manor, but the
majority would be accompanying Lady Rockwell and her young
charge to London. Mrs. Perkins, the housekeeper, had been sent
ahead with several housemaids and a few footmen to ready the
house in town the last week in January, and Sarah and Lady
Rockwell followed with their entourage a few days later.

The journey to London took six days, but soon they were
settled in Lady Rockwell's home in Cavendish Square. It was
large and comfortable with expensive, though somewhat

outdated, furnishings. Lady Rockwell lost no time in seeking a private tutor for Sarah's blossoming artistic skills. A Dutchman by the name of Jansen Meijer was given the position, and Sarah awoke on the morning of her first lesson with a great deal of excitement.

Though completely uninformed regarding the gentleman employed to train her, Sarah secretly envisioned a handsome, talented young man, destined to fall madly in love with her during the course of her lessons. She rehearsed in her mind several romantic scenes they might share, and thought of ways in which she might politely but firmly refuse his ardent declaration of love and his desire to marry her. With senses and heart aflutter, she entered the drawing room to see if the real Mr. Meijer was anything like the romanticized version in her head.

He could not have been more different.

Jansen Meijer turned out to be a short, balding man more than twice her age. He had a bulbous nose and keen black eyes that were quick to find fault in his new pupil.

"Your proportions are all wrong," he stated when he first saw her work. "You are not drawing caricatures; you must learn to be exact in your execution."

He rolled his r's when he spoke, and the harsher sound made his criticism sting even more. Flipping through her small portfolio, he clucked his tongue and shook his head, frowning. Sarah bit her lip, shrinking away from the censure. Finally he stopped on a small watercolor she had painted the week before they left Leicestershire. It was a depiction of a tiny sparrow huddled on a frosted branch, no doubt lost on its way south towards warmer climes.

Mr. Meijer narrowed his eyes. He cocked his head and harrumphed, and Sarah was surprised when instead of another cutting remark he said, "This is good. You have captured the brightness of his eye and the detail in his feathers. Not easy to do with birds."

Sarah sighed in relief and smiled timidly at the gentleman, but he did not smile back.

"It is good," he said gruffly, "but it, too, can be improved. You have much to learn."

The two hours following this declaration were gruesome. Nothing Sarah did was right in the eyes of her tutor. Her hand was too heavy. Her grip was too firm. Her paint was too thick, and then it was too thin. Again and again Sarah corrected herself, and again and again Mr. Meijer found something else to fault.

"You may have a pretty face, Miss Mendenhall," he said in parting when the morning was spent, "but you will never paint a pretty picture unless you can apply yourself."

It was the final straw. As soon as the door shut behind his rotund form, Sarah fell to her knees beside the settee and burst into tears. Lady Rockwell, who had deposited herself in a far corner of the room during Sarah's lesson, came forward. She sat beside Sarah and gently stroked her head.

"I am sorry, my dear," she said. "He was rather harsh, I think."

"He... he..." Sarah's voice caught on a sob. "He said I had no talent. He said m-my work was rub-rub-rubbish," she choked.

"There now, hush," the countess soothed. "He did not mean what he said."

"Of c-course he meant it!"

43

"Nonsense! Though I find his manners undeniably lacking in refinement, he is one of the best tutors to be had. Exceptional masters are always the most critical where they see the most potential."

Sarah was not convinced, but gradually her sobs subsided. She dried her tears and sat beside the countess on the sofa. Lady Rockwell took her hand, giving it a squeeze.

"Do not lose faith in yourself so quickly, *Meine Kind.* Give yourself some time, and accept the help of others. I would not have encouraged you in painting had I not thought you capable of great things."

She patted Sarah's cheek fondly, then retired to her room to dress.

Sarah's lessons continued through the cold, bleak weeks of February. Though she tried with all her might to please her tutor, Mr. Meijer always found something to criticize. If it had not been for the quiet dinner parties and social gatherings she attended in the evenings, Sarah would have found life very depressing.

Sarah had painting lessons twice weekly, and on the other mornings the ladies made calls and accepted visitors. In the evenings they went to parties or the theatre. As more and more families arrived in town, the livelier their excursions became, and consequently, the livelier Sarah became. All her life she had dreamed of a season in London, and now she would finally have it.

Though Parliament had been in session since January and

families continued to pour in from the country, there remained an unofficial restraint against society. It was nearly tangible—a buzzing, thrumming current of expectation and anticipation hung over the town. Finally, on the Monday before Lady Day, it was announced that vouchers were available for the opening of Almack's the following Wednesday.

The Season had begun.

"The entire *ton* will be at Almack's next week," Lady Rockwell told Sarah when news of the opening ball reached Cavendish Square.

"And are we to be among them?" Sarah asked, her stomach fluttering.

"Of course. It is a very exclusive club, but we shall not have any trouble in securing our invitation. Lady Cavanaugh is a friend of mine, and as one of the patronesses of Almack's, she will ensure that we are given vouchers."

Sarah dressed with particular care when the night of her long-awaited début arrived. She vacillated between the ivory and sapphire gowns, as well as a pretty pink silk she had acquired since arriving in London. While the blue gown was stunning and she had worn it on a few occasions, she did not want to appear ostentatious. Not many young ladies wore such bold colors, after all. She finally decided upon the ivory silk.

"Oh, Lady Rockwell, how excited I am!" she said as their carriage pulled up in front of the club.

Her companion smiled. "I hope the evening meets with your expectations."

Sarah laughed. "My only expectation is for a wonderful evening, and I am sure to receive *that*."

They entered the crowded rooms at half past eight, and Sarah gasped at the size and opulence of the establishment. The main ballroom was enormous. Massive chandeliers dripped from the ceiling, their crystals winking and flashing in the candlelight. Two large balconies overlooking the dance floor jutted out from either end of the room, and along the wall hung long, velvet draperies with golden tassels. Gilded chairs and ornate statues lined the walls. Sarah looked around her in awe, the murmuring sound of hundreds of tongues and swishing ballgowns echoing off the coffered ceiling.

She felt quite insignificant.

Glancing around, she wished she had chosen the peacock blue gown instead of the creamy silk she wore. The women in the room wore dresses in every imaginable shade. Pale pink, golden yellow, rich burgundy—the variety of colors was endless. The gentlemen's garments were equally as colorful, and she spied several waistcoats in navy, crimson, orange, and green. Sarah looked down at herself and frowned. She had not worn the blue because she did not want to appear too conspicuous, but now she feared she may not be noticed at all.

The press of bodies in the room scarcely allowed for much movement, but at last Sarah and the countess managed to find their way to a group of Lady Rockwell's friends and associates. A large woman saw their approach and called out to them cheerfully.

"Lady Rockwell! Miss Mendenhall! How delightful to see you."

"How do you do, Mrs. Ashby?" the countess said.

"Oh, quite well, quite well, thank you," came the reply. She was a handsome woman with a jolly face, and though she was a bit stout now, Sarah could see that she had been a beauty in her day.

"And Lady Mills? I trust you are in good health?" Lady Rockwell inquired of another.

"I am well," the lady replied with a smile. "And what is more, my son Peter is well." The way she said it immediately piqued Sarah's attention.

"I do not believe I have had the pleasure of meeting your son. Is he in attendance this evening?" Sarah asked politely.

Lady Mills nodded. "He is there, dancing with Miss McBride."

She gestured towards a tall, gangly fellow with blondish hair and a simpering mouth. He was dancing the quadrille with an elegant young lady, but he appeared rather bored. Lady Mills smiled possessively.

"Miss McBride has a fortune of fifteen thousand pounds," she said grandly.

"If only she had the looks to accompany it," Mrs. Ashby said in an aside to Sarah. Sarah was not sure whether she should look shocked or amused at this comment, until Mrs. Ashby winked at her.

"Are they engaged?" Lady Rockwell enquired.

"Not *yet*," Lady Mills said with meaning. "But I would not be surprised if an announcement was forthcoming."

It was common knowledge among the established London families that the Mills were anxious to see their eldest son married. Their family had a baronetcy, but their fortune was running out—thanks in part to the unchecked frivolity of the son whom she was praising. It was obvious that Lady Mills wanted the match very much.

Sarah looked back at the dancing couple, but for all Lady Mills's fine airs and confident words, she detected no regard in either young person. Miss McBride was very plain, and she moved stiffly within the steps of the dance, seeming anxious to get away. Peter Mills was lazily scanning the crowd as if calculating who his next partner would be.

Just then two young gentlemen approached and bowed to the gathered ladies. "Mr. Morris and Mr. Carlisle!" Mrs. Ashby sang out. "Have you come to ask me to dance?"

Everyone laughed, for it was clear from their admiring looks that the gentlemen came to enquire after Sarah. She smiled demurely and curtsied to each in turn as they were introduced.

"Mr. Morris, how is your mother?" Lady Rockwell asked.

"She is laid up with the gout at present, Lady Rockwell, but hopes to accompany us to the assembly rooms soon."

While his friend was speaking, Mr. Carlisle sidled up to Sarah and spoke low in her ear. "Have the old crows been setting you up, Miss Mendenhall?"

Sarah laughed. "No, indeed. They have been very kind. Although I confess that I am anxious to dance—I have not been to a ball in ages and oh, how my feet long for it!"

"Then you have not danced yet this evening?" he asked, surprised.

"No, we have only just arrived."

Mr. Carlisle looked triumphant. "Then allow me the pleasure of being your first partner," he said with an elegant bow. Sarah granted him a dazzling smile as she took his arm.

Sarah soon forgot all about her fears, so lively and amiable was her partner. He asked after her family and how she was liking London, and as her initial shyness wore off her natural charm shone through. She showered him with smiles and anecdotes about her adventures in India, the two of them laughing as she recounted the first time she rode an elephant. She was charming and sweet, and by the end of half an hour he was quite headlong in love with her. He escorted her back to her chaperon, ignoring the glaring look of his friend Mr. Morris in the process. He bent to kiss her hand and began to ask if he might call on her, when another young man stepped forward and asked her to dance. Sarah recognized him as William Stafford, having met him at a party the week prior. She immediately accepted and was whisked away to dance once more.

The quadrille was lively, and Sarah found her partner to be quite agreeable. A bit more formal and stiff than Mr. Carlisle, but he was a pleasant fellow and a beautiful dancer. When he returned Sarah to Lady Rockwell at the end of the dance, she noticed that Peter Mills was there with Miss McBride on his arm. Introductions were made all around, and leaving his supposed intended in the clutches of his mother, Peter asked Sarah if she would care to dance.

Sarah immediately accepted, anxious to discover whether her observations were correct. Peter led her to the dance floor, complimenting her on her grace and poise.

"Thank you, but I am not nearly as elegant as Miss McBride seems to be," she said coyly. Peter laughed.

"Let me guess: my mother has been telling everyone within hearing that Miss McBride and myself are engaged."

"*Soon* to be engaged," Sarah corrected. She looked up at him and saw a look of amused annoyance on his face. "Is it not so?"

"No, it is not," he said as the dance started.

"Does Miss McBride know?" Sarah inquired. He smirked at her.

"Yes, but our families have not yet caught on. My mother would like to see me the husband of a fortune, and her mother, the wife of a baronet."

Sarah nodded. "I see. But neither of you are disposed to please your mothers?"

"Are you?" he asked brashly.

"I have no mother," she replied candidly. He drew back, surprised.

"Forgive me," he stammered. "I did not know."

"It is all right," she smiled at him. "My mother and father died when I was very young. My brother Charles is my guardian now."

"Ahh, I see. And would you be inclined to ask your brother's opinion about whom you should marry?"

Sarah was thoughtful. "Yes, I believe I should ask his opinion." Her look turned impish and her eyes sparkled mischievously. "Though I cannot say that I would follow his advice."

Peter laughed. "Then you know precisely what I mean. Miss McBride is rich enough, to be sure, but have you ever met with such a sallow face as hers?"

Sarah's jaw dropped. Had he just insulted a lady in her presence? Before she could collect her senses he continued.

"No, I would much rather have a pretty wife—one whom I

could bear to look at. And though she does have a handsome fortune, there are plenty of eligible young ladies with money *and* beauty, are there not?" He looked at her suggestively, and Sarah shook her head.

"You flatter me, Mr. Mills. Though I possess a fair amount of beauty, I am no heiress."

"What is your connection to Lady Rockwell, then?"

"She is the grandmother of my very dear friend Katherine, who was lately married to my brother Charles. They returned to our home in India last summer, but I have chosen to remain here, as a companion to the countess."

"But have you no fortune of your own? Surely you must, if your brother married the granddaughter of a countess."

Sarah frowned, indignant. "Katherine married Charles because they loved each other, not for social or monetary reasons."

Peter contemplated her answer, a calculating look in his eyes. She did not like his preoccupation with money and appearances, and determined to set him down further if she could. Tossing her head, she declared, "And to be frank, no; I have no fortune. Though I have no intention of marrying at present, my affections and three thousand pounds are all that I shall bring to that union—which I am *sure* will be sufficient for the man *I* intend to marry."

Her partner smiled, amused, but Sarah could not shake her uneasiness and was glad when the set ended. She returned to Lady Rockwell, anxious to forget her partner.

She did not stay with her patroness for long. Word had traveled quickly that Lady Rockwell's beautiful young charge was amiable, witty, and full of charm, and the gentlemen clamored to have a chance to dance with the pretty brunette and taste of her smiles. Several young ladies in the room were already looking at her through narrowed eyes, trying to determine how much competition she would be, their mothers staring haughtily down their noses at her with hawkish dislike.

Oblivious to the stir she was causing, Sarah enjoyed the evening with the vigor and delight one can only find in the young. Everything she saw and experienced was locked away in her girlish heart to be thought over and dreamed of for months and years to come. Even the stale refreshments and watered down lemonade were ambrosia to her tongue, for it meant that she was a guest at Almack's, the most prestigious club of London society. Her first ball of her first season in London was everything she wished it would be and more, and when at last the night had worn away even the early morning hours, she returned with Lady Rockwell to Cavendish Square with a contented heart.

"Well, *Fräulein?*" Lady Rockwell asked as they emerged from the carriage outside her front door. "Was it everything you hoped for?"

"No, Lady Rockwell," Sarah sighed dreamily. "It was *ever* so much more!"

Chapter 6

March 1834
London, England

Rex alighted from the carriage, staring sullenly up at his residence on Park Street. He had exhausted nearly all of his remaining funds to pay the rent on the fashionable house for the season, but he knew he must keep up appearances. Now that his uncle had cut off his allowance and inheritance, Rex needed to find and marry a woman of wealth *before* she discovered that his own fortune was gone.

He entered the house and handed his hat and coat to his valet. "Tell Mrs. Jenkins to send up some tea and cakes," he said, making his way upstairs. Finding a fire in the sitting room raised his spirits a bit, and soon Mrs. Jenkins shuffled in carrying a tea tray loaded with hot scones, fresh butter, and sweet preserves. Rex smiled at the familiar sight.

"Mrs. Jenkins, you are a vision," he said gallantly. The matronly housekeeper turned pink but narrowed her eyes.

"I'll 'ave none of your lip now, Master Jameson. I turned you over my knee when you was a babe an' I can do it again," she said sharply. Rex laughed.

"Dear Mrs. Jenkins, I tremble in your presence. Forgive me of my impudence, and accept my apologies." She scowled at him, but there was a fondness in her eyes as she did so.

"Go on with you, then," she said brusquely, setting the tray on a side table. "Eat up while ev'rythin' is good an' 'ot."

Rex needed no second bidding. The journey from Summerwood was scarcely twenty miles, but he was sufficiently hungry to make quick work of the light meal. He poured himself some tea and then gestured for her to take the tray away. "Please send Walters up at once," he asked as she bustled out of the room. She nodded, and he strode to the window.

February in London was cold and wet, but March was completely insufferable. One day a chilly drizzle might fall from the oppressive gray sky, and the next it would be sunny and warm. On this, the twenty-seventh of March, the sun had shone bravely through a thin veil of clouds nearly all day, but had at last succumbed to the gathering storm as it dipped below the horizon. Rex drew back the curtain and surveyed the damp street below. A carriage drove past, carrying nameless passengers to unknown destinations. He wondered idly if the occupants were blissfully on their way to attend the theatre or a ball, or if some corrupt personage rode inside the curtained equipage.

"You wished to see me, sir?"

The voice of his valet caused Rex to turn. "Yes, Walters, I did. I shall be going to White's tonight, and I need you to lay out my best suit." He drained his teacup and set it down on the sill.

"And send my card to Lady Fawkes. I shall be paying her a visit to secure my voucher to Almack's for the Season." His valet bowed, and Rex turned to look out the window once more. The streets were again deserted, and a few heavy raindrops were beginning to speckle the uneven cobbles. He shivered. He was not looking forward to going out tonight.

"Jameson! I wondered when you would be making an appearance in town."

A tall gentleman with ruddy curls stood as Rex entered the room, smiling at him.

"Frederick, old friend! How do you do?"

The two friends clasped hands, and Rex was invited to the table where two other gentlemen sat.

"Jameson Rex, this is Edward Murphy and Charles Stanton." The gentlemen acknowledged each other and took their seats.

"Stanton was just telling us what is happening in the House of Commons."

Rex perked up. He did not hold a seat himself, but he was interested in politics and enjoyed knowing what was decided during each session.

"Aye, they are trying to improve the child labor laws."

"In what way?"

"Setting a minimum age for the sweeps. Boys as young as six are being hauled off and forced to work. You know the conditions for them."

The men at the table nodded grimly. The life of a chimney

sweep was dangerous, and cruel. Rex frowned.

"Deplorable. I am glad to hear that something is to be done about it. Children should be cherished and nurtured, not forced into labor when they are hardly out of the cradle."

Mr. Murphy and Mr. Stanton exchanged looks. Frederick Neild cleared his throat, and Rex's eyes darted between the gentlemen in confusion. Something was amiss.

"Rex, take a turn with me. There is something I should like to ask you," Frederick said, standing.

A chill that had nothing to do with the frigid night air stole over him, but Rex nodded and stood. He bid farewell to the two men at the table, and joined his friend in acquiring drinks at the far end of the room. Through an open doorway to their left Rex saw the gaming tables set up, the men gathered around them laughing and conversing quite loudly.

"How is Mrs. Neild?" Rex asked when they were alone. His friend smiled.

"She is well. Nearing her confinement."

Frederick had been married for two years and already had a little boy. Rex clapped him on the shoulder and smiled.

"You have my congratulations. I hope all goes well."

"Thank you," Frederick replied, ducking his head. "Camilla is a strong woman, and little Fred is a healthy boy. I am sure it will be all right."

Rex nodded, the thought of Mary during her confinement cutting sharply through his memory. Frederick shifted his feet, casting a glance back at the other gentlemen. Rex narrowed his eyes.

"Out with it, Neild."

His friend shook his head, clearly uncomfortable. "It is nothing. Only... well, we were talking of children..." His voice trailed off and he looked at Rex expectantly.

Rex's face went pale. The room spun around him, and the sounds from the crowd grew muffled and dim, as if he were trapped underwater. *He knows*, thought Rex. *He knows about Caroline.* Rex shook his head, dazed. He thought of the other two men, and the look they had shared—they obviously knew as well. How did they know? How had Caroline's existence become common knowledge?

"Rex?"

Frederick was watching him nervously. He and Rex had been friends for more than a decade, and his youthful face was clouded with concern. Rex attempted a smile, hoping to reassure him, but all he managed was a grimace.

"What have you heard?"

Frederick sighed. "They say you have a child. A little girl." He hesitated. "And no wife."

"Who says?"

"Everyone. I have heard it from three or four sources already."

Rex dropped into a nearby chair, and Frederick sat down beside him. The slump of his shoulders and the graveness in his eyes made Rex look as if he had aged ten years. "How did they find out?" he murmured to himself.

Though it was clearly a rhetorical question, his friend answered anyway. "How is anything discovered? Gossiping servants, most likely."

Rex shook his head. His household was fiercely loyal, he

knew that nothing could have been discovered through them. But his uncle's servants, perhaps? Had he verbally lambasted Rex within their hearing? It did not matter. The damage was done, and he must now accept the consequences.

"What else have you heard?" he asked, piecing together his control once more.

"That is all."

Rex breathed a sigh of relief. Perhaps his loss of fortune would remain unknown, at least until he could find a bride.

A bride.

A sick feeling knotted in his gut, and he turned to his friend. "I need to get married. As soon as possible."

His friend was taken aback. "What about the girl's mother?"

Rex sighed, closing his eyes. "She is dead," he said softly.

Frederick nodded, and after a moment Rex looked up at him. "Am I beyond hope, then?" he asked.

His friend grimaced. "Not past *all* hope, perhaps," he said doubtfully. "But you may have a hard time finding a lady willing to accept another woman's place—and her child."

Rex knew his friend was right. It would not be easy to find such a lady, but find one he must. He got to his feet, and his friend stood beside him. "Thank you, Frederick. I bid you good night."

Frederick clapped Rex on the shoulder as if to say "good luck" before turning away. Rex walked through the open door near him and into the gaming room.

With Caroline's existence common knowledge, he would have to change tactics. Rex was not a stranger to disappointment, nor was he afraid of the difficulties now before him. He strolled around the room, considering his options.

A burst of raucous laughter assaulted his ears, and he turned towards the source. A group of gentlemen were laughing and talking quite close to him, obviously inebriated. His gaze landed on the one man he recognized: Peter Mills.

On seeing his former schoolmate, an idea flew into his head which he almost at once dismissed. Turning away, he tried to banish the errant thought, but it persisted. He paused, considering. *Desperate times, desperate measures,* he thought. Turning back, he strode resolutely towards the table where Peter Mills sat.

His comrades were just leaving, and Rex sat down in one of their empty chairs. "Hello, Mills. I trust you are well?"

Peter Mills stared at him, and Rex chuckled.

"Come now, you cannot pretend that we are mere acquaintances? We were at school together, after all. That seems claim enough for you, since you accost me nearly every year that I am in town, intent on seeking the bottom of my pocketbook."

The man next to him grinned, clearly more at ease with their connection laid bare. "That is true. But I do not recall the last time *you* sought out *my* company."

Rex inclined his head, his blue-gray eyes dancing. "And yet, here I am."

"Here you are."

Peter leaned back in his chair, stroking his mustache as he regarded the man opposite. Rex stared, unflinching, back at him. Though Peter belonged to an old, respectable family, he had earned the reputation of being shifty and somewhat of a rake. He was loose with his money and his morals, and often with those belonging to others as well.

"What are you doing with yourself these days?" Rex asked.

Peter waved his hand vaguely in the air. "Oh, the usual. Trying to have as much fun as I can before I settle down."

"I thought you would have learned your lesson after the fiasco with Miss Grant."

Peter rolled his eyes. "That was ages ago—nearly two years past! Besides, she was an ignorant girl to think I would actually marry her. I am glad her family took her away—it saved me a lot of trouble," he grumbled.

Rex stiffened. To hear the callous way in which Peter flippantly regarded the virtue of a young lady was repulsive. His eyes narrowed, and Peter smiled smugly.

"I have grown wiser, you see. No more green girls straight from the schoolroom for me, no sir! I find I do not get into scrapes with the more, shall we say, *experienced* ladies." He smirked at Rex. "*You* know how that is."

Rex stiffened. He knew what Peter was implying, but he tried to act as if he did not.

"What do you mean?" he asked, picking up the drink he had been served.

Peter feigned indifference as he set his own glass down, examining his fingernails. "Only that I heard you had a lady on the side. And from what I gather, she could not possibly be green, to have remained anonymous for so long." He raised an eyebrow at Rex, a knowing look in his eyes that disgusted his companion.

Rex stared at his glass and said nothing. Peter leaned towards him.

"Is it true, then?"

Rex looked up. "Is what true?"

"Is there a lady?"

Rex sat back in his seat, weighing his words carefully. "What have you heard?"

Peter shrugged. "Not so much about a lady," he admitted, "but there *is* talk of a little girl."

Rex nodded silently, and Peter's eyes widened. "I cannot believe it. Mr. Jameson Rex, the high and mighty gentleman, full of noble ideals and sentimental lectures?" His mocking tone dared Rex to challenge him, but as furious as Rex was, he knew he could not. The gleeful look on Peter's face filled him with disgust.

"Who is she?" Peter asked, unashamed.

"She is my concern, not yours," Rex snapped.

"But if you are caring for her, she must be your child..." Peter hinted, grinning wickedly.

Rex's eyes flashed with anger, but he reigned it in. Losing his temper would do no good, and after all, it was not Peter he was angry with. He blew out his breath in frustration. "I will not be able to care for her much longer. My uncle has cut me off."

"Completely?"

"Yes. My allowance and inheritance—gone."

Whistling quietly, Peter sat back, and Rex chuckled darkly. "I am afraid my pocketbook will not do you any good this year," he said sarcastically.

There was a moment of silence while Peter mulled this over. Finally he sat forward.

"So, what are you going to do?" he asked with interest.

Rex looked up at him. Peter Mills was a spoiled dandy. He was fairly good-looking and had fashionable taste, but his arrogant manner and loose morals often got him into trouble. All of his friends knew that Peter had no desire to marry, and so long as his father and his comrades lined his pockets, he likely never would.

But Rex also knew that Peter Mills had connections that might help him. Among Peter's varied acquaintance were many wealthy women friends—with as little desire to marry as he himself possessed. Women whose wealth and status in society meant that most people turned a blind eye to their actions.

The thought that had formed in Rex's mind as he first observed Peter Mills had initially filled him with abhorrence, but he knew that Peter could help him in ways that others could not. His stomach turned as he considered what he was about to undertake. *Desperate times*, he rationalized again.

All this had passed in a moment, and Peter was still leaning forward, waiting for Rex's reply.

"I plan to marry an heiress, of course," Rex said with forced calm.

"An heiress!"

"Certainly," Rex continued, feigning disinterest. "Is that not what *you* plan to do someday?"

"Yes," his companion hesitated. "But you will not likely find many of the ladies with whom you are acquainted very willing, what with the rumors floating around."

Rex narrowed his eyes. "Perhaps not in my current set of acquaintance. But surely there are *some* heiresses who would be willing?" he asked suggestively, raising an eyebrow.

Surprise flashed across Peter's face, but then he grinned. "There might be a few of those around, though it may take a bit of persuading to get them to settle down. I would be happy to introduce you to them, if you like."

Rex studied the man opposite. Peter was draped over the chair, a half-empty glass in his hand and a smug look on his face.

Rex nodded. "I am counting on it," he said grimly.

Chapter 7

"Another bouquet has arrived for you, Miss Mendenhall."

Sarah's eyes met Lady Rockwell's over the dinner table and she smiled. The older woman shook her silvery head in disbelief.

"How many admirers have you managed to acquire in the last month, Miss Mendenhall?"

"Oh, I lost count last week. A dozen, at least," she answered gleefully.

"Take care, *Fräulein*," Lady Rockwell said, frowning. "They may feel you are in earnest in your encouragements."

Sarah laid down her fork and looked quizzically at the countess. "*Am* I encouraging them?"

Lady Rockwell hesitated. As much as she felt the need to lecture her young charge, she had no real reproof to give. Lady Rockwell's quick eyes had watched her carefully in their social gatherings, worried that she might find her protégé to be a vicious flirt. But she was not. Sarah Mendenhall was lively, sweet, graceful, and kind. The exotic nature of her upbringing and girlish exuberance made her even more attractive, and the gentlemen flocked to her side like moths to a flame. Naturally this delighted the débutante, and she reveled in the cards and flowers that flooded the house. But she did not play silly games with them, as many of her counterparts did.

"Not exactly," Lady Rockwell countered. "But they may not be aware of your resolve. They may think that your affections may yet be won."

Sarah shook her head. "I have made it no secret that I will not enter into an engagement this year, and I cannot help it if the young men prefer my company over others. I am merely trying to enjoy myself; they are simply along for the ride."

Lady Rockwell sighed and shook her head.

"We have been invited to the Thatchers this evening, along with several other families," she said after a moment. "Is Mr. Jeremy Thatcher among your conquests?"

"Hmm," Sarah tapped her nose thoughtfully. "I danced with him at the Lovell's last week, and I believe he sent me flowers. But he has not offered for me yet."

"Offered for you! *Um Himmels Willen!* How can you even suggest such a thing?" Lady Rockwell cried incredulously.

"Well, Fred Grimshaw proposed to me last week, but of course I turned him down," Sarah replied benignly, returning to her meal. Lady Rockwell stared at her in mute astonishment. When her companion did not reply, Sarah looked up. Laughing at the shock on her benefactor's face, she explained.

"Of course I did not take him seriously, Lady Rockwell. Freddy is a lovesick little puppy dog; very sweet and amusing, but he has no idea what he is about. In fact, I am a little concerned he might be taken in." She frowned, and a tiny dent appeared between her eyebrows that made her look like a pouting child. The ridiculousness of hearing her refer to a man more than five years her senior in such a way got the better of Lady Rockwell, and she laughed.

"My dear Miss Mendenhall, I am sorry I ever doubted your abilities to hold your own in London society," she said.

Sarah's eyes twinkled merrily as she reached across the table and squeezed the older woman's hand. "Apology accepted, Lady Rockwell. I am happy to have earned your confidence."

A card arrived as they were finishing their meal, and Lady Rockwell read it while sipping her tea.

"It appears the Willis's are having a ball," Lady Rockwell said, reading a card.

"A ball! How wonderful!" Sarah looked up from her plate with starry eyes. "When is it to be?"

"On Tuesday next," Lady Rockwell replied, glancing up. Sarah's face fell.

"That is the night we had planned to attend the opera."

Lady Rockwell surveyed her young friend. "Well? Would you like to see the opera, or attend the ball?" She laughed at the martyred look on Sarah's face. "A difficult decision, to be sure," she teased. But Sarah squared her shoulders.

"Let us go to the ball," she declared resolutely. "We can attend the opera some other time."

Lady Rockwell chuckled. "Very well. I shall respond to the Willis's invitation in the affirmative, and we shall enjoy *Fra Diavolo* another time."

They finished their dinner and retired to the drawing room. Lady Rockwell sat down to pen their acceptance, and Sarah pulled out her notebook and began to sketch the new vase of flowers that had arrived. A half hour later, the butler announced the arrival of Dr. Matthews.

"Thank you, Lawrence. Please show him into my private parlor; I shall be up directly."

The butler nodded and left, but Sarah looked up, concerned.

"Is something ailing you, Lady Rockwell?"

"Age, my dear. It is merely the years catching up with me." Sighing, she allowed herself a worried frown. "My heart is not what it used to be. The trip to India to fetch Katherine took a far greater toll than I realized."

Sarah set her pencil down and crossed over to the countess, touching her shoulder gently. "Is there anything I can do?"

Her patroness chuckled. "Do not worry yourself over me, *Mein Kind*. I shall be well. Dr. Matthews's visits are merely a precaution; I am not at death's door yet." She patted Sarah's hand and stood. "I shall leave you to your drawing."

"Miss Mendenhall, you are an absolute vision tonight."

Jeremy Thatcher brushed his lips across the back of Sarah's gloved hand. She smiled sweetly up at him.

"Thank you, Mr. Thatcher. It is always a pleasure to see you."

"The pleasure is all mine, Miss Mendenhall, to have your lovely face before me once more."

Sarah laughed. "Take care, Mr. Thatcher—it appears that Miss Elizabeth Brooks does not like what you are saying to me." She nodded at a young lady standing across the room from them, whose dark eyes were looking daggers in their direction.

Mr. Thatcher flushed faintly, but he turned gallantly away and replied, "I care not what Miss Elizabeth thinks—it is *you* I wish to please tonight."

"Oh no, this will never do!" Sarah trilled. "I will not allow you to snub dear Miss Elizabeth on my account. Goodbye, Mr. Thatcher."

Sarah sailed away, leaving the way clear for Miss Elizabeth to swoop in and nurse Jeremy Thatcher's wounded heart. She made her way across the room, where several other guests were gathered.

"Ah, Miss Mendenhall! Come here, my dear," Mrs. Ashby called to her. She was standing next to a woman Sarah knew only by sight as Mrs. Reed, and a young lady whom Sarah presumed to be one of her daughters.

"Are you acquainted with Mrs. Reed?" the jolly Mrs. Ashby asked. Sarah curtsied, smiling demurely.

"I believe I am. How do you do, Mrs. Reed?"

"How do you do, Miss Mendenhall. This is my daughter, Rosemary." The young ladies curtsied and murmured their greetings to one another.

"I understand that you are taking painting lessons, Miss Mendenhall," Rosemary said politely.

Her mother sniffed. "*My* daughters have taken lessons since they were ten years old."

Sarah flushed. "Of course. But I did not have that pleasure.

There was not the opportunity for me to take lessons in India, you see."

"Oh, yes, India. It must have been dreadful growing up in such an uncivilized nation!"

Mrs. Reed turned to Mrs Ashby and began a diatribe of all the horrendous stories she had ever heard spoken about India. Sarah was mortified. Embarrassed and angry over Mrs. Reed's words, she knew not how to respond. Rosemary saw her agitation and leaned forward.

"You must forgive my mother, Miss Mendenhall," she said quietly. "She is quite jealous of you, you see."

Sarah was taken aback at her words. "Whatever do you mean?"

Rosemary colored slightly. "Oh, it is nothing. She only wishes I had as many admirers as you do."

Sarah knew not what to say to such a declaration, but thankfully Rosemary went on. "And do not feel bad about not having painting lessons until now. Even after nine years of lessons, my work still looks atrocious!"

Sarah smiled, beginning to thaw. "I am sure you are too modest, Miss Reed, but thank you. You are very kind."

Rosemary smiled shyly back at her. "Are you at all fond of music, Miss Mendenhall?"

"Indeed, I am!"

"Do you play then, and sing?"

Laughing lightly, Sarah shook her head. "No, not at all. I can sing when I must, but I fear I lack the talent to play for company. Do you play yourself, Miss Reed?"

"Rosemary is very accomplished on the pianoforte," her

mother interjected proudly, having turned her attention once more to the young ladies. Blushing, Rosemary ducked her head.

"I would love to hear you play sometime," Sarah said, smiling warmly at her.

Rosemary nodded. "I should like that very much."

The conversation then turned to other pleasantries. Sarah complimented Rosemary on her gown, which Mrs. Reed took as an invitation to give a detailed account of her daughter's new wardrobe. While she was speaking, Sarah observed Peter Mills slinking into the room. His calculating eyes scanned the crowd, and when they rested on Sarah he smirked. She turned away quickly, not wanting to draw his attention.

But she was too late. He sauntered over to where the group was gathered and bent his head towards Sarah's ear.

"Miss Mendenhall, you look absolutely bewitching when you are being coy," he murmured. Sarah frowned, annoyed.

"I was not being coy, I was trying to avoid you." Her frankness caused the young man to burst out laughing, and the ladies around them looked at him in surprise. He continued to chuckle, but swept an elegant bow for them.

"Forgive me, dear ladies, but Miss Mendenhall said something extremely amusing." He looked at Sarah and raised one eyebrow, and to her dismay the women gave each other knowing looks and moved away. Only Rosemary appeared apprehensive as she left. Peter looked smug, and Sarah blushed in agitation.

"Come now, Miss Mendenhall. You will not run away from me as well, will you?" he asked, suppressing a grin. Sarah scowled at him, but did not move away. If she did not speak with him now, he would only corner her again later. She thought it best to get it over with.

"I met Fred Grimshaw over at White's," he said conspiratorially. "He looked quite put out, poor boy."

Sarah tried to ignore him, but Peter Mills was clearly waiting for a response. She sighed in aggravation.

"He really did it to himself. I was sorry indeed to have to refuse him, but I told him not to think seriously of me."

"Have you told Jeremy Thatcher that as well?" Peter asked with a wicked glint in his eye. Sarah huffed.

"I am beginning to think that all you London gentlemen care for is the chance to fall in love with a pretty face," she declared petulantly. Peter laughed.

"It is true that we have a fondness for pretty young women," he said with a wink. "But not all of us fall in love so easily." He looked her up and down for a moment, the hunger in his eyes barely concealed. "For some of us, it requires a bit of persuasion."

Sarah was incensed. "If you think for one moment that I am *that* kind of lady, you are grossly mistaken."

She turned on her heel and stalked off, anger and disgust burning her cheeks. She felt dirty, and wished she had never allowed Peter Mills to draw her into conversation.

The evening wore on, and Sarah found that she could almost forget the unpleasant run-in she had had with with Peter Mills. She sought the company of Rosemary Reed again, finding that her gentle smile and cultured voice had a calming influence over her. She had to endure the haughty looks of Rosemary's mother, but since Rosemary herself was patient and kind, Sarah felt mostly at ease in their presence.

Supper was served at nine o'clock, and Sarah had nearly forgotten the unfortunate affair from earlier when another disagreeable event occurred.

"I understand that Miss Mendenhall is very fond of music," Miss Elizabeth Brooks declared to the assembled party. "Since she is new to our midst, we have not had the pleasure of hearing her play for us. Miss Mendenhall, would you be so inclined as to favor us with a song?"

Sarah blanched, and Miss Elizabeth looked triumphant. *She must have overheard me speaking to Miss Reed!* Sarah thought. Lady Rockwell looked at her uneasily. No doubt the older woman was recalling the failed piano lessons she had attempted with her young charge. But Sarah tossed her head and did her best to appear unruffled. Trilling a laugh, she replied, "Oh dear me, no! I am sure there are far superior musicians in the room than myself."

"Come, Miss Mendenhall, I am sure you are too modest. I insist on hearing you!"

A murmured chorus of assent rippled through the crowd, and Miss Elizabeth smiled darkly. Sarah ground her teeth together.

She cast her eyes around and caught the countess's eye, who was sitting beside Mrs. Reed. Suddenly an idea flew into Sarah's head, and she turned back to face Miss Elizabeth.

"Very well," Sarah sighed dramatically. An expression of alarm flashed across Lady Rockwell's face, but before she could intercede Sarah spoke again. "Miss Reed, would you be so good as to accompany me?"

Surprise and pleasure mingled on the young lady's face, but she quickly agreed. The pair made their way to the pianoforte in the corner of the room, and Miss Reed sat down while Sarah stood beside her.

"Do you know Playel's *Aria?*" Sarah whispered anxiously. Rosemary nodded, and Sarah grew weak with relief. If she had not known the song, the entire charade would have gone up in smoke. Rosemary placed her hands on the instrument and began to play.

What Sarah Mendenhall lacked in instrumental execution she made up for in vocal abilities. Her soprano voice was sweet and steady, and in their early music lessons Lady Rockwell had been pleased to discover that her pitch was nearly perfect. It was lucky for Sarah that Miss Reed was such an accomplished pianist and knew the piece well. Sarah sang beautifully, and the duet was met with thunderous applause at its conclusion. Miss Elizabeth sat in sulky silence, not only because Sarah had bested her, but because she seemed to have gained even more admirers during her performance. Sarah managed to wriggle away from the dandies that flocked to her side and squeezed Rosemary's hand.

"Miss Reed, thank you *so* much for coming to my rescue!" she gushed. "I do not know what I would have done if you had refused to help me." The relief was evident in Sarah's voice, and her new friend smiled shyly up at her.

"It was my pleasure, Miss Mendenhall."

"Your mother was right—you are an excellent musician."

Rosemary blushed and looked down. "You are very kind."

"Do say that you will come visit me," Sarah whispered as Mrs. Reed came to claim Rosemary's attention. "I should so like to make your better acquaintance."

Rosemary smiled and nodded as her mother drew her away. Sarah let her go with a cheerful wave, but she was soon drawn back to the flattering young gentlemen who clamored for her attention.

Across the room, Peter Mills leaned casually against the wall and watched the scene before him with amusement. Another young gentleman came and stood beside him, following his gaze. Turning to Peter, the gentleman smiled.

"Is not Miss Mendenhall the most enchanting creature you ever beheld?" His voice betrayed his admiration, and Peter turned his lazy eyes upon him.

"She is certainly causing quite a stir in society," he agreed. He looked back towards Sarah, whose musical laughter could be heard across the large room. Her cobalt eyes were bright with excitement; she obviously enjoyed the attentions of her many admirers, despite her flippant regard for any of them. She turned her head and caught Peter's eye just then, and he winked at her.

Sarah deliberately turned her head.

Chapter 8

One week later

The melodic sounds of a string quintet floated softly through the still night air. Rex's carriage pulled up in front of the Willises' home, and he drew a deep breath. Tonight marked his first public appearance since his arrival in town, and if he was being honest with himself, he knew he had been dreading it. His object and desire for coming to town had been the same every year, but each year he had been disappointed. Would this season follow like all the others?

Alighting from the carriage, he glanced up at the house. Light poured from every window, flooding the street with counterfeit warmth. Squaring his shoulders, he walked resolutely up to the front door and knocked.

He handed the butler his invitation and was shown into the drawing room. A few surprised looks met his entrance, but he smiled and nodded to those whom he knew. Two matrons stood to his right whispering to one another, throwing disapproving looks in his direction. He ignored them as he milled about, acknowledging his acquaintances before making his way into the ballroom.

Rex knew he would be received differently in town now that news had spread about Caroline. Though improper relations were not uncommon, having an illegitimate child was heavily frowned upon. The persons involved often exiled themselves to the country, in order to avoid the vicious backlash of a hypocritical society. But that was not an option for Rex. More than saving his pride, he needed to save Caroline, and he was willing to endure whatever humiliation or embarrassment might come his way in order to do so.

Among the gentlemen of his acquaintance, Rex had been received in much the same way as he had in former years. There were a few guffaws and back-slapping, and a couple of knowing looks and winks, which he had anticipated. But when the patronesses of Almack's denied his application for a voucher, he knew that among the matronly set at least, he should expect more than a few condescending looks and disapproving whispers. Rex took it all in stride. As far as he could tell, people only knew about the existence of Caroline, and very little else. Though certain of receiving a snub if he attempted to court any woman of his former acquaintance, he still had good looks, charm, and the appearance of wealth on his side, which was sufficient enough to entice less sanctimonious women to marry him. He only hoped to be able to find one with enough money to help him out of his predicament.

He stood along the wall, watching the couples dancing and scanning the crowd for anyone he knew, or anyone he *should* know. The Thatchers were there, of course, and he observed Miss Elizabeth Brooks dancing with their son, Jeremy. The Reeds and the Staffords, being two of the oldest families in London, were also there in sufficient numbers, but there were several new faces with whom he was completely unfamiliar. A bewitching redhead stood close to Mrs. Ashby, and dancing near him in the set was a charming brunette with lively blue eyes and a trilling laugh.

Rex stepped away from a passing footman and saw Peter Mills slouching along the wall in his direction. His eyes narrowed. Rex did not particularly like his company, but under the present circumstances, he knew that a man with Peter Mills's connections was invaluable.

"See anything you like?" Peter asked him with a sly smile. Rex ignored the innuendo and nodded towards the dance floor.

"What can you tell me about the ladies here tonight?" he asked.

Peter crossed his arms and faced the room, suddenly business-like. "Miss Louisa Brooks has twelve thousand pounds, but is as good as engaged to the Earl of Somerset. Her sister is attached to Thatcher, but she may be won over. Miss McBride has recently inherited fifteen, but even for that I do not believe she is worth it." He frowned. "Mrs. Ashby's niece is visiting from Northampton, and though I have not yet made her personal acquaintance, I have heard that she has ten or fifteen as well."

"Who is the young lady dancing with Augustus Carlisle?" Rex asked, eyeing the pretty brunette again. Peter's eyes lit up.

"Ah, you have landed on the single most sought after belle of the season," Peter said with a smug smile.

Rex raised his eyebrows, clearly impressed. "She is very

pretty. And must have a handsome dowry if what you say is true."

But Peter was shaking his head. "No, indeed. A mere three thousand pounds is all she has to offer, and yet the gentlemen are wild about her."

"Only three thousand?" Rex repeated, surprised. He turned to watch her dance down the set, seeing how lightly she stepped and how gracefully she moved. Her eyes were bright and her smile lit up the room. He narrowed his eyes, looking deeper. She had a turned up nose, brilliant blue eyes, and an abundance of chestnut hair, curled and braided in extravagant loops on her head. She laughed, and the sound reached over the murmuring crowd and fell upon his ears like fairy music.

Mesmerized, he turned to the man beside him. "Who is she?" he asked again. Peter smirked.

"Miss Sarah Mendenhall, lately of Calcutta, India." Rex frowned, and Peter nodded across the room at the silver-haired matron watching the young débutante. "She is staying with Margaret Greenwood, the Countess of Rockwell."

Rex looked thoughtful. "She has connections, then."

Peter shrugged. "Connec*tion*," he corrected. "Her family is completely obscure. Her older brother married Lady Rockwell's granddaughter, from what I understand, and though the countess is her benefactor at present, she has attached no financial endowment to Miss Mendenhall." His look turned bored. "I cannot fathom what the young pups see in her."

Laughing, Rex turned to face him. "It sounds to me like someone has been snubbed by society's pet." His eyes held an accusing look, though he was obviously amused.

Peter rolled his eyes. "I knew she would never be a conquest of mine, so I am not greatly disappointed."

A surge of anger and revulsion welled up inside of Rex, and he hated Peter Mills in that instant. Desperate for a distraction, he cast his eyes around the room, and again they landed on Miss Mendenhall.

So many of the eligible young ladies of society were forgettable—even the handsome ones. They all seemed the same, year after year. But something about Sarah was different. Something in her air was so bewitching, so distinctive. And yet, aside from her eyes, none of her features were what society would call striking. Brown hair, a freckled nose, a small mouth, and a petite form. But when they were all of them combined into one cheerful, vibrant young lady, the effect was tremendous.

Sarah Mendenhall was absolutely extraordinary.

Rex watched her for several moments, until he was once again in command of his feelings. Sighing, he tore his eyes away from her.

"I need to marry money, Peter. And soon." He turned and scanned the room. "If Miss Mendenhall has no fortune, I will not be wasting my time chasing after her. Evidently there are plenty of young men to do that," he added dryly.

Peter was twisting one side of his sandy mustache, deep in thought. A sly smile crept across his face, and suddenly he snapped his fingers, slapping Rex on the back. "I have it. Five thousand pounds."

"Pardon?"

"Five thousand pounds says you cannot make Miss Sarah Mendenhall fall in love with you."

"You are out of your mind," Rex replied, looking away.

Peter chuckled. "No, I am pining for amusement, and this may turn out to be even more amusing than watching Freddy Grimshaw make a fool of himself."

Turning back with a shrewd look on his face, Rex studied him. "Why?"

Peter shrugged. "I just told you. I want to be amused." He smiled crookedly, a wicked glint in his eyes. "Consider it a business proposition, Rex. You need the money; I need the entertainment."

"And what of Miss Mendenhall?"

Peter shrugged again. "What of her? She has suitors enough, if she had a mind to settle down. If you cannot succeed, she will be no worse off. And if you do," he chuckled darkly, and Rex raised an eyebrow at him. "Well, she shall get a taste of her own medicine then, I suppose."

Rex turned away, disgusted. Men like Peter Mills would never know the value of a woman, would never understand what it meant to love and be loved by one of the fairer sex. His thoughts turned to Mary, and his gut twisted. Peter spoke of conquests, and Rex hated him for it.

But he hated himself more.

Though Rex had loved Mary with every fiber of his being, that is what she had been—a conquest.

Rex shook his head, striving to clear himself from the pain and guilt that gripped his heart. Peter was right, in one respect at least. Rex needed money. His situation demanded that he marry this season, but what if he did not? What would happen to Caroline if his money ran out? Peter's reasons for extending the wager were contemptible, to be sure, but Rex's reasons for accepting it need not be. Surely the welfare of a sweet, innocent child justified a little flirtation...

Rex squared his shoulders and held out his hand.

"Five thousand pounds," he said, shaking Peter's hand firmly. His comrade chuckled, clapping a hand on Rex's shoulder.

"Come, let me introduce you."

To say that Sarah was enjoying herself would be an understatement. She was rapture personified, and every dance brought more delight than the one before. She was never without a partner, and never had to wait more than two minutes for refreshment, so numerous were her admirers and so anxious to oblige. Taking a seat next to Rosemary, she laughed breathlessly.

"Oh Miss Reed, is this not the most wonderful night of your life?"

Rosemary smiled. "It is a marvelous ball," she said. "But where are your beaux? They have been trailing after you all night," she finished with a laugh.

"I have managed to escape them at last," Sarah replied with false annoyance. But her eyes twinkled merrily, and Rosemary laughed again.

"You like having them around, admit it," she said to her friend, nudging her playfully. Sarah giggled.

"Of course I do! Though I *did* want to slip away and see you for a moment. I am so glad you came to visit me this week, for you are just the sort of friend for whom I have been longing." She squeezed her arm affectionately. "Are you enjoying yourself?

Tell me, which of them are your favorites?" she asked conspiratorially, sidling up to Rosemary and looking out over the room. Rosemary blushed.

"I have not as many to choose from as you," she said modestly.

"Enough to have a preference though, if I am not mistaken," came the reply. Scrutinizing the colored waistcoats filling the dance hall, Sarah nodded at a few of them.

"I like Freddy Grimshaw, though I have already refused him once," Sarah said. "And Augustus Carlisle is so diverting! I declare, he had me laughing the entire time we were dancing. But there are quite a few gentlemen here tonight with whom I am not yet acquainted."

Rosemary followed her eyes, and smiled when she saw where they were trained. "That is my cousin, Anthony Reed. He has just taken a commission in the North, so you will not be able to bewitch him for long," she teased.

Sarah smiled, nodding at another guest. "And who is that gentleman? Standing with Peter Mills."

Rosemary had to wait for a couple in the set to pass before she could answer, but her face was grave when she did. "That is Mr. Jameson Rex, who until this year was one of the most eligible bachelors in town."

Sarah was intrigued. "What made him so eligible?"

"Well, he is handsome, for one thing," Rosemary said. Sarah could see that for herself. He was tall and dark, with chiseled features and a strong jaw. His figure was trim and his clothes tailored to accent his lean frame. Sarah noticed that hers was not the only pair of female eyes trained on his face, and she turned back to Rosemary, clearly impressed.

"The ladies must be positively wild for him!" she said, admiration reflected in her voice.

"Well... some are. He has a very nice estate in Surrey, and he is due to inherit a large fortune from his uncle as well."

"No wonder he is so eligible," Sarah murmured.

"*Was*," Rosemary corrected her.

Sarah turned to face her. "What happened to make him less desirable?"

Rosemary glanced around, then bent her head towards her friend. Sarah leaned in, anxious to hear some new gossip.

"His uncle discovered a little girl at his estate," Rosemary said solemnly. "She was calling him Papa."

Sarah's eyes grew wide. "He has a child?"

Rosemary nodded.

"But has he never been married?"

Her friend shook her head.

Sarah turned away, troubled. An unmarried gentleman, harboring a girl? What sort of man would have the audacity to raise an illegitimate child? She frowned.

"How old is the girl?"

"I believe she is four or five years old."

"And no one had any idea of her existence until now?" Sarah replied incredulously. Her friend shook her head.

Sarah was thoughtful. "But how could that be? Certainly *someone* would have known about her..." Surely there was some cause or explanation for his actions, but what?

Sarah turned back to get a better look at the gentleman in question. He was smiling now, and the change in his features was subtle but pleasing. Though at first glance his handsome face had appeared quite stern, there was a softening around his eyes when he smiled. She found herself wondering what color they were, and wishing she were closer. Suddenly he turned and looked straight into Sarah's eyes. She gasped and turned away, but not before she saw a similar look of surprise reflected in his own face.

"Well, he is certainly very handsome," she stammered to Rosemary, blushing. She pulled at her gloves, resisting the urge to peek over her shoulder to see if he was still watching her.

He was.

"Ah, Miss Mendenhall!"

Sarah was returning on the arm of William Stafford when Mrs. Ashby greeted her. Peter Mills and Jameson Rex now stood beside her niece, Mary Anne, with whom Sarah had been getting better acquainted before she was asked to dance. She thanked Mr. Stafford, who excused himself and withdrew. Determined to be polite, Sarah nodded and smiled at Peter.

"Mr. Mills, how are you this evening?"

"Better now that you have graced me with one of your smiles, Miss Mendenhall," he said gallantly, bowing low. Sarah wanted to roll her eyes but managed a little laugh instead.

"We were just making the acquaintance of Mrs. Ashby's niece," Peter continued, nodding towards the pretty redhead. "And since my friend expressed a wish to know you as well, I promised to introduce him to you. Miss Mendenhall, may I present Mr. Jameson Rex."

Sarah turned to the tall, handsome man standing beside Peter. Despite his somewhat sober appearance, he had a pleasing face, framed on three sides by jet black hair and side whiskers. Standing before him, Sarah could now see that his eyes were gray —no, blue. They held a hint of amusement, as if there were a teasing remark poised on his lips. She smiled, looking up at him through her lashes as she curtsied, and the corners of his mouth drew up as well.

"I am pleased to make your acquaintance, sir," she said. His smile grew ever so slightly as he bowed.

"Not so pleased as I am, Miss Mendenhall."

His voice was deep and his tone respectful, without a hint of flirtatious suggestion. It was a refreshing change for Sarah, and she liked it very much.

The current in the room shifted as the musicians began to play another song. Sarah clasped her hands together, her blue eyes shining with delight.

"Oh, the waltz!" she said with longing.

"May I have the pleasure, Miss Mendenhall?" Rex asked cordially.

Sarah promptly accepted, taking his arm and following him to the dance floor. Rex put his right hand on her waist and her heart jumped. While she reveled in the romantic steps and the graceful turns of the waltz, she was still unaccustomed to the closeness of her partner during the dance. She placed her right hand in his left and looked up at his face. A faint smile played around his lips, and the look of merriment in his eyes grew to fill his entire expression. It intrigued her; she wanted to know what he found so amusing.

Rex led them gracefully through the opening steps. He was a divine dancer, and Sarah noted his strong grip and confident manner as he led her first one way, then another. She glanced around the room at the other dancers every few moments, but Rex never took his eyes off her face. After several minutes she could stand the silence no longer.

"What do you find so fascinating in my face, Mr. Rex?" she asked, unashamed. He raised one eyebrow and grinned crookedly at her.

"I am merely trying to discover what it is that has the whole of London in a turmoil. As far as I can tell, there is nothing extraordinary about you."

Sarah gasped, narrowing her eyes at him. "I believe that is the first time a gentleman has ever dared insult me," she said with false indignation. But the amusement in her eyes could not be contained, and Rex winked.

"You are certainly charming when you pretend to be angry," he said. "I will give you that. But what else is there? How have you managed to ensnare half the male population of London in less than a month?"

Sarah smiled slyly. Dropping her eyes for a moment, she then looked up at him through her lashes. "Do you expect a lady to give away *all* of her secrets, Mr. Rex?" she asked a little breathlessly, her eyes intent on his face. For a moment Rex was stunned, and then he laughed.

"Well done, my dear!" he cried. "I believe I am beginning to understand your appeal. You are charming, flirtatious, coy, beautiful... and if I understand correctly, are playing hard to get."

He raised one eyebrow at her in question, but she scoffed.

"I am *not* a flirt," she said emphatically. "That was merely for your own benefit, and to teach you the consequences of being impudent to pretty young women. And furthermore," she continued, as Rex shook his head, chuckling, "I am not playing hard to get. This is my first season in London, and I intend to enjoy myself fully and completely. An engagement will only tie me down, and though I have no reservations about matrimony in general, I absolutely refuse to be drawn in this year."

"Very good, very good," he said. His eyes were brimming with hidden laughter, and Sarah noted how much more handsome he looked when he smiled in earnest. "I can fully appreciate your hesitation, as I have never been in a great hurry to marry myself."

"And what have your reasons been, sir?"

He shrugged. "I have not found the right lady," he said candidly. Sarah considered his answer in light of what she had discovered about him, and knew not what to think.

They had been waltzing for some time, weaving in and out of other couples, completely synchronous in their steps and movements. Rex led with such calm assurance, such graceful expertise that Sarah felt as if she were dancing on air. They were silent for a time, each of them studying their partner as if trying to piece together a puzzle. Presently Rex spoke.

"I understand you are lately from India, Miss Mendenhall."

Sarah's face lit up. "Yes, indeed. I have spent all my life in India."

"What brings you to England?"

Her look softened. "My brother, who came intent on winning the heart of the woman he loved." She explained that her dear friend Katherine Greenwood—the Countess of Rockwell's granddaughter—had spent nearly a year with them at their indigo plantation in Calcutta. Sarah's brother Charles had fallen in love with her there, and when Katherine returned to England, he followed in order to ask for her hand.

"They were married last May," Sarah continued, sighing at the memory. "And in August they left for India. But the countess grew fond of me, and asked if I would stay on as her companion." She smiled. "I have dreamed of London all my life, so I was happy to oblige."

"What about London intrigues you?" Rex asked, genuinely interested.

"Why, everything! The people, the town, the shopping..."

"Society?" Rex supplied.

"Precisely," Sarah said, smiling up into his eyes. He returned her smile, searching her face for a moment.

"Do you not miss India at all?" he finally asked.

Sarah opened her mouth to assure him that indeed, she did not, but his look was so intense, his question so sincere that she paused. "I suppose I do," she confessed after a moment, surprising even herself. "I never thought I would, since all my life I have wished for England."

"What do you miss about it?" he asked, his deep voice gentle.

Sarah grew thoughtful. "The beauty of the land. The cries of the birds." Suddenly her eyes grew bright. "And the flowers! So much variety and color. I never thought to cherish them when they were always before me, but now that they are not, I wish I had."

"Which are your favorites?"

"Probably jasmine. Their blossoms are so small and delicate, and their fragrance so delicious..." Her voice trailed off. "Yes, of all that I remember, it is jasmine that I miss most."

She looked up at him with a contented smile, and in that moment Rex saw what had bewitched all the others. The woman in his arms was honest, sincere, and completely unaffected. She had not been spoiled by pleasure and society, and the innocence she exuded was delightfully refreshing.

Rex would have to watch himself.

The dance ended just then, and he released his partner. He had not realized that throughout the waltz he had been drawing her ever closer, and their bodies had nearly been touching when he stepped away and bowed to her. Sarah's cheeks were faintly flushed, and her eyes were bright as she curtsied.

"Thank you for the dance, Miss Mendenhall," he said, holding out his arm. She took it with a smile.

"I am glad you asked me," she said frankly. Rex raised his eyebrows, surprised, but as they rejoined their party just then, he said nothing.

The couple were complimented on how well they danced, and Sarah felt a thrill of pleasure course through her. She had enjoyed the waltz with Rex, and found him even more fascinating than before. She kept glancing at his face, and when Rosemary joined them a short time later, she gave Sarah a significant look. When at last Peter and Rex excused themselves, Sarah watched them go with a sigh. It was only after they walked away that she realized Rex was the first gentleman, since her arrival in London, who had *not* asked to see her again.

Chapter 9

"Miss Rosemary Reed to see you, miss."

Sarah looked up from her painting and smiled at the butler. "Thank you, Lawrence. Please show her in."

Lady Rockwell came to stand behind Sarah, examining her work before Sarah put it away. The picture emerging from the canvas was of the tree outside the drawing room window. Tiny green buds sprouted along the knobby gray branches, and in the distance a flowering dogwood tree blossomed.

"Your work grows better every day, my dear."

Sarah let out her breath in a half sigh, half laugh. "I wish that Mr. Meijer felt the same. It seems the harder I work, the less pleased he is with my progress."

"That may be true, but would you have pushed yourself as hard if he had not been such an exacting tutor?"

Sarah smiled. "Perhaps not."

The countess chuckled. "*Indeed* not. I know your disposition far too well, Miss Mendenhall, for it is not unlike my own once was."

Sarah stared. "You were once as I am?"

"Not quite so popular, but just as silly and headstrong at times." The countess laughed when Sarah pretended to be affronted. "Never mind, *Mein Kind*. You know how fond I am of you." She patted Sarah's cheek affectionately and left the room.

Sarah removed her smock before putting her paints away, and soon the door opened again to admit her guest. Sarah went to meet her, extending her hands to clasp those of Rosemary's.

"I am *so* glad you have come, Miss Reed!" Sarah exclaimed, leading her to the settee. "Lady Rockwell is a fine companion, but she is not *you*."

Rosemary's cheeks turned pink, and she smiled fondly at her friend. "I was anxious to get away. Mama has been dragging me around with her all morning and I thought I should never have escaped."

"Where have you been?" Sarah asked with interest.

"Oh, just visiting. We stopped to see Mrs. Ashby and her niece, as well as the Hamptons, the Walkers, and my Aunt Eugene—Anthony's mother."

"We stayed home this morning," Sarah said with complacency. "We have been out visiting so often that Lady Rockwell said we must remain at home in order to allow the visits to be repaid."

"Who has called?"

"A few of Lady Rockwell's friends came by this morning: Lady Derby and Mrs. MacFarland. But then Miss Elizabeth Brooks came by with her mother, and oh! The sour looks they kept giving me! As if I had poured lemon juice in their tea," Sarah giggled. "Jeremy Thatcher came in while they were here, and you should have seen the look on Miss Elizabeth's face! She was white as a ghost, and poor Mr. Thatcher was as red as a pumpkin."

"Poor Miss Elizabeth," Rosemary said with feeling. "She was so sure of Mr. Thatcher's affections."

Sarah waved her hand vaguely in the air. "They are still hers, I am sure. Jeremy Thatcher has only had his head turned because I am new in town and a bit more lively than Miss Elizabeth. But he has been courting her for two seasons now, has he not? They will make a match of it yet, I am sure, for I have told Mr. Thatcher off a time or two already."

"I cannot imagine how you do it."

"Do what?"

"Speak with such candor and frankness to your gentleman friends."

Sarah shrugged. "They are all of them a little lovesick, but I have not had my head turned by a single one of them, and I do not intend to. I see them all as my friends, and a jolly set they are, too."

Rosemary shook her head, still quite in awe. The talk turned to sundry other subjects: how many new gowns Rosemary had had made up for the season, if they were attending the ball at Almack's next Wednesday, and what exactly Mrs. Reed thought about Mr. Nelson, whom Sarah knew to be a favorite of Rosemary's. Her friend blushed when Sarah asked this, but was spared having to answer by a knock at the door.

Lawrence came in carrying a large bouquet of flowers and a

card on a silver salver. "This has just arrived for you, miss," he said, stopping in front of Sarah and bowing slightly. Sarah cried out in delight and clapped her hands.

"Oh, how lovely. Miss Reed, have you ever seen such delicious carnations?" She took the card and smiled at the butler. "Please put them in some water and place them with the others, Lawrence."

"Others?" Rosemary asked as Lawrence quit the room.

"Yes, there have been three other bouquets sent this morning alone," Sarah smiled happily, oblivious to the astonished look on her friend's face. "One from Freddy Grimshaw, of course (he sends one every day), one from William Stafford, and one from Peter Mills, which I nearly threw out, but the roses were *so* divine. I simply did not have the heart."

"I wonder who this one is from?" Rosemary asked, remembering to be polite.

"I do not know," Sarah replied as she turned the note over in her hands. The script was clean and elegant, but it was not a hand she recognized. She broke the seal and unfolded the note, which was written on a slip of fine, thin paper. Spreading it open, she read the contents aloud.

" 'To Miss Mendenhall, with my sincere compliments.' "

"Is it not signed?" Rosemary asked, leaning forward. Sarah shook her head.

"No, not at all. Not even his initials."

"Here, let me see."

Sarah handed the note to Rosemary, who scrutinized the writing. She turned the paper over in her hands and studied the seal. Suddenly she cried out.

"That is the Rex family crest!" She looked up at Sarah with wonder. "Jameson Rex sent you flowers."

"Jameson Rex?" Sarah asked with amusement. "Hmm. I would not have thought it of him. He did not seem to be much impressed with me," she murmured, thinking over their conversation at the ball and remembering that he had not asked to see her again.

"I think he must be," her friend replied with some trepidation.

Lawrence reentered the room just then, carrying a large crystal vase overflowing with pink blossoms. He set it down on a marble-topped table near one of the windows, which held three other vases filled with flowers. Sarah smiled, looking over at the table filled with blooms. There were roses from Peter, orchids from Mr. Stafford, daisies and chrysanthemums from Freddy, and now carnations from Rex. Her eyes skipped from vase to vase, thinking of the men who sent them. Her gaze lingered on the rosy blossoms most recently received, and her mind went back to the ball the previous evening, and the dance she had shared with Rex. There was something discordant in his manner that unsettled her, but she could not yet put her finger on it.

She tapped her nose thoughtfully. He was certainly intriguing, and though Sarah did not think it wise to encourage his attentions, she decided not to reject them, either. Surely there was more to Jameson Rex than anyone knew, and Sarah was determined to discover what it was.

The following evening Sarah and Lady Rockwell attended the theatre with the Ramseys. Lady Rockwell's box had a fine view of the stage, and Sarah was most anxious to watch the performance, but it seemed that Edward Ramsey had other plans.

"You look positively divine this evening, Miss Mendenhall," he said as she entered the box, bowing low and kissing her gloved hand. Sarah wore her pink satin evening gown, a string of pearls clasped around her throat and woven into her rich brown tresses. Her bright blue eyes were rendered even more vivid in contrast to her attire, and she smiled sweetly at him.

"Thank you, Mr. Ramsey, you are most kind."

Edward Ramsey's chest puffed out like a peacock. He was an ordinary sort of man; a bit too thin for fashion and possessing a forgettable face.

"Would you care for some refreshment before the show?" he asked.

"No, thank you."

Sarah took her seat near the front of the box, peering over the balcony at the people gathering in the seats below. She was glad to see that Miss Elizabeth Brooks was seated next to Mr. Jeremy Thatcher and his mother, and she observed Mrs. Ashby seated with her niece a few rows behind them. Sarah smiled and waved at them and Mrs. Ashby waved jovially back. The box opposite them held several members of the Stafford family, and Sarah nodded politely in their direction.

"Have you seen *It Takes Two* before, Miss Mendenhall?" Mr. Ramsey asked.

"No, I have not yet had the pleasure."

"Well," he continued, seating himself beside her. "It is a

wonderful little show about a man named Mr. Thurgood and a woman named Mrs. Tuttle, who conspire to bring their children together in *matrimony*," he said the word slowly, drawing it out, "though the young people themselves have no desire to be joined."

"It sounds fascinating," Sarah said politely, still scanning the crowd for anyone else she might know.

"Oh, it is, as you will soon judge for yourself. You see, Miss Tuttle and Mr. Thurgood (the younger one, that is) have no desire to be *married*," he looked at Sarah meaningfully, "but they cannot convince their parents of this. So they hatch a plan to fool their elders that throws everything into a turmoil."

"Indeed!" was all Sarah could manage to say.

"Yes. But of course their plan does not turn out they way they wish. In the second act—"

"Mr. Ramsey," Sarah interjected, striving to hide her annoyance, "I really would like to see how the play unfolds by watching it myself."

He looked surprised at being interrupted, but soon recovered himself, smiling at her condescendingly and moving his chair just a bit closer to her own. "Of course, Miss Mendenhall," he said, his voice low in an attempt at intimacy. "But as the plot is undeniably complicated, allow me to interject at times, in order to explain what happens from scene to scene which allows the *marriage* to eventually take place." His nondescript eyes gazed into her own in a way that was surely meant to be romantic, but Sarah found his look so comical that she turned away, coughing into her handkerchief in order to hide a sudden attack of giggles.

"Miss Mendenhall, what is the matter?" he asked with alarm.

"Nothing, nothing," she tried to assure him, coughing so hard that tears began to form in her eyes.

"Is there anything I can do?"

"A glass of water, please," she gasped.

As soon as he had left, Sarah stopped coughing and allowed herself a hearty laugh. Lady Rockwell shot her a severe look, but it took Sarah several minutes longer to recover completely. She sat up, wiping the tears from her eyes and holding her side as she strove to catch her breath.

"May I ask what you find so amusing, Miss Mendenhall?"

The deep voice of Jameson Rex sounded in her ear, and Sarah looked up quickly. He was standing just behind her, and she was so surprised at seeing him suddenly appear that she swallowed the laugh beginning to form and hiccuped instead.

"Oh dear, Mr. Rex, you startled me!" she said.

"My apologies, but I observed you and Lady Rockwell as you came in, and I wished to pay my respects."

"Please, do sit down," she offered politely, clearing her throat and smiling at him. "I shall be happy to tell you what I was laughing at."

He bowed and took the seat next to her. The contrast between him and its former occupant was so great that another fit of giggles threatened to erupt, but she managed to hold them in check. She could not contain her grin, however, and she radiated such playful energy that Rex found himself smiling as widely as she was. She glanced quickly around them, then leaned in so as not to be overheard.

"Edward Ramsey has been trying to make me fall in love with him."

97

"Oh?"

"Yes." She giggled. "But he has no idea how to go about it, poor man. He keeps dropping hints about *marriage* and *matrimony*... as if saying the words enough will make me think of entering into it with him!"

Rex managed a sympathetic chuckle. "Poor devil. He will soon join the ranks of the other brokenhearted snubs of Miss Sarah Mendenhall."

Sarah waved her hand impatiently in the air. "There is no such thing. None of the men I have discouraged are truly in love with me, and I am not in love with any of them."

Amused, Rex sat back in his chair, folding his arms across his chest. "They have all been going about it wrong, have they?"

"Going about what wrong?"

"Making you fall in love with them."

A more modest girl would have blushed and changed the subject, but Sarah took his question to heart. "Yes, I suppose they have," she said thoughtfully.

Rex burst out laughing, and both Mrs. Ramsey and Lady Rockwell looked in their direction with disapproval. Sarah knew that Lady Rockwell did not like Jameson Rex, but as she had not forbidden Sarah from associating with him, she felt no unease.

"Then tell me, Miss Mendenhall," Rex said, a crooked smile on his face, "how *would* a gentleman go about making you fall in love with him?"

"Goodness, how should I know?" Sarah asked. "I have never been in love before, and have no idea how it is done."

Rex seemed amused by her answer. "But have you no sense of your personal tastes, your own likes and dislikes, to give you an understanding of how it might happen?"

"None whatsoever," she replied easily. "I suspect I shall never know when I am in love. One day, a man will simply ask for my hand and I shall accept." She laughed airily, and he shook his head in disbelief.

"Unbelievable," he said. His eyes were full of mirth, and though Sarah liked the admiration she saw there, she did not think it wise to encourage him further. She smiled at him.

"It was very kind of you to come and say hello," she said with a tone of gentle dismissal. Rex took the hint and stood, bowing low.

"Believe me, Miss Mendenhall, the pleasure was entirely on my side." He leaned in ever so slightly. "But do not be too hard on young Ramsey—you have no idea how enchanting you really are," he said in an undertone. Before Sarah's face could register her surprise, he turned and was gone.

It was not long before Edward Ramsey returned with a glass of water for her, and she took it gratefully. Sipping the drink, she mulled over the man and the conversation she had just encountered. Though the lights dimmed, the curtain opened, and Edward Ramsey continued to whisper ineffectual compliments in her ear, Sarah was oblivious to them all.

She was thinking of Jameson Rex.

Chapter 10

April gave way to May, and soon the drab, gray raindrops falling from the sky lost their icy chill. Spring had arrived in London, and brought with it not only rain but an abundance of flowers. Daffodils and crocuses bloomed in every garden, and Sarah saw the beauty emerging from the damp, black earth with gladness.

Rosemary called in Cavendish Square one drizzly morning to invite Sarah to go shopping. She was surprised when it was only Lady Rockwell that met her in the drawing room.

"Is Miss Mendenhall unwell?" she asked with concern.

"No, but she has not yet finished with her tutor. Come, have some tea—she will join us shortly."

The last hour had been another grueling, disheartening lesson for Sarah. Mr. Meijer lectured her until she was on the verge of tears. "You have forgotten," he scolded. "You have made some pretty paintings and think you are an expert, but you are not! Look at this." He jabbed a finger harshly at a watercolor she had recently completed: a depiction of the carnations Rex had sent. "These blossoms are atrocious. You did not even bother to form the petals, but scribbled over the blobs and call it a flower—bah!"

Sarah clenched her teeth together to keep a sob from escaping.

"Now, see this, here," Mr. Meijer continued, his tone softening somewhat. He gestured to the unfinished picture currently before her. It was the scene from the window, with the knobby branches and dogwood tree blooming in the distance. It had been the main subject of her lesson that morning and was nearly finished. "This has potential. This is good." He turned and looked intently into her face. "But this is where you begin to be impatient in all the others! You *must not* rush the art! Let it come to you."

Sarah gulped and nodded, and her tutor sighed. "That is enough for today. We shall try again next week."

Ten minutes later Sarah joined Lady Rockwell and Rosemary in the drawing room. When asked about her lesson, she shook her head and refused to comment. Anger and frustration still burned within her, though it was difficult to determine if the majority of her displeasure was directed at Mr. Meijer or herself. She was grateful when Rosemary stated the reason for her visit, and gladly agreed to accompany her.

Sarah sighed as the carriage door closed behind them. "Oh, Miss Reed," she said dramatically. "I fear I shall never learn to paint properly."

"Of course you will! Your work is lovely, and far superior to

101

anything I have produced."

Sarah managed a faint smile. "Thank you, dear, that is very kind. But never mind—I wish to forget about art for the moment and enjoy myself. Where are we off to this morning?"

"Mama asked me to pick up her new hat, and I would like very much to get another pair of evening gloves. Beth soiled my best pair last week and I simply cannot get the stains out."

They chatted as the carriage rolled southward to Bond Street, where the fashionable shops of London butted against one another in expensive little rows. London was bursting with occupants now that Parliament and the Season were in full cry, and the street was bustling with carriages full of other eager shoppers.

They pulled up in front of Mrs. Reed's favorite milliner's, and one of the footmen helped the ladies down from the carriage. The road was slick from the night's rain, and their pattens made little tinkling sounds as they approached the door of the shop. Suddenly Sarah slipped, and with a cry of dismay found herself falling backwards onto the wet cobbles.

A strong arm shot out from the crowd and caught her elbow, and though Sarah's feet still slid from beneath her, she did not land on her backside in the mud as she anticipated, so firm was the grip on her arm.

"Careful now; here, take my hand," a masculine voice instructed.

The voice was deep and authoritative, but gentle in tone and address. Sarah looked up, taking Rex's other hand. She smiled gratefully at him.

"Thank you, Mr. Rex," she said with feeling, finding her

footing once more. She reached for Rosemary, and Rex released her into her friend's care.

"Are you hurt?" he asked, concern lacing his voice.

"No. Thanks to your quick reflexes, nothing but my pride has been damaged," Sarah replied with a little laugh. A smile tugged at the corner of Rex's mouth, but he merely nodded and tipped his hat.

"I am glad to hear it," he said. "Is there somewhere I may escort you, to ensure your safe arrival?"

"Thank you, but no; this is where we are bound." Sarah smiled and nodded at the shop before them.

Rex bowed. "Then I shall bid you farewell. Good day, Miss Mendenhall; good day, Miss Reed." Touching his hat once again to each of them, he smiled and strode off.

Sarah watched him go, and Rosemary slipped an arm through hers. "How fortunate that Mr. Rex was passing just at that moment!" she said, as the ladies drew up to the front door. "I hate to think what a dreadful fall you would have taken had he not caught you."

They spent the next half hour browsing the various articles of fashion and dress which excite and delight young ladies of their age. Rosemary collected her mother's hat, and found a new pair of ivory evening gloves for herself. Sarah scrutinized a daring little cap of scarlet felt, with feathers and ribbons sticking cock-eyed from the side of it.

"You are not going to purchase it," Rosemary asked, wariness coloring her voice.

Sarah laughed and plucked it from the table. Removing her bonnet, she set the cap at a jaunty angle over one eye.

"There! How do I look?"

Her friend laughed, but her look was admiring. "It is far more fetching on you than I imagine it would be on me."

"It *is* rather becoming, is it not?" Sarah replied, gazing at her reflection in a small glass that hung on the wall. "I have no idea when I shall wear it, since Lady Rockwell would surely disapprove, but I believe I shall get it nonetheless." She removed the ostentatious headpiece and took it to the counter. After paying the clerk, the ladies gathered their parcels and left the shop. A light rain was falling when they emerged, and Rosemary groaned.

"Oh, dear. We have been longer than I realized; Oscar must have taken the horses for a walk. Can you see them anywhere?"

"No, not at all," Sarah replied, looking up and down the street for a sign of the Reed's coach. "We may as well go back inside until he comes around again."

"But what if he turns the corner and does not see us waiting? He may continue on..." Rosemary's voice trailed off as she gnawed on her lip, not sure what to do.

"Then I shall stay out here and watch for him."

"Oh, no! You will catch your death of cold," her friend protested.

"And you shall ruin your mother's new hat if you stand outside another minute." Sarah handed her parcels to Rosemary and shooed her friend back to the warmth and dryness of the shop, assuring her that she would only be a moment.

The minutes ticked by while Sarah waited in the chilly drizzle, scanning the road in either direction for a sign of Oscar and the carriage. Other shoppers, sheltered from the rain by sleek black umbrellas, glanced at her sideways as they passed. Sarah smiled and nodded at them benignly, as if standing alone in the dreary spring rain were a natural thing for a young lady to do. Before long she began to feel the cold and dampness seeping through her skirts and dripping from her hair, but there was still no sign of the carriage.

Suddenly the rain was blotted out, and a low chuckle caused her to turn. Jameson Rex was standing beside her once more, holding his umbrella aloft to cover them both.

"It appears you are in need of assistance again, Miss Mendenhall," he said, his blue-gray eyes dancing merrily under the brim of his top hat. She smiled easily, matching his tone and teasing address.

"But of course, Mr. Rex. What better things have you to do today than rescue me?" she said sweetly. Rex laughed.

"How is it that you find me again, sir?" she asked after a moment. She narrowed her eyes in mock severity. "Are you following me?"

Still chuckling, Rex shook his head. "Indeed, I cannot acknowledge such a scheme, though I confess it is tempting." He winked at her. "No, I was patronizing the haberdasher's down the lane, and happened to be coming and going the same time as yourself."

He glanced around, a slight frown creasing his brow. "But where is Miss Reed? Surely she has not left you here..." Concern clouded his features, and Sarah sprang instantly to her friend's defense.

"No, indeed. When Miss Reed and I were finished with our business, we discovered the carriage had gone—Oscar must have taken the horses to walk so they will not freeze—and I volunteered to watch for them while she went back inside."

"Of course you did."

He was obviously amused at her predicament, but before she could reply he continued. "But seeing as how your carriage has not yet returned, please allow me to call a cab for both yourself and Miss Reed."

Sarah tried to object, but he was already hailing a passing coach, and insisted on helping Sarah into the hackney. He told the driver to wait as he went into the shop in search of Miss Reed. They emerged shortly after, and it seemed to Sarah that Rosemary was protesting the arrangement as well. Rex was insistent, however, and soon the ladies found themselves on their way home; Rex having paid their fare and given them assurance that he would watch for their coachman and send him on his way after them.

Rosemary sat in nervous agitation as the carriage bounced along the street. "What will Mother say when I return home without the coach?" she fretted.

"You will tell her that Oscar took the horses to walk, and Jameson Rex paid for a hackney so that we would not have to wait in the rain," Sarah said brazenly.

"Oh no, I could not!" Rosemary sounded appalled. "Mother does not at all approve of Mr. Rex. If she hears I have been in company with him... alone..." She shuddered, but Sarah scoffed.

"You were not alone; I have been with you the entire time."

Rosemary gave her a doubtful look, as if to convey that the notion of being with Sarah and Rex at the same time would not help to persuade her mother that nothing clandestine had happened between them. Sarah ignored her.

"Besides, there was nothing improper in what happened."

Her friend still did not look convinced, and Sarah shook her head in exasperation. "Leave Mr. Rex out of it then, if you like; simply tell your mother we were tired of waiting and hired a coach to take us home."

Rosemary considered for a moment, then smiled and nodded as she accepted the plan. The rain continued to fall as the coach rolled along the slippery streets.

"It is no wonder you have caught a cold," Lady Rockwell scolded.

Sarah came down to breakfast the next morning with a red nose and an aching head. The countess, who had sent Sarah back to bed at once, finished her breakfast alone. Now Lady Rockwell stood beside her, and from the look on the countess's face, Sarah knew she was in for a lecture.

"First you ran off without taking your umbrella, even though you knew it had been raining all night. Then you bought yourself an outrageous hat, which no respectable lady would ever wish to be seen in. And when at last you did arrive home, not only were you dripping wet, but you came in a hackney coach that Jameson Rex hired for you! *Was denkst du!*" Her tone made Sarah wince. The situation sounded so much worse coming from Lady Rockwell's lips.

"Standing in the rain, watching for the carriage," Lady Rockwell muttered. "What on earth were you thinking of?"

Sarah sighed. "Please do not shout at me, Lady Rockwell;

107

my head aches so."

"I am not shouting," the elderly woman replied, checking herself. She sat down in a chair facing the bed where her young charge lay. Betsy bathed Sarah's feverish brow with a cold cloth, and Lady Rockwell shook her head.

"Why did you not wait in the shop with Miss Reed?" Lady Rockwell asked again, though Sarah had already explained the reasons to her. "You would not have caught a chill, and you would not have run into Jameson Rex again."

It was clear from her tone which calamity Lady Rockwell believed to be the worse. Sarah merely sighed, knowing an answer was not expected. The older woman continued.

"I do not like the attentions he has been paying you, Miss Mendenhall," she declared. "Nor do I like the encouragement you have given him."

"I have not encouraged him," Sarah protested with a frown. "Has my behavior towards Mr. Rex been anything more than the conduct I have displayed towards other young gentlemen?"

Lady Rockwell was silent as she considered the question. Sarah met her piercing gaze with stubborn assurance, knowing what her answer would be. At last Lady Rockwell sighed.

"No, I suppose not," she answered reluctantly as Sarah lay back against the pillows. "But that does not mean that Mr. Rex understands your behavior; he may feel that you are soliciting his attentions."

"Mr. Rex is perfectly aware that I have no intention of accepting any proposal, from any young man," Sarah responded in a tired voice, throwing an arm carelessly across her face.

"There are plenty of women willing to accept the attentions

of a man without accepting anything else," Lady Rockwell said in an undertone. "Just promise me that you will be careful," she said more clearly. Sarah's arm dropped and she turned her head to look at the older woman.

"I promise, Lady Rockwell," she murmured. Sitting up, she looked at her guardian in earnest. "I do not doubt that there are many young women who have fallen for Mr. Rex's charms and attentions, but I assure you I shall not be one of them."

Lady Rockwell watched her for a long moment, searching Sarah's face. The pretty brunette gazed steadily back at her, a stubborn set to her lips. The look was very familiar to Lady Rockwell, who remembered looking and feeling much the same when she was young. At last the countess rose to her feet.

"Very well. Get some rest," she said gruffly. "We will not be able to attend Almack's this evening, but perhaps you will be well enough for the Stafford's party on Saturday night." She turned and left the room, leaving Sarah to convalesce in peace.

Chapter 11

A few days spent in bed soon set Sarah to rights, and though she lamented the lost evening at Almack's, she was looking forward to the Stafford's party with great interest. She dressed with care, choosing the peacock blue gown and a simple silver necklace as her only adornment. Betsy did her hair, and Sarah gazed in satisfaction at her reflection when her toilet was complete.

"You look lovely, miss," Betsy breathed, her eyes wide with admiration.

Sarah turned from the glass and brushed a soft kiss on her abigail's cheek. "You are a dear, Betsy. Thank you for your help."

Surprise and pleasure mingled on Betsy's face, but she merely ducked her head and busied herself tidying up.

Sarah felt as if she were floating on air as she went down to the drawing room a short time later. Lady Rockwell was already waiting, and soon they were tucked into the carriage and on their way to the party. Sarah watched out the misty window, where a nearly full moon reflected off the thick fog which filled the street, casting eerie shadows into the alleys and backways along their journey. She shivered.

They arrived just as the clock struck eight, but there was already a sizable number gathered in the grand house. The ladies were shown into one of the large drawing rooms on the second floor. Gilded mirrors and delicate tapestries lined the walls, and the vaulted ceilings were hung with crystal chandeliers that sparkled and shone like rainbow jewels. Sarah left her chaperon and crossed the room to greet Rosemary, who stood conversing with her mother and one of her sisters in a corner.

"Miss Reed, you look beautiful," Sarah greeted her friend, planting airy kisses on either cheek as the two young ladies embraced. Rosemary's cheeks flushed with pleasure as she returned the compliment.

"Thank you, Miss Mendenhall, but I pale in comparison to yourself," she said with awed admiration. "Wherever did you get such a gown?"

"Lady Rockwell had it made for me. Is it not stunning?" She took a step back and turned from side to side, smiling demurely at them. Rosemary laughed, Mrs. Reed sniffed, and the younger Miss Reed looked on in worshipful adoration.

"Stunning," Rosemary repeated.

The two friends linked arms and began to walk the perimeter of the room, chatting with each other about their families and the other parties and gatherings they planned on attending. The heads of several guests turned as they passed, drawn to the bold, beautiful gown and the pretty woman who wore it, but the friends were too engrossed in one another to notice. Sarah wanted to hear all about the ball at Almack's that she had missed, though Rosemary assured her it was very dull.

"Half the *ton* was at Madame Olivier's, I understand," Rosemary sighed.

"Who is Madame Olivier? Does she run another assembly hall?"

Astonished, Rosemary stopped walking. "Why, have you not heard of it?"

Sarah shook her head, and Rosemary smiled in delight. She knew how much Sarah relished good gossip, and it was a treat to be able to tell her something new. Rosemary led them to a small bench out of the way where they could converse undisturbed.

"Madame Antoinette Olivier runs a very fashionable place in Mayfair, along Piccadilly," Rosemary began, enjoying her role as informant to her eager friend. "She established it years ago, and it has grown quite popular."

"The French actress?"

"Yes, though she does not perform anymore—she is so busy running the rooms now. You see, as a singer and an actress, Madame Olivier's gatherings are a bit more... er, *stimulating* than the assemblies at Almack's."

"In what way?" Sarah asked breathlessly.

Rosemary glanced briefly around to make sure her mother was not listening, then leaned in and spoke softly.

"While she *does* give proper parties and dances like any other establishment, Madame Olivier is famous for one thing only: her masquerade balls."

Sarah drew in her breath, her eyes alight with excitement. "A masquerade! Oh, what a lark! Have you been to one yourself?"

"Goodness, no," Rosemary denied emphatically. "Mama would have a fit if I ever stepped foot in Madame Olivier's rooms."

"But, why?"

"Because with everyone wearing a mask, you cannot know who your partner is."

Sarah suddenly remembered Lady Rockwell's injunction: *Never dance with a gentleman you do not know or to whom you have not been introduced.* She frowned. "Have you never wished to go?"

Rosemary hesitated, not sure what answer to give. Sarah could see both the response she wanted to give and the response she felt she should give fighting for dominance in her friend's eyes, and she laughed triumphantly.

"You *have* wished to attend!" she breathed. Rosemary blushed and shook her head, but Sarah leaned in and spoke low in her ear.

"I don't blame you," she whispered conspiratorially. "For I should like to go the first opportunity I can." She drew back with a fierce look, daring her friend to believe her. Rosemary looked aghast.

"Lady Rockwell will never let you..." she began, but Sarah tossed her head.

"Lady Rockwell need *never know*," she countered, smiling mischievously. She turned abruptly, glancing around the room and remarking on the number gathered therein, but the brightness in her eyes convinced Rosemary that Sarah was not at all interested in the party surrounding them—she was forming a scheme to get them both to the masquerade.

The party was a gay affair, and all the principal families in London were in attendance. Rex was deep in a political argument with several members of parliament, though he held no seat himself. Peter Mills stood beside him, looking thoroughly bored with the conversation and glancing around the room in search of more lively entertainment. His eyes were drawn to the dazzling gown which Sarah wore, and his gaze lingered on the two young women. They sat slightly apart from the rest with their heads drawn together in an obviously intimate conversation. Peter smirked—what could they be talking of?

He turned from Rex and meandered across the room, bowing to his acquaintance as he passed and exchanging a few words with friends. He passed the two young ladies, who seemed oblivious to everything around them, and stationed himself a few feet away; his back to them, gazing out of a window at the dark night.

"Goodness, no," he heard Rosemary whisper emphatically. "Mama would have a fit if I ever stepped foot in Madame Olivier's rooms."

"Have you never wished to go?" Sarah's voice responded.

Madame Olivier? Peter stood perfectly still, straining to hear their conversation over the hum of a dozen others. He heard the hiss of a low, feminine voice, and turned ever so slightly to glance at them from the corner of his eye.

Sarah was gazing at her friend, a look of defiant

determination on her face. "Lady Rockwell need *never know*," he thought he heard her say. Suddenly they were talking of the party, laughing gaily and striving no more to conceal their conversation. Turning away from them, he replayed the conversation in his mind. A slow smile spread across his face as he turned in search of Rex. He saw him standing where he had left him. Anxious to disclose what he had learned, Peter strode purposefully across the room.

Rex was speaking when Peter walked up, but he caught Peter's eye and a silent communication passed between them. When Mr. Stafford picked up the conversation, Rex glanced at Peter, who leaned in and spoke quietly.

"I have it on good authority that Miss Mendenhall would like to visit Madame Olivier's establishment."

Rex narrowed his eyes. "How good is your authority?" he murmured.

"I heard it from Miss Mendenhall herself."

Surprised, Rex excused himself from the other conversation and turned fully towards Peter, each of them stepping away for more privacy.

"Lady Rockwell will never approve," Rex frowned.

"Of course not. But I do not think she is planning to ask for the countess's permission." Peter briefly related to him what he had seen and heard.

Rex rubbed his chin thoughtfully. "It will take some planning, but I think I can manage it."

"If any man can pull off such a clandestine scheme, it is you."

Resentment boiled up inside of Rex at his words, but his

handsome face showed no sign of unrest.

"Where is Miss Mendenhall now?" he asked, scanning the room.

His gaze fell upon her just as Peter nodded in her direction, and for a moment time seemed suspended. Her magnificent blue gown stood out among the creams and pinks in the room like a bird of paradise: beautiful, elegant, and more stunning than all the others. Sarah was encircled by a loose gathering of friends and admirers, laughing and talking with gay animation. Beauty and happiness radiated from her like sunlight, drawing everyone near to feel of her warmth. She laughed, and the tinkling notes reached his ears like the chiming of fairy bells, breaking his reverie. Drawing a breath, Rex tore his eyes from her face. Peter chuckled beside him.

"Oh, dear," he clucked accusingly. "Has Miss Mendenhall cast a spell over the unconquerable Jameson Rex?"

Rex rolled his eyes for his comrade's benefit. "Of course not. I am merely studying my opponent." He smiled wryly, and Peter laughed, clapping him on the shoulder.

"Good man, good man. I am happy to see you are taking to the sport."

Rex nodded curtly and turned away. "You shall have your sport," he muttered under his breath as he drew away.

He approached the throng surrounding Miss Mendenhall, and was happy to see that he immediately caught her attention. Her vivid blue eyes sparkled with merriment and Rex again found himself lost in her gaze. She was surrounded on all sides by admirers, and Rex was contemplating how to get her alone when she greeted him.

"And here is Mr. Rex," Sarah sang out, flashing him a smile that would dazzle any man. "I beg you will all forgive me, but I have promised this gentleman a turn about the room, and I see he has come to claim my attentions."

Rex most certainly had *not* obtained any such promise from her, but he bowed and smiled, playing along. The gentlemen surrounding Sarah were forced to stand back as she took Rex's proffered arm, and the two of them walked away.

As soon as they were clear of the crowd, Sarah heaved a sigh of relief. "Thank you, Mr. Rex. Your arriving just at that moment was Providential."

Amused, Rex raised his eyebrows. "I am happy to be of service, Miss Mendenhall, but tell me—why were you so keen to escape?"

"One can only handle so much of a good thing, you know," she said with a coy smile. "Do you not ever tire of having women thrown at your feet and hanging from your arm yourself?"

Rex chuckled. "I do not seem to have as great a number of admirers as you do, Miss Mendenhall."

"Not this year, perhaps. But Miss Reed told me you were the most sought after bachelor in town before—" She suddenly stopped, mortified to find herself speaking thus to Jameson Rex. Her face flushed crimson and she looked away, wishing her words unsaid.

Surprisingly, Rex laughed. "Is that so? The most sought after bachelor in town, hmm," he mused. "Peter Mills will be disappointed to hear that."

Sarah ventured a peek at his face. His gray-blue eyes were brimming with amusement, and relief flooded her mind as she realized he was not offended.

"Mr. Rex, I beg you will forgive me," she began, tripping over her words in her haste to apologize. "I cannot believe that I —"

"Think nothing of it, Miss Mendenhall," he interrupted, smiling at her.

Sarah's cheeks burned with shame, and she walked in agonizing silence beside him for several moments. At last Rex broke the silence.

"What else did Miss Reed tell you about myself?" he asked easily.

Sarah groaned inwardly. If only she had held her tongue! She glanced at him again, but there was no anger in his face, only genuine curiosity. She sighed.

"I suppose I should tell you, though it might upset you to hear it."

Rex laughed darkly. "I highly doubt that, Miss Mendenhall. In all likelihood I have already heard it."

She considered his response, and decided he was probably right. "She told me that a young girl was discovered at your estate, and that the child was calling you 'Papa.' "

He nodded slowly. When she did not continue, he looked down at her. "And?"

Shrugging her shoulders, Sarah added, "That was all."

He stopped and turned to her, his face serious. "Did she not also tell you that I have never been married?"

Sarah squirmed under his gaze. "Well, yes, she did," she admitted, "but you told me as much yourself, sir."

"Did I?"

"Yes, indeed. When we danced together, at the Willises' ball."

Surprised, Rex thought back to his interactions with Sarah on that night. He reflected on their first meeting, and what he had disclosed during the dance they had shared. Slowly he nodded.

"So I did," he said at last, recalling their conversation.

Sarah blew out her breath in one big huff. "There. Now all that is behind us, perhaps we might enjoy ourselves?" She looked up at him expectantly, a smile in her eyes and her voice.

"But is the reputation of a lady such as yourself quite safe, do you think, in the company of a scoundrel such as I?" he asked in mock astonishment. Sarah rolled her eyes and laughed, grateful to see that his mood had lightened.

"I am in no very great danger, I believe," she replied playfully.

He narrowed his eyes, and his mouth turned up on one side. His crooked grin and piercing gaze were enough to make any young lady swoon, and Sarah hardly expected the next words he spoke.

"But what if I *were* to endanger your reputation? On purpose?"

For a moment Sarah's blood ran cold. But despite his rakish look, Sarah could detect a playful spark in his gray eyes, and she decided to play along.

"Well now, that changes things," she said slowly, her smile fading and her face serious. Glancing around, she whispered, "What did you have in mind?"

Rex threw back his head and laughed, and Sarah joined in, delighted at the pleasure her unexpected response gave him.

When at last he gained control of his voice once more, he shook his head, a look of admiration in his steely eyes.

"You, my dear, are amazing." He was still chuckling, but as their laughter died down, his eyes turned serious. "But in truth, I was quite in earnest. I fear I have something to propose that, should you choose to accept, may jeopardize your reputation."

Confused, Sarah said nothing. Keeping his eyes locked on her face, he murmured. "I understand you wish to attend a masquerade ball at Madame Olivier's."

First surprise and then bewilderment played across her features as he waited patiently for Sarah to speak. At last she asked, "How did you know?"

Rex winked at her. "We rakes have our way of knowing these things."

She laughed lightly, but lowering her voice said, "You are right. I have heard that Madame Olivier is famous for her masquerade balls, and I am determined to attend one." She watched him closely, measuring how much he knew. He met her gaze with his own, a hint of a smile playing about his straight lips and no sign of surprise in his eyes. Sarah's heart pounded as she asked, "Will you help me?"

Rex watched her face intently, purposely remaining silent long enough to see a shadow of uncertainty creep into her eyes. His eyes never strayed from her own, and the intensity burning within them made Sarah feel as if his look might consume her in an instant. Abruptly he smiled, that crooked grin she was learning to appreciate.

"My dear, I thought you would never ask," he said.

Chapter 12

Sarah waited impatiently as Betsy put the finishing touches to her hair. "That will do, Betsy," she said curtly.

"Can I 'elp you with anythin' else, miss?"

"No, Betsy, thank you. Tell Lady Rockwell I shall be down directly." Her maid curtsied and turned to leave. "Oh, and Betsy?"

Though her servant paused and looked back at her, Sarah kept her face turned away. "Please let Lawrence know that Miss Reed will be calling for me at nine. She has a little cold, so she will not likely come inside—just tell him to inform me when the carriage arrives, please."

Betsy acknowledged her directions and left the room. Finally alone, Sarah turned again to look at her reflection. She was wearing a creamy silk gown with tiny rosebuds embroidered on it, scattered across the full skirt in clusters of three or four. The crimson blossoms made her own rosy cheeks appear even more brilliant. *Lady Rockwell will think I am painted*, she thought to herself, frowning. But there was no help for it. Her excitement for the evening, coupled with her nerves, lent a high flush to her cheeks, and she trembled as she considered what she was about to undertake.

Ten days had passed since the party at the Staffords. Ten days since Jameson Rex had agreed to help Sarah attend a masquerade ball at Madame Olivier's. Ten days of careful planning and whispered conversations with Rosemary, who had only agreed to the scheme because she was more frightened of *not* knowing what happened to Sarah than she was of her own mother.

Rex had told Sarah to be ready for his carriage at nine o'clock sharp on Tuesday, and to make sure she had an alibi to give to Lady Rockwell. It had not been difficult to convince Rosemary that the easiest alibi was for Sarah to tell Lady Rockwell she was going out with Mrs. and Miss Reed, and for Rosemary to tell *her* mother she was going out with Sarah and the countess.

"But where shall I tell her we are going?" Rosemary lamented.

"Tell her we have been invited to an exclusive dinner in Berkeley Square, and that as my particular friend I wish for you to accompany me."

Rosemary looked alarmed. "I have never told a falsehood to my mother before."

"Do you want to go to the masquerade or not?" Sarah asked impatiently. Rosemary nodded, though she still looked like a frightened child.

"And be sure to bring your mask. I will call for you a little after nine o'clock."

"But how are you going to get away?"

"Never you mind," was all Sarah said. Rosemary was too nervous to press the matter, so she let it drop.

In truth, Sarah did not dare tell her friend that Jameson Rex would be calling for her himself. She had enough sense of propriety to know that even if nothing happened between them, if it were discovered that she had spent time alone, after dark, in an enclosed carriage with Jameson Rex, her reputation would be ruined. She swallowed hard as she thought of the implications of her actions, but her desire to attend the masquerade ball was so great that she pushed aside her worries, focusing only on the delight the evening was sure to elicit.

Now the night of the masquerade had arrived. Turning from her reflection, Sarah strode to her wardrobe. She pulled out her muff and her fur wrap, grabbing Betsy's mending basket as she turned to sit down on the bed. Carefully, Sarah clipped the threads along the bottom seam of her wrap, just a few inches wide. She retrieved the crimson sash she had purchased a few days earlier and carefully slid it inside the seam. Rising from the bed, she pulled the gaudy scarlet cap out of her hatbox and placed it carefully inside her muff. It looked a little lumpy underneath the downy white fur, but if Sarah held her wrap carefully over the arm carrying her muff, it was hardly noticeable.

Glancing at the clock, Sarah saw that there were only fifteen minutes left in the hour. Quickly she grabbed her reticule, then her mask from its hiding place beneath her bed. She and Rosemary had purchased their masks only three days earlier, and since that moment Sarah had felt fully the danger and excitement of what they were doing. The mask she had chosen was made of black taffeta, with ivory and crimson ribbons streaming from the sides. Tiny white seed pearls were stitched in perfect rows around the edge of the mask with silver thread, and it sparkled in the candlelight as she carefully placed it in her handbag.

Her heart was pounding as she made her way down to the drawing room. The ruffles and lace on her gown made soft swishing sounds as she walked, and Lady Rockwell looked up from her place on the sofa as Sarah entered the room.

"You look very nice this evening, Miss Mendenhall," Lady Rockwell complimented her.

"Thank you," Sarah replied, a little breathless.

"When will you be leaving?"

"Mrs. and Miss Reed will call for me at nine," Sarah said, glancing at the clock on the mantel. It was five minutes before the hour.

"I still do not understand why you want to go see that awful play again."

Sarah forced a laugh, though it sounded shrill in her ears. "Rosemary has not yet seen *It Takes Two*, and I did not fully understand it the first time we went, what with Edward Ramsey whispering in my ear the whole time."

Lady Rockwell studied her as she spoke, suspicion gnawing at the countess. Sarah's eyes were bright, her cheeks were flushed, and her hands trembled as she smoothed the folds of her skirt—a clear sign that something was amiss. What was she up to?

Sarah said no more, however, and Lady Rockwell was silent as she returned to her needlework. Soon the wheels of a carriage were heard crunching on the gravel drive outside, and both women looked up at the sound. Sarah's face grew pale.

"Have you remembered your opera glasses?"

"I have them here," Sarah whispered, patting her reticule absently. Lady Rockwell narrowed her eyes.

"What is the matter, *Fräulein?* You look as though you might faint!"

"No, no; I am well," Sarah answered brightly, turning away from the countess. She watched the door expectantly, and a moment later Lawrence entered the room.

"The carriage has arrived, Miss Mendenhall," he said, bowing politely.

"Thank you, Lawrence. Goodnight, Lady Rockwell," Sarah sang out as she sailed from the room.

"Miss Mendenhall—" Lady Rockwell began, rising from her place on the sofa.

But Sarah was already gone.

Sarah stood in the entrance hall, carefully maneuvering her wrap onto her shoulders and her hands into her muff so as not to disclose what was hidden inside them. She had not dared make the attempt in the drawing room with Lady Rockwell looking on, and every moment she expected to hear the swish of her ladyship's skirts coming down the hall. Sarah had heard the countess call out her name as she left the room, but the terrified débutante knew that Lady Rockwell must suspect something was amiss, and Sarah dared not face her again.

With her wrap and her muff in place, Lawrence opened the door for Sarah, and the footman standing by the carriage sprang to attention. He placed a gloved hand on the handle of the door, waiting for her approach before opening it. Sarah took a few steps down from the front door, suddenly feeling as though she were marching to her death.

Nonsense! she scolded herself, drawing a deep breath. *It is only Jameson Rex in the carriage.* Abruptly she froze, her foot suspended above the step beneath her, her mind racing frantically to outpace the frenzied beating of her heart. If the rumors about Jameson Rex were true (and all evidence pointed to them being so), he had lured some poor, misguided woman to her demise, perhaps in much the same way as Sarah was herself being lured. For a moment her heart stopped, then it thundered ahead at such speed that the blood pounded in her ears. Did she dare get in the carriage? Would Jameson Rex whisk her away to be his mistress as well?

Suddenly the footman turned the handle and the door to the carriage swung open. Somehow Sarah had made it down the steps and now stood facing the gaping hole of the open doorway, her fate inches ahead of her in the darkened coach. Breathless she waited, hovering between what was safe and what she was beginning to feel was certain ruin, until a familiar voice broke through the darkness.

"For heaven's sake, get in the carriage, Miss Mendenhall—the night air is freezing!"

Sarah gasped as recognition dawned, and the shock propelled her forward into the black abyss, not even reaching for the footman's hand as she climbed into the waiting vehicle.

"Mrs. Ashby! Whatever are you doing here!" Sarah sputtered.

"Did you not wish to attend the masquerade ball at Madame Olivier's this evening?" the large woman asked, her tone bewildered. Mrs. Ashby's niece sat in quiet stillness beside her, and Sarah looked from one to the other, trying to make out their faces in the gloom.

"Why, yes, of course, but... but how did *you* know?"

The jovial woman sitting across from her chuckled. "My dear, who would not wish to attend a lively masquerade over a stuffy, high-end ball?" She laughed, and Sarah realized that Mrs. Ashby was very discreetly acknowledging the anonymity which Sarah's clandestine arrangement required. She smiled, and her heart lifted from the dread and worry which had filled her only moments before. She settled herself into her seat as the carriage lurched forward.

"Mary Anne here is quite wild about the masquerades, are you not, my dear?" Mrs. Ashby continued. "We much prefer them to the dreary affairs at Almack's."

Sarah smiled in the darkness. "I do not mind the balls at Almack's, but I confess that I am quite looking forward to this evening."

Mrs. Ashby shifted her large figure in her seat, rocking the carriage slightly. "I thought as much. And dear Miss Reed! I confess to never have thought *she* would fancy a masquerade ball, but the more, the merrier, I always say." Sarah could hear the smile in her voice, even if she could not see it.

The carriage soon drew up in front of the Reed's home, and Sarah turned to her chaperon. "I believe I shall go in for

Rosemary myself," she said.

"Just as you please," came the placid response.

Sarah sprang from the coach, taking the footman's hand only for a moment to ensure she did not slip, then climbed the short flight of steps to knock on the front door. She was shown inside by the butler, who went to call Miss Reed.

A few minutes later he returned, informing Sarah that Miss Reed had suddenly taken ill and would not be able to accompany her.

"Miss Reed is ill?" Sarah repeated, gaping at him.

"Yes, miss."

Sarah paused, thoughtful. Rosemary had been perfectly well the prior afternoon. She bit her lip, quickly forming a plan. Turning to the butler, she sighed dramatically. "I am *so* sorry to hear that she is unwell, for she was *so* looking forward to this evening! Do you think... might I see her for a moment?"

He hesitated, so she reached out and laid a hand very gently on his arm. "I only want to speak to my *dear* friend for a moment —only a moment."

The butler knew Sarah quite well, as she and Rosemary had been intimate for several weeks now. She smiled sweetly at the graying gentleman, praying that her powers of persuasion would not fail her. At last he consented.

"Very well. This way, Miss Mendenhall."

Sarah followed him to a long corridor on the third floor, where he left her with a bow outside of Rosemary's room. As soon as he had turned the corner at the end of the hall, Sarah rapped on the door sharply, not waiting for an invitation to enter.

"Rosemary! For heaven's sake, what are you doing?"

Rosemary gasped, startled not only by Sarah's abrupt entrance but by her tone and address; her friend had never called her by her Christian name before. She was sitting at her vanity in her dressing gown and slippers, and the sight made Sarah's cheeks burn.

"I cannot do it, Miss Mendenhall—I simply cannot do it!"

"What do you mean you cannot do it? We have been planning this for weeks!"

"I know," Rosemary choked, turning away. "But I feel so ill... I cannot bear to go through with it."

"And had you any intention of informing *me* of your plans to abandon our scheme?" Sarah spat.

Rosemary looked at her friend, stunned. She had never seen this side of Sarah before, and the fire that flashed in her friend's eyes made her shrink even more.

"I am sorry," she whispered, fighting back tears. "But surely you will not—"

"If you think that I will relinquish my desire to attend a masquerade ball at Madame Olivier's simply because you do not have the backbone to accompany me, you are *much* mistaken."

Rosemary burst into tears, and the anger that had flared to life in Sarah's breast abruptly burnt itself out. Sighing, she walked over to her friend and knelt beside her.

"Forgive me, Miss Reed," she said stiffly, her voice somewhat strained. "I spoke harshly, when there was no reason to cause you such pain."

Rosemary sniffed, drying her eyes on her handkerchief. "No, you were right; I have no backbone. Not when it comes to my mother."

Sarah was silent, and after several moments she stood.

"Is there nothing I can say to convince you to come with me?" she asked, more gently than before. But Rosemary shook her head.

"Very well. I shall bid you goodnight then, Miss Reed."

Sarah turned to leave. Her hand was on the door when her friend called out, "Sarah!" Surprised, Sarah turned just as Rosemary arrived beside her and threw her arms around her neck. "Forgive me," she sobbed.

Any lingering anger on Sarah's part evaporated in that instant. Patting her gently, Sarah replied, "Of course, dearest, if you will forgive me as well."

Rosemary nodded, and the friends embraced. "I shall send you word tomorrow," Sarah assured her as they drew apart. Rosemary smiled tentatively.

"I shall look forward to it."

Sarah gave her friend a final nod, then turned and left the room.

Chapter 13

The carriage ride to Piccadilly was not long, and Sarah barely had time to remove the crimson sash from her wrap, tie it around her waist, and don her mask and hat before they reached their destination. Mrs. Ashby did not seem surprised to hear that Miss Reed would not be joining them, and Sarah tried not to let it bother her. She was determined to enjoy herself even without her friend, and feeling that her reputation was now quite safe under the escort of Mrs. Ashby, she emerged from the carriage, breathless with excitement, into the splendidly decorated halls of Madame Olivier's.

The rooms were bursting with light from scores of candelabras and chandeliers which hung from the walls and the high ceilings. Dozens of guests mingled and mixed in the dance hall, their masked faces blending into anonymity.

Mrs. Ashby gave the footman at the door their tickets, and the three ladies entered the main ballroom. In the corner, a small orchestra was playing a lively tune. The masked revelers turned and marched first one way and then another, filling the room with their laughter and conversation. The air was heavy with mystery and intrigue, and Sarah quivered with anticipation.

A tall, lanky man in a dove-colored suit and a navy mask approached them. He bowed to Sarah and asked, "May I have the pleasure of the next dance, miss?"

Sarah gasped. It was Edward Ramsey! She had no idea that he was the sort of man to enjoy a masquerade ball, and coupled with the memory of his ridiculous antics at the theatre, it was all she could do not to burst out laughing. Not trusting her voice, and afraid of being discovered herself, she merely nodded and curtsied, and he bowed before turning away.

"Oh, Mrs. Ashby," Sarah whispered to her chaperon when he had gone. "How on earth am I supposed to keep my identity a secret? What if someone tells Lady Rockwell of my being here?"

The large woman shrugged. "Those who know you well may recognize your voice, but many will not. It does not signify, however—it is an unspoken rule that whether or not you know anyone, the identities of guests at a masquerade are not to be revealed by others."

Sarah felt a little better on hearing this, and soon another song started and Mr. Ramsey returned to claim her hand. Mary Anne had been solicited by a man in a black suit and a scarlet waistcoat, who joined the same set as Sarah and her partner.

The dance began, and Sarah learned firsthand how difficult it is to dance with a man when both your identities are supposed to be a secret. Intent on keeping herself unknown to her partner, she merely laughed and nodded when he tried to converse with her.

The result was that Edward Ramsey thought his partner a silly, ignorant girl and paid no more attention to her the rest of the evening, which was precisely what Sarah wished for.

The night wore on, and Sarah danced with several partners. Most of them she did not recognize. Though she had never considered herself overly romantic, Sarah felt as though a spell had been cast over the occupants of the ballroom. The cloaked figures and masked faces swirling around her lent an air of romance to the entire evening, and Sarah felt certain that if she were ever to lose her head or her heart to a man, it would be at such a ball.

Shortly before midnight she was approached by a gentleman clad completely in black. He moved with surety and elegance, and Sarah waited for him to speak to see if she could discover his identity. But he bowed mutely before her and held out his hand, silently inviting her to dance. Something about the stranger sent a chill down Sarah's spine, but the air in the room had woven its spell, and Sarah found she could not resist. She nodded and placed her gloved hand in his own.

They walked slowly around the room, watching the other guests while they waited for the next dance to begin. The mystery of the evening wove its terrible magic over them, and Sarah's heart beat strangely in her chest. When another dance started, her partner led her, trembling, onto the floor.

The music indicated that the dance was a waltz, and Sarah found herself in the arms of the stranger, feeling more and more uneasy. She tried to engage him in conversation, but he remained stoically silent, spinning and twirling her artfully across the floor. It seemed as though he was deliberately leading her further and further from her chaperon. By the time Sarah realized this, they were in a far corner of the darkened room. In the shadows, a door stood open like a gaping mouth, ready to swallow both Sarah and her partner. Immediately she released his hand and attempted to back away from him, but the stranger grabbed her wrist and wrapped an arm around her waist, pulling her into the darkness.

"Let me go!" Sarah cried, trying to pry his fingers from her wrist. But the stranger laughed humorlessly.

"I think not," he said, his voice low. "I have been waiting for this opportunity all evening; you will not deny me my pleasure now."

Something about his voice was chillingly familiar, and Sarah struggled again to free herself.

"You will not get away with this. I... I shall scream if you do not release me!"

"No, you will not," he sneered, abruptly pulling her close and clapping a hand over her mouth. Sarah struggled against her captor, but he was strong, and his hand covered not only her mouth but her nose as well. She wriggled in his grasp, but her struggle was in vain. Every moment his grip grew tighter and she grew weaker, fighting for every breath. He had nearly succeeded in dragging her completely through the open door when another voice rang out from the blackness.

"Release her—now!" a masculine voice commanded.

The stranger whipped around, and his grip on Sarah momentarily faltered. She pulled against him at just the right moment, and found herself snatched from one pair of arms into another, shoved roughly into the corner so that her back was against the wall. She tried to scream but choked on a sob, the body of her new captor pressing against her. She pushed against his back and he instantly gave way, and she suddenly realized that the body and arms around her did not hold her captive. She was closely tucked between the wall and the back of another gentleman, whose arms reached backward to encircle her but who faced the man in black.

The gentleman was protecting her.

"You are no better than I am," the stranger in black sneered. "Every man in the room has been watching her with hungry eyes —I merely got to her first!"

Sarah trembled at his words, and the protective arms around her tightened a little.

"Leave. Now," the gentleman ordered, his voice murderously low.

The waltz had ended and several couples were looking curiously over at them. The man in black glanced around, then finally let out his breath and stalked away. Sarah felt faint with relief, but the arms around her remained stiff, the gentleman's broad shoulders tight. After several moments, he slowly lowered his arms and stepped away from her, turning to face her for the first time.

"Are you all right?" he asked gently.

Sarah glanced up at her rescuer, recognizing the scarlet waistcoat of the man who had solicited Mary Anne upon their arrival.

"Yes," she replied weakly. "Thank you."

He nodded curtly, then held out his hand. "You should sit down. May I escort you to a chair?" His voice was deep, and laced with concern. She nodded.

Carefully she took his arm, and he led her slowly to the nearest chair. The distance was not far, but Sarah trembled with every step, her nerves stretched nearly to breaking. She sighed in relief when her weight was off her legs, feeling herself grow calmer now that she was in a well-lit portion of the room. She looked up at her benefactor and managed a shaky smile.

"Thank you, sir. A thousand times, I thank you. I do not know what I would have done had it not been for you."

"You are most welcome, Miss Mendenhall."

A jolt coursed through Sarah as she heard her name spoken. She had not been paying very great attention to the identity of her savior before, but now she looked up at his masked face in an effort to discover his identity.

The smoky blue eyes of Jameson Rex stared intently back at her.

"Mr. Rex," she murmured. As recognition dawned in Sarah's face, a tiny smile revealed itself below his black mask. He nodded once in acknowledgment, but then his face grew somber.

"You have been able to recognize me—can you tell me if you recognized the man in black?"

Sarah hesitated. Peter Mills's lazy smile and wandering eyes flashed into her mind, but she shook her head. It might have been him, but she was not sure.

"It would be a terrible thing to accuse any gentleman of, but especially since I cannot be sure of his identity, I have no name to give you."

Rex nodded at her answer, and Sarah wondered if his mind was on Peter Mills as well. She shuddered, then frowned as a new thought arose.

"But, how did you know it was me? How did you come to my rescue?"

It was difficult to tell in the dim light, but Sarah thought she saw his face flush. "I recognized you almost instantly," he confessed, a hint of a smile playing around his mouth.

"But I am wearing a mask."

"Your beauty cannot be masked."

She narrowed her eyes at him, and he stared benignly back at her. Suddenly she gasped. "You asked Mrs. Ashby to escort me here this evening!" she cried triumphantly. He chuckled, nodding.

"Yes, I did, and I knew *her* the moment she entered the room. I recognized her niece as well, so my powers of reasoning left me to conclude that you were the other young lady in her company," he finished, the merriment in his eyes only barely concealed.

Sarah smiled, feeling far more at ease now. Turning to glance across the room, she spotted Mrs. Ashby sitting down in an alcove near the orchestra. Rex followed her gaze.

"Would you like me to take you back to your escort, or would you care to dance?"

Surprised, Sarah studied his face. It was hesitant, as if he feared that her ordeal had robbed her of any pleasure the night had provided. She smiled gently to put him at ease.

"A dance would be lovely."

His eyes grew bright behind his disguise, and he held his arm out to Sarah, who took it without a word.

Walking beside him, Sarah felt a current of emotion pass through her. She glanced up at his face, remembering the press of his body against her own and his arms wrapped protectively around her. She blushed, feeling suddenly shy in his presence, the intimate moments of his gallantry burned into her mind.

He led her slowly on to the dance floor, careful to stay in the lightest portion of the room and nearer to her chaperon than before. Sarah was grateful for his thoughtfulness. The encounter with the man in black had unnerved her, but standing on the dance floor across from Rex, she felt her initial excitement returning. Rex's face betrayed no emotion as he gazed at Sarah, waiting for the music to start. She stared nervously back at him, her smiling lips gently parted, her heart beating wildly in her chest.

The electricity in the room was nearly tangible as the dance began. Sarah had not noticed how warm it had become, but she suddenly found it difficult to breathe in the dim, candlelit air. Her eyes were trained on Rex's face as they drew first together and then apart in the steps of the dance. He, too, was watching her intently, and when they came together again, she felt him draw her close in order to whisper in her ear.

"Miss Mendenhall, there is something I have been wanting to ask you."

Sarah exhaled slowly, feeling slightly dizzy. "Yes?"

"Where on earth did you get that ridiculous hat?"

A laugh burst forth from Sarah's lips, and the tension that was building between them seemed to evaporate.

"I bought it the day you rescued me on Bond Street," she giggled.

He chuckled. "I did not realize you needed rescuing from your purchases that day, as well."

She swatted him playfully on the arm, and the dance pulled

them apart again. She watched as he turned with another guest; a stout woman in a plum-colored gown. As they came together once more she asked, "You did not tell me before—how did you know I needed help?"

His jaw tightened, but one corner of his mouth pulled up. "I have been watching you all evening," he breathed as he took her in his arms once more. "I could scarcely take my eyes off you. But then suddenly, you were gone. I had to find you."

Sarah shivered, the hair on the back of her neck rising.

"I am not the only man who has been watching you this evening, either. More than a dozen dandies have been talking about the ravishing beauty in the ivory gown."

Sarah drew away, scrutinizing him. "Why are you flattering me, Mr. Rex?"

"Why do *you* think I am flattering you?"

Sarah considered his question. They were standing apart, facing each other at the bottom of the set, for once not moving as they waited for the top couple to descend. She studied him: his chiseled jaw, his crooked smile, his blue-gray eyes, so piercing in their intensity. Suddenly a thought struck her, and her face clouded.

"I hope you are not trying to make me fall in love with you," she said with a frown.

"Would it offend you so if I said that I was?"

"Most definitely."

"Then I will not say it," he said, winking at her. The lead couple passed, and they came together again. Rex watched her with the same intense look as before, but Sarah's petulant demeanor kept him silent. Soon the dance ended, and they bowed to one another. He stepped beside her and took her hand, placing it in the crook of his arm.

"Miss Mendenhall, you have made it very clear that you have no intention of falling in love or accepting a proposal this season. Is it not so?"

"Yes," she answered warily, watching him through guarded eyes.

"And has it never occurred to you that I enjoy your company precisely for that reason?"

Surprise flitted across her face, but he went on before she could respond.

"It is no secret that I have been on the hunt for a wife for many years. But I have grown weary of the game, and it is refreshing to enjoy the company of a young lady without being afraid that she will misunderstand my attentions."

Sarah nodded thoughtfully. "If that is the case, I am glad to hear it. I believe I feel the same way about you," she answered. "Knowing that you understand I am not to be won over, and with the understanding that your reputation eliminates *you* from the list of eligible men whom I could even be enticed to marry, it is pleasant to have a companion with whom I may converse without raising suspicion."

Rex laughed. "Your frankness does you credit, my dear. I am glad we understand one another," he responded, an amused note in his voice. He flashed his crooked smile, and Sarah smiled, comfortable once more.

The ordeal from earlier had drained Sarah more than she realized, and she was glad when Rex finally escorted her back to Mrs. Ashby. It had frightened her as well, and though Rex remained nearby for the rest of the evening, Sarah did not dance again.

The masquerade lasted until the early hours of the morning. Rex handed Sarah up into the carriage, and she thanked him again for everything he had done.

"It was my pleasure, Miss Mendenhall," he said, brushing his lips against the back of her gloved hand.

She smiled, and the door was shut. Rex stood for several minutes, watching the carriage drive out of sight and considering the young woman who was conveyed away therein. He then returned to his rooms on Park Street, far more solemn than when he had left them earlier in the evening.

Sitting in front of his fire, Rex watched the flames licking at the dry wood. It crackled and popped in flashes of brilliant color, a mesmerizing display of nature's fireworks. But soon his thoughts turned once again to Miss Mendenhall, and he sighed. Of two things he was growing ever more certain, and he was not sure which of the two revelations disturbed him most. Firstly, that Sarah Mendenhall could not be won by means of flattery or seduction. Hers was a disposition totally unlike the other young ladies of London, and it should not have surprised him that the way and means of wooing her would not be the same, either. It had, however, and he realized that he would need to change his tactics if he were to win her affections and Peter Mills's five thousand pounds.

And secondly, that Sarah herself was far more bewitching than he had anticipated. Rex's situation was nearly desperate; he could not afford to lose his heart to her when he knew full well that he must marry an heiress, and soon. He sat before the fire long into the night, until he at last drifted off to sleep in his chair, thinking of the lady whose spell had been cast over the whole of London; a spell which Rex felt himself slipping beneath.

Chapter 14

Sarah awoke in high spirits the next morning. Coming down to breakfast, she looked as light and cheerful as the sun peeking through the clouds outside the window.

"*Guten Morgan, Fräulein.* How was the theatre?" Lady Rockwell asked as the meal began.

Sarah's smile faded. She had completely forgotten that an account of the evening's events would be desired by Lady Rockwell. Having never been party to anything that had required such deliberate scheming, Sarah squirmed, suddenly aware of the many falsehoods she had told, and the others which would be required in order to maintain her ruse. Her disposition had never tended towards deceitfulness, and her present predicament made her feel most uncomfortable.

"I... do not know," she said at last, her voice timid, her eyes averted. Lady Rockwell stared at her.

"What do you mean you do not know? Did you not attend

the theatre with Mrs. and Miss Reed last night?"

Shifting uncomfortably in her seat, Sarah refused to meet the older woman's gaze. Two choices lay before her: continue her deception, or tell Lady Rockwell the truth. Neither choice was very appealing, for she was sure to meet with disapproval from either, but since her attendance at the masquerade had been chaperoned by a respectable woman (one of Lady Rockwell's own friends, at that), she hoped she would be forgiven. Surely it could not have been a *very* great scandal... could it?

Lady Rockwell peered at Sarah, still waiting for a reply.

"No," Sarah finally acknowledged, drawing out the word so that it became two syllables. "I did not."

Lady Rockwell placed her utensils firmly on the table. "Miss Mendenhall," she said in a stern voice. Sarah peeked at her in chagrin. The anger she saw flashing in her guardian's eyes frightened her, but since she had already confessed that she was not at the theatre, there was nothing to do but make a clean breast of it.

"Explain yourself," Lady Rockwell ordered severely.

"I did not attend the theatre with Mrs. and Miss Reed," she began meekly, striving to meet the older woman's gaze and failing miserably in the attempt. "I went somewhere else instead. I am sorry to have deceived you; it was very wrong of me, and I apologize."

The moments ticked by in agonizing silence as Sarah waited for the reproof she knew was coming.

"Where were you?"

Lady Rockwell's voice was quiet, but the tone in which she spoke made it feel like a blow. Sarah took a deep breath and looked up, forcing herself to meet the gaze she felt on her face.

"I went to a masquerade ball at Madame Olivier's, with Mrs. Ashby and her niece."

Sarah threw the words across the table, hastily retreating into her meal and taking a few quick bites of food to avoid any immediate questions. But the bread stuck in her throat like cotton, and she could hardly swallow the bite of egg which followed.

Lady Rockwell watched her in silence for several moments. Then she, too, lifted her fork and began to eat. But she cut her food slowly; she ate deliberately; and with every forkful that was lifted to her lips, Sarah felt less and less hungry.

The meal continued in this manner until at last Sarah could eat no more. She laid down her knife and stared numbly at her plate, thoroughly miserable. Lady Rockwell raised the last bite of her own breakfast to her mouth, wiping her lips and her fingers and placing the cloth silently on the table. She took a drink and set the glass slowly back in its place. Only then did she clear her throat and address the unhappy young woman before her.

"It is clear that you had a reason for keeping your plans from my knowledge," she began. "I assume it was because you feared my reaction had I known your designs." She looked at Sarah expectantly, and the girl across from her nodded obediently, her eyes brimming with tears.

The countess sighed. "Come now Miss Mendenhall, I am not *very* angry with you, though I confess to be greatly disappointed."

Sarah looked tentatively up at her, and seeing that Lady Rockwell's stern features had softened considerably, Sarah relaxed a little bit.

"Will you tell me about it?"

Again Sarah hesitated. If she revealed Jameson Rex's involvement in the scheme, Lady Rockwell was sure to fly into a rage. Regardless of the fact that he had not actually escorted Sarah to or from Madame Olivier's, he was the reason she had even been able to attend. Sarah was certain that Lady Rockwell would be furious if she knew his role in the plot, even if he *had* rescued her.

The entire incident with the ebony-clad stranger was another reason for her hesitation. Though Sarah had been rescued, it was precisely the sort of thing which the countess had warned her about. She therefore resolved to satisfy Lady Rockwell's curiosity inasmuch as she could leave Jameson Rex—and the deplorable stranger—out of the story completely.

"At the Stafford's party a few weeks past, Miss Reed told me about Madame Olivier's masquerade balls. Since Miss Reed said that her mother would not allow her to attend one, I did not think that you would allow it, either." She dropped her eyes to her lap, her cheeks burning. "We agreed on a plan to attend one together this week, but in the end Miss Reed decided not to accompany me."

Lady Rockwell sniffed. "I am happy to hear that Miss Reed, at least, has some sense of decency and propriety." Sarah winced at the accusation, but the countess continued. "You are right—I do not approve of masquerade balls in general. The very idea breaks one of the cardinal rules of refined society: never dance with a man whom you do not know!"

She was silent for a moment, and Sarah peeked at her when she did not continue. Lady Rockwell was not smiling, but the lines around her eyes and mouth had softened, and Sarah exhaled.

"But I suppose that since you were chaperoned by a respectable woman, we may consider that your reputation remains intact. I daresay there were others of our acquaintance in attendance as well. It is clear that you are sorry, and I see no need to discuss this issue further."

"Oh, yes, indeed, Lady Rockwell," Sarah was quick to interject. "There were many of our acquaintance there. In fact, you would not believe who—"

"Miss Mendenhall," Lady Rockwell broke in severely. "We will not discuss this any longer. And furthermore," she added, her tone implying the finality of what she was about to say, "you are not to attend any more masquerades, nor deceive me as to your whereabouts again. If I cannot trust you to conduct yourself with due respect and propriety, I shall have no choice but to send you back to your brother in India. *Verstehst du?* Is that clear?"

"Yes, Lady Rockwell," Sarah answered meekly.

"Oh, my dear Miss Mendenhall, how glad I was to receive your note!"

The door had scarcely shut behind Rosemary when she flew to Sarah's side and grasped her arm. "Are you well? Have you been... harmed at all?" she asked hesitantly. Sarah's look softened when she saw the genuine concern in her friend's face. Rosemary may not have very much gumption, but she certainly had a good deal of compassion.

"No, dearest, I am well. I was escorted to and from the ball by Mrs. Ashby and her niece."

"Mrs. Ashby?" Rosemary repeated with surprise. "I did not know that she was at all interested in the affairs at Madame Olivier's."

"Neither did I," Sarah confessed. "But she and her niece attend the masquerades quite often, I understand."

"Are you planning to go again?"

Sarah shuddered, thinking of her narrow escape. "No. It was extremely diverting, but for my own part, I prefer to dance with gentleman of whose identity I can be certain."

"Did anyone recognize you last night?"

Sarah grinned. "Jameson Rex called me by name."

"Jameson Rex?" her friend replied, incredulous.

"Yes." Sarah proceeded to tell her friend all about her dance with Rex in the early morning hours. Rosemary looked both envious and afraid, and Sarah could not help wondering if Rosemary wished she had accompanied Sarah after all.

"It all sounds very romantic," Rosemary sighed at the end of Sarah's tale. "But do you really think it was wise of you to go? What will Lady Rockwell say if she discovers where you were?"

"She already knows," Sarah sighed. "I told her this morning over breakfast, and although she was very disappointed, she was not nearly as angry as I thought she might be."

Their conversation turned to other matters then, and the next quarter hour was spent quite pleasantly. At the conclusion of her visit, Rosemary embraced her friend.

"Oh Miss Mendenhall, I am so glad you are safe. And I am happy that you enjoyed yourself."

"Dearest Rosemary—may I call you Rosemary? And you must call me Sarah. No more of this "Miss" stuff for us. We have been through the refiner's fire together, and have earned the right to call each other by our Christian names, have we not?"

Rosemary nodded, her cheeks pink with pleasure. "I should like that very much, Miss— Sarah," she finished, blushing at her mishap. But Sarah laughed, and kissed her friend airily on the cheek.

"You will get used to it soon enough," she said, linking her arm with her Rosemary's and walking with her towards the door. "And though we must speak with propriety and decorum in public, I am glad that I may call you Rosemary when we are alone."

They embraced again, and Sarah waved until the carriage carrying her friend was out of sight. She then made her way to the sitting room, but was surprised to find it empty. Calling the butler, she asked where Lady Rockwell might be found.

"She is meeting with Dr. Matthews at present," he said.

Guilt washed over Sarah, and she wondered if her antics had put a strain upon the countess. But the old butler smiled at her worried frown.

"Never mind, miss. Lady Rockwell is made of firmer stuff than you or I suppose," he said, leaving the room.

Sarah swallowed her fear, sitting down on the settee and smoothing her skirts. Moments later, however, she arose and went to the window. The day had begun with a shower, and tiny droplets of water hung suspended on the leaves and branches of the trees. Every once in a while the sun would peek through a break in the clouds, illuminating the dewdrops like a thousand flashing diamonds. It was very pretty, and Sarah suddenly felt the urge to paint the sight.

She crossed the room to retrieve her sketchbook when her eye caught sight of an opened letter sitting on the desk. Remembering that it had arrived from Katherine several days earlier pierced her with guilt. Though she had been thrilled to hear from her brother's wife, she put off sending a reply and had quickly forgotten altogether. Replacing her sketchpad and pencil, she sat down at the desk instead, determined to pen a reply to her sister-in-law.

Looking out the window, Sarah chewed absently on her bottom lip as she considered what she might write. Her mind wandered back over the events of the last few weeks, and she smiled as she put her pen to the paper.

My dearest Katherine,

I sincerely hope this letter finds you well. What a happy event to hear from you! I am glad your journey home was swift and uneventful, and that Charles is treating you well. Dare I hope that your next letter will bring me news that I may anticipate the arrival of a dear little niece or nephew? Forgive my impertinence; I am sure your grandmother would be appalled if she knew I had asked you such a question.

London is as diverting a place as I thought it would be. I still cannot believe you never cared for it! I am sure that if you and I would have spent a Season here together, you would have found it as enjoyable as I have. There are no elephants here to frighten you, as you are well aware.

Lady Rockwell has finally given up on my music lessons, and instead I am a slave to the brush. She has hired a Dutchman to oversee my artistic education, and he is quite a demanding master. Though you would not expect that my work improves from the way he rants at me, I believe my little talent is blossoming, and it makes my heart glad. You know what a fondness I have for beautiful things, and now I have the ability to capture their likeness forever.

Our evenings are full of dances, parties, and dinners, and I have more beaux than I know what to do with. Lady Rockwell says it is positively shameful how the young men fall all over themselves for me, but they are certainly a jolly set, and I am glad to have their company. Though I am not opposed to matrimony in general, I am determined to enjoy myself this season, and refuse to be drawn in by any of them.

Give my love to Charles, and be sure to write back as soon as you are able, though I cannot guarantee I will return the favor. My interest in reading and writing has not yet improved, but I will struggle to endure, for your sake.

Yours,

Sarah

Chapter 15

The spring had been unseasonably cool, and in the last several weeks there had only been a handful of days pleasant enough to enjoy the morning air in Hyde Park. It appeared that Winter refused to release his icy grip on the city, but as the days grew steadily longer and warmer, he finally succumbed. The sooty gray air no longer clung to the inside of Sarah's lungs, and beneath her feet the damp, muddy streets at last began to dry. Clusters of tiny rosebuds burst forth in the front garden, their tight little blossoms hiding yellow and crimson petals. Sarah could not wait until they bloomed; they would make lovely subjects for her paintings.

It was on a fine day late in May that an unexpected caller arrived in Cavendish Square. Lady Rockwell and Sarah were in the sitting room discussing their plans for the day, when Lawrence entered the room and announced the arrival of Jameson Rex. The gentleman bowed as he was introduced, and took the seat that was cordially offered to him by the countess.

"I hope I am not intruding," he asked as he sat down, looking from one lady to the other.

"Not at all," Sarah responded cheerily. "Lady Rockwell and I were just discussing our agenda today."

"And have you anything to look forward to?"

"Not until this evening. We shall attend the ball at Almack's, of course. Will you be in attendance, sir?"

"I am afraid I will not have the pleasure."

"Are you engaged elsewhere?"

"No, but I was not so fortunate as to secure a voucher this year." Though he smiled, the tone of his response at once led Sarah to understanding, and she blushed for having put him in such an awkward situation.

"Oh," she stammered, looking from him to Lady Rockwell, who sat quietly knitting in an armchair by the fire. The older woman sniffed.

"I am sure that your evening will afford you a great deal of pleasure," Rex said. "But as there are several hours until your attentions will be claimed by more fortunate gentlemen than myself, I have come to invite you to take a drive with me in my new curricle. It is a very fine day, and I would be glad of your company."

"Oh, how wonderful!" Sarah clapped her hands. "I should be delighted. Lady Rockwell?" she asked, "is that agreeable to you? Have you any need of my company this morning?"

The countess turned and looked solemnly at her young charge, but Sarah either would not or could not understand her meaning. Her bright eyes fairly danced with excitement, oblivious to the warning Lady Rockwell tried to convey. At last the countess sighed.

"No, you go along. I shall rest at home this morning."

Sarah beamed, and Rex chuckled as he stood. "It is settled, then. I shall bring the curricle around and wait for you in the drive." He bowed politely to the countess, flashed a crooked smile at Sarah, then turned and was gone. Sarah was on her feet and nearly out the door in the same instant, but Lady Rockwell's voice called her back.

"Miss Mendenhall!"

Sarah turned, hesitating. "Come here," came the command, and Sarah obediently went back to the countess's side. Lady Rockwell must have seen her worried expression, for she chuckled quietly.

"I will not revoke my permission, if that is what you fear."

Sarah visibly relaxed. "Thank you, Lady Rockwell," she said with feeling.

"I will not revoke my permission, but I warn you to be careful," the countess said, all hint of lightheartedness now gone. The smile on Sarah's face faded.

"Jameson Rex is handsome, wealthy, and obviously interested in you," she began, watching Sarah closely for a reaction. "But his reputation is unpardonable. You must be on your guard."

Sarah smiled affectionately at her. "Dear Lady Rockwell, you are kind to remind me. But need I remind *you* that my heart is untouchable? My soul belongs to London, for this Season at least, and no man—however handsome or wealthy or even titled he may be—shall break my resolve, or lead me into ruin, as may be the case. There. Are you satisfied?"

Her blue eyes sparkled as she looked down on Lady Rockwell, who sighed, shaking her head.

"I suppose I must be, when you declare yourself so resolutely. But I worry. More stalwart hearts than yours have been carried away by a handsome face, *Fräulein,*" she said, looking doubtfully up at her. But Sarah only laughed, and bent to brush a kiss on her wrinkled old cheek.

"I daresay they have, Lady Rockwell. But you must trust that mine will not be among them." She waved goodbye and danced from the room, before Lady Rockwell even had time to recover from the shock of being kissed.

"What are their names?"

Rex and Sarah were driving along one of the principal paths in Hyde Park when Sarah asked about the horses. They were a matched pair of gelding bays, with black stockings and muzzles, and ebony manes and tails.

"Francis is the one on the left, and Finnigan is the one on the right."

"How long have you had them?"

"A few years now, but they have only been broken the last twelvemonth. Finnigan can be a bit spirited, but I think he has finally settled down and become accustomed to the harness."

Rex held the reins loosely in his hands, and only now and then tightened one or the other in order to lead the horses where he wanted. Sarah watched his gloved hands with fascination.

"It looks easy enough."

Rex laughed. "Not as easy as it seems, but it is not difficult once you learn how."

"Will you teach me?"

The eagerness in Sarah's voice could not be mistaken, and Rex smiled. "I wondered when you would ask me that. But I must forbear. Driving is not a skill that elegant young ladies need learn."

Sarah scoffed, indignant. "There are plenty of young ladies who know how to drive a team of horses. I never had need of it in India—indeed, I never even thought of it! But now I think it would be grand to drive myself around in a little gig, with a pretty chestnut mare and a little green-painted carriage."

"There is more to driving a horse and buggy than looking fashionable while doing so," Rex chuckled.

Sarah huffed in mock exasperation but said nothing more. She watched Rex out of the corner of her eye, his handsome profile rendered even more striking in the clear, warm air. The corner of his mouth was drawn up in a crooked grin, and his gray-blue eyes were bright and happy. He turned and caught her looking at him.

"What mischief are you concocting in that pretty little head of yours?" he asked in his rich baritone voice. Sarah laughed; a happy, trilling sound that rang in the air around them.

"I am determining what course I should pursue in order to convince you to teach me how to drive."

Rex laughed himself, a hint of mischief dancing in his own eyes. "Only one course will provide you with the outcome you desire, my lady."

"And which one is that, pray tell?"

They turned a corner just then, and Sarah watched as Rex expertly guided the horses around the narrow bend. He glanced over at her, a rakish grin on his face. "Tell me which of the young men in your pocket you like best of all."

Sarah gasped, then laughed as she slapped him playfully on the arm. "How abominable you are! You know that a lady would never speak of such things to a gentleman." But the set of her mouth and the twinkle in her eye led Rex to understand she might be persuaded.

"Come now, Miss Mendenhall, do not play coy with me. Surely you have a dozen or more to choose from. Is it Freddy Grimshaw?"

Sarah wrinkled her nose. "Have you really such a low opinion of my taste in men?"

"Ah-ha!" Rex cried triumphantly. "So you *do* have a favorite! Or at least, you prefer men who are not Fred Grimshaw."

Sarah blushed, shaking her head. "You are impossible!"

"Impossible to get the better of, I daresay," he replied with a wink.

She narrowed her eyes. The challenge was obvious in his tone, and when he looked back at her she could see it in his eyes as well. She tossed her head.

"Very well, you are right. I do have a favorite."

Rex smiled in self-satisfaction. "He must be very different from poor Freddy," he said.

Sarah allowed herself a smile. "He is."

Rex was silent for a moment, considering. Looking over at

her with a serious expression, he asked, "Edward Ramsey?"

Sarah burst out laughing, and Rex joined her. "Poor Edward! But no, this gentleman is *much* more handsome." Sarah watched him with mild eyes, her mouth drawn up in a half smile as she anticipated his next barb.

"Hmm," Rex mused. "More handsome than Edward Ramsey and less ridiculous than Fred Grimshaw."

Sarah giggled.

"I have it!" Rex snapped the reins in his excitement and the horses jumped into a faster trot. He reined them back slowly, then gave Sarah an expectant look.

"Jeremy Thatcher?"

"Too dull," Sarah replied with a bored look.

"Michael Elliot?"

"Too forceful."

"Marshall Todd?"

"Too freckled," she giggled.

Rex groaned.

"The gentleman I am thinking of is handsome, kind, and full of wit," Sarah supplied. "He is fearless and vivacious, and an excellent dancer. I have yet to find his equal among his peers."

Intrigued, Rex looked over at her. She was gazing at him intently, her vivid blue eyes boring into his own.

"If I did not know better," he said slowly, "I would suspect you were speaking of me." He narrowed his eyes at her. "Are you attempting to flatter me into concession?"

"Only if it is working," she whispered, a wicked glint in her eyes.

Rex threw his head back and laughed. "Indeed it is, Miss

Mendenhall," he said at last, admiration coloring his words. "Your powers of persuasion are unparalleled."

"I am glad to hear it," she declared triumphantly, a smug smile upon her face. "Now, how do we begin?"

"We begin by taking you home," he chuckled. When Sarah protested, he smiled gently at her. "Never mind, my dear. The hour is getting late, and Lady Rockwell will begin to wonder where you are. But I will call for you tomorrow, and we shall have our first lesson then."

Chapter 16

Peter Mills leaned lazily against the cold brick building, keeping his eye on the doorway at the end of the street. The traffic was not heavy, and his vigil was soon rewarded by the sight of a carriage, which slowed as it passed him and came to a stop in front of the jet black door he was watching. Adjusting his hat, Peter crossed the street quickly. His gait was casual and his steps deliberate as he neared the carriage, where the footman was just helping a lady out of the vehicle.

To say that the woman was beautiful would not do her credit. She was strikingly handsome, with flawless, porcelain skin and hair so dark it was nearly black. Her large eyes appeared even more doe-like by her straight, petite features, and her generous bosom and tiny waist made her womanly figure even more fine. She smiled as Peter tipped his hat, and held her hand out to him.

"Peter Mills," the woman crooned, her voice like velvet. "I wondered when our paths would cross again."

"Not soon enough for my pining heart, Lady Isabella," he returned, kissing her gloved hand.

She laughed, taking his arm. "Come inside. I have only just arrived—but you knew that, did you not?" She cast him a sly smile, and he winked at her. Laughing, she led the way into the house.

Lady Isabella Gray's rooms in Grosvenor Square were very grand. The only child of the Marquess of Stafford, she had been born to a life of privilege. Though the title and estate fell to a cousin after her father's death, a generous sum had been left to her in his will. She had been raised without a mother (her own having run off with an Irishman when Isabella was small), and so had no one to please but herself.

And please herself she most certainly did.

Accustomed to all the finest that money could buy, her rooms in London left nothing to be desired. An enormous crystal chandelier hung in the opulent entryway, and the marble floors they walked upon were polished to perfection. Leaving her mantle and gloves with a footman at the door, Lady Isabella led Peter to the luxurious drawing room on the second floor, which was filled with over-stuffed furniture and gaudy ornamentation. Peter lounged across the velvet settee, perfectly at ease in his surroundings. A maid clad in a black dress and starched white apron brought in a tray of tea and biscuits, and only after she had poured the refreshment and been dismissed did Isabella speak.

"Tell me, Peter dear, how did you know I was in town? I have scarcely been in London two days." Her ebony eyes were coy as she glanced at him over her teacup, and he smiled silkily in reply.

"I make it my business to know these things, my lady."

She laughed—a deep, throaty sound that was as rich as cream. "Ah, Peter," she purred. "Ever the flattering gentleman."

He raised his cup in acknowledgment as she continued. "If you will not tell me how you knew of my arrival, I trust you will at least tell me what your purpose is in coming to call?"

"Must one have a reason for calling upon the most beautiful woman in town?"

"No, but one usually does."

Peter chuckled, but he set his cup and saucer on a side table and leaned back, regarding her thoughtfully.

"Tell me, do you know Jameson Rex?"

She laughed. "*Everyone* knows Jameson Rex, darling," she said lazily. But Peter could detect a spark of interest burning in her eyes, and he smiled knowingly.

"Ah, yes. I had forgotten how well you *do* know him, Isabella."

She arched her delicate eyebrows, ignoring the implication. "I know him well enough, I daresay. Why do you ask?"

He shrugged. "I simply wondered if you might like me to introduce you again to his notice."

"And why do you suppose I should like to be noticed by Jameson Rex?"

"I assumed that was why you came to town."

"Because Jameson Rex is here?" she scoffed.

"No, because Jameson Rex is looking for a wife."

She waved him off impatiently. "Jameson has had plenty of opportunities to marry. He comes to town every year, and every year the old cats throw their daughters at his head. But he has

162

never paid them any mind. Why should this year be any different?"

"Because this year he is determined to marry—and before the season is over."

She narrowed her eyes, wary. "Why?"

Peter sat up, surprised. "Have you not heard?"

"About the child? Of course I have." But Peter was shaking his head.

"Not about the girl. About his uncle. Rex has been cut off completely."

Her teacup rattled on the saucer as Lady Isabella set it down abruptly. "Completely?" she repeated, incredulous. Peter nodded, and a slow smile crept over her face.

"At last," she breathed.

Peter chuckled, and she eyed him shrewdly. "And why are *you* so interested in the affair?"

"Is it not enough to wish that my friend make an advantageous match?"

"Not, perhaps, for any other man," she answered, smirking at him. "But I know you, Peter Mills. What game are you playing?"

"One for which I hope you will forgive me," he said, unashamed. "You see, Rex and I made a little wager, and I should like to see whether he would rather win the bet, or win *you*."

She raised an eyebrow at him, and he grinned wickedly.

"Besides, I promised Rex that I would introduce to his notice the eligible ladies of my, shall we say, more *intimate* acquaintance."

His eyes travelled up and down her figure, and she smiled seductively at him.

"Care to enter the competition?" he asked.

Lady Isabella picked up her saucer again, taking a lazy sip of tea. When she lowered the cup from her lips, Peter could see that they were set in determination.

"Darling," she said, her sultry voice dripping, "There will *be* no competition."

The ball held in honor of the Whitman's youngest daughter would be talked about for years to come as one of the highlights of the London season. A very old, wealthy family, the Whitmans were well-liked not only for their social position, but for their generous natures and quiet affability. It seemed the whole of London's esteemed society were invited for the coming-out of Miss Eliza Whitman, and on the evening of her début ball the house was filled to overflowing.

Sarah stood beside Lady Rockwell, smiling politely at the matronly women they conversed with and trying not to appear too bored. When Rosemary entered the room and caught Sarah's eye, Sarah excused herself to join her friend.

"My dearest Rosemary!" she cried, brushing a feathery kiss on her friend's cheek. "I had nearly despaired of seeing you tonight. I am glad you did not disappoint me."

"How silly you are! I told you yesterday we were planning to come."

"Yes, but that was before Mr. Nelson invited you to attend the theatre with him and his mother," Sarah said with a sly smile.

Rosemary's face flushed, but she smiled as she shook her

head. "We were already engaged for this evening, and Mama would not like to disappoint the Whitmans."

"Even though we both know *you* would have rather gone with Mr. Nelson," Sarah laughed.

Rosemary ignored her teasing friend and looked about the room. "I cannot believe how many people are here!"

"Yes, it is quite the crush," Sarah said with amusement.

"And have you made any new acquaintance?"

"Not yet, although there is one guest in particular I am dying to meet. Who is the lady with Jameson Rex, do you know?"

Rosemary turned to where Sarah indicated, and saw a dark-haired beauty on Rex's arm. Peter Mills stood on his other side, and Rosemary furrowed her brow. "I do not know," she said uncertainly. "She looks somewhat familiar, but I cannot recall from where."

Frowning, Sarah tried to study the lady without appearing to stare. She was by far one of the most handsome women in the room, though she was certainly past the blush of innocent youth. Sarah guessed her age to be about twenty-five, and was surprised to see her hanging on Rex's arm with an air of possession in her manners.

"She seems very familiar with Mr. Rex," Sarah commented.

"I told you before—Jameson Rex has been a favorite among the ladies for years. Perhaps she is a former—" Suddenly she stopped. The lady in question had her head tipped back, laughing at something Rex had said, and the sound carried across the room to Rosemary's waiting ears. The woman's voice had a deep, rich timbre, so low it almost sounded like a man's. Recognition dawned, and Rosemary's eyebrows rose.

"Lady Isabella Gray," she said softly. Sarah turned to her expectantly, and her friend explained. "I know her now. She has not been to London for several years, preferring Bath and the country to town life. At least, that is the reason I have heard. But I am sure it is as much to escape her scandalous reputation as anything else." Rosemary's face was grave. "She is beautiful, to be sure, but she is by no means polite society."

"Is she not?" Sarah asked, surprised. "She seems very fashionable."

"Oh yes, she is quite fashionable, but not at all respectable! She was a model of propriety in her earlier years, but then something happened... I am not quite sure what, as it was all hushed up and I did not hear much about it. And then her father died, and suddenly it seemed as if she had no more inclination to *be* respectable. She is quite wealthy, you know, so she has lived to please herself. And the men she entertains," Rosemary added.

She turned away in disgust, but Sarah looked back towards Lady Isabella, curious to see how Rex responded to her advances. He stood casually at her side, not seeming to notice or care how Lady Isabella leaned on his arm, or laid a hand on his chest when she laughed. He seemed perfectly at ease, being neither attracted nor repulsed by the ebony-haired beauty on his arm. In truth, Peter Mills seemed more drawn to her provocative looks and demure smiles than Rex did, but Rex himself certainly looked comfortable. Suddenly he looked up, and his eyes met Sarah's across the room.

Sarah blushed, instantly wishing she had not allowed her curiosity to overcome her sensibilities. Rex nodded in greeting, his amused smile apparent even from the distance, and Sarah nodded curtly in reply, turning away just as Lady Isabella looked in her direction. Rosemary had moved away from her while Sarah sat in reverie, and she turned in search of her friend.

Rosemary stood visiting with Mrs. Ashby and her niece. Sarah tried to join in the conversation, but her mind was racing with unanswered questions about Jameson Rex and his lovely guest. She was unusually quiet, and soon drew the attention of the gregarious Mrs. Ashby.

"You seem out of sorts tonight, Miss Mendenhall," the lady observed.

"Oh! No, not at all," replied Sarah, a little too cheerfully.

"Ah! But of course you are! Mary Anne, does not Miss Mendenhall seem out of spirits?" The pretty young redhead opened her mouth, but her aunt rode over her before she had a chance to reply. "I can see the reason clear enough my dear: you are bored with us, and surely wish to be dancing!" A set was just beginning to form, and Mrs. Ashby cast her eyes around in search of a partner.

"Oh no, Mrs. Ashby, I certainly do not wish to dance," Sarah rebuked her. Her head was in a muddle, and the last thing she wanted was to attempt the steps of a dance when she was most likely to fall flat on her face due to inattention.

"Nonsense! All young ladies like to dance," Mrs. Ashby declared. "Ah! Mr. Thatcher!" she called to a passing gentleman, not seeing through the crowd that Miss Elizabeth Brooks was already on his arm.

"Mr. Thatcher, surely you have a desire to dance, do you not?"

"Indeed I do, ma'am!"

"Then you must dance with our dear Miss Mendenhall."

She turned and bestowed an angelic smile upon Sarah, who was as red as a beet from embarrassment and anger. Mr. Thatcher, equally embarrassed, stammered his apologies and indicated to Miss Brooks, whose venomous eyes were trained on Sarah's face. Mrs. Ashby laughed, excusing the couple with a wave of her hand and looking around again for another partner.

"Let me see, who can we get for you..."

"Mrs. Ashby, please! I assure you that I have no desire to dance at present."

"Of course you do!"

"Please, Mrs. Ashby," Rosemary interjected, attempting to come to her friend's aid. "I do not think—"

"Here we are! Mr. Mills, sir," Mrs. Ashby sang out, addressing the man who was sauntering in their direction. "Have *you* a wish to dance with our sweet young friend tonight?"

"Mrs. Ashby!" Sarah cried desperately.

"It would be my pleasure," Peter replied in his silkiest voice. "I crossed the room with no other purpose." His lazy eyes took in Sarah's flushed countenance and added, "If I may have the honor, Miss Mendenhall?"

Outraged and completely mortified, Sarah nodded in mute reply and took his arm. He led her onto the floor and into position. She glared at him, her anger towards Mrs. Ashby finding vent in his apathetic visage.

"I am only dancing with you to escape that insufferable busy-body," she said acidly.

He laughed. "But of course!"

She sniffed, clearly annoyed at his disinterest. His eyes

roamed over her figure, and she shuddered, wishing she had refused. They were silent for a time, and as her anger ebbed, her curiosity took over. Since she was already committed to dancing with him, she determined to find out what she could about Lady Isabella.

"I do not have the pleasure of knowing the lady with whom you were conversing," she said, assuming an air of indifference.

"Lady Isabella Gray," he said languidly, turning. Sarah followed his gaze and saw that the lady in question was dancing with Rex a short distance from them.

Despite what Rosemary had revealed about Lady Isabella, Sarah could not help admiring her. With a keen eye for fashion, Sarah knew at first glance that Lady Isabella belonged to that breed of *haute couture* women to whom all of society look for guidance. Her milky throat glistened with diamonds, and her sleek ebony hair was done up in the latest style. The deep purple gown she wore exposed her delicate shoulders, setting off her creamy complexion with striking contrast, while long white gloves blended almost seamlessly into her porcelain skin. Sarah sighed at her loveliness.

"Lady Isabella Gray," she repeated, more to herself than her partner. "And how is she acquainted with Mr. Rex?"

"I believe they have long been acquaintances."

"Indeed!" Sarah looked past her partner to gaze at the couple once more. Lady Isabella danced as gracefully as a swan, and Rex led her with the ease of one long comfortable with his partner. Sarah bit her lip, turning back to Mr. Mills.

"Has she been in town long?"

His eyes narrowed, and a suspicious smile lifted the corners of his mouth. "Why do you ask?"

Sarah shrugged. "I do not recall having seen her before this evening, for she is certainly handsome enough that I should remember her if I had."

"Yes, she is quite the handsomest woman of my acquaintance—if I dare make such a declaration in the presence of society's pet."

His mocking smile was almost too much for Sarah to endure, even if she wished for more information about Lady Isabella. She wanted to slap the silly grin from off his face and never see him again. Instead, she tossed her head and smiled at him between her teeth.

"I believe I must agree with you, Mr. Mills. She is enchanting, and I should dearly like to make her better acquaintance."

"Would you, indeed?"

"Yes, I would. But your manners are so atrocious that I know I cannot rely upon *you* for an introduction."

He laughed; a jeering, leering chuckle that told Sarah the barb had struck a nerve. "Indeed, you are mistaken. I would be very happy to introduce you to her notice."

Sarah forced a smile, not about to accept any favors from Peter Mills. "Thank you, sir, but I am sure I will have the pleasure soon enough without you having to put yourself out. Good evening."

She sailed away before the crowd had even finished applauding the end of the dance, intent on putting as much distance between herself and Peter Mills's wandering eyes as possible. So swift was she in her flight that Sarah, not mindful where she was going, passed within inches of Jameson Rex and his bewitching partner. She turned her head away, but not before she saw him bestow a smile and a kiss upon Lady Isabella's gloved hand.

Chapter 17

Rex smiled to himself as he snapped the reins, whipping the horses into a faster trot. The last two hours had again been spent instructing Sarah on the proper way to handle the reins, and he knew that the pair were a bit on edge. They could sense the unfamiliar hands that had led them, as well as the nervousness those hands felt in being in control. But Rex was as patient a teacher as he was a driver, and Sarah had soon relaxed. Their second lesson in St. James Park had gone well, and having just escorted Miss Mendenhall home, Rex was wondering how to spend the remainder of his afternoon. He needed time to think, so he turned his horses into Hyde Park, resolving to take a few turns around the green to clear his head.

A letter had arrived from Mrs. Partridge the previous day, and while it contained no radical news, it had the effect of unsettling his nerves and bringing his purpose for coming to town back into sharper focus. He needed to find a wife. Caroline needed a mother. They both needed money, and while Miss Mendenhall was amusing, she was not what he was looking for. He shook his head, a smile tugging at the corner of his mouth. No, Miss Mendenhall certainly would not do for a wife. She was too sweet, too young, too impulsive, too trusting, too naïve, and most importantly—too poor.

His smile faded. He would never have given her a second thought were it not for the wager Peter Mills had made with him, but because of the bet between them, Rex had been spending considerable time in Miss Mendenhall's company. The more time he spent with her, the more distant his true goal became, however much he rationalized that it was time well spent. He told himself she was bound to fall in love with him eventually, and when she did he could claim the five thousand pounds from Peter and get down to his real purpose: to find and marry an heiress. But now that Lady Isabella was in the picture, all of that changed.

Lady Isabella Gray had walked into his life as abruptly as he had walked out of hers nearly a decade earlier. She was young, then—only sixteen years old—and Rex had courted her with the passion and vigor of lovesick youth. He had been a favorite of the late marquess, and the announcement of his betrothal to Lady Isabella had been anticipated every day. But the more intimate he became with her, the more he found in her a lust for power and an appetite for wealth that even her father's fortune and position could not satisfy. Though she declared her love for Rex and her desire to marry him, she ran off after the Duke of Charlesworth the minute he showed an interest in the beautiful young heiress. The duke drank of her charms and showered her with promises as empty as the rooms in which she found herself after he had tired of her. Lady Isabella was ruined. She returned to Bath in disgrace, begging for Rex's forgiveness and pleading with him to take her to wife as they had planned.

But Rex had refused. He walked away from Isabella, his heart and his pride hurt but his eyes open, grateful for his escape. He had never once looked back. Years later, after the marquess died and Isabella came into her inheritance, she waltzed back into society, flaunting her money and her loose reputation at any young cad who would have her. She cared nothing for what was said of her; money spoke louder than words, and all but the most pious of social circles were open to her because of it. Their paths had crossed occasionally in the years since then, but all intimacy between them was lost. They were nothing but nodding acquaintances.

Until now.

Rex heaved a sigh, rubbing his forehead. He had never wished to renew his relationship with Lady Isabella, but he could not deny the fortuitous timing of her reappearance in his life. He needed a wife with money, a woman who could overlook the sins of his past and the whispers of society and marry him, for Caroline's sake.

He clenched his jaw. *This is for Caroline.* He would do whatever was necessary in order to secure the capital he needed to protect her. But was marrying Lady Isabella the answer? She had money in abundance, but had she any heart? Would she care at all for Caroline? Rex knew that Isabella had a marked preference for town life over a quiet life in the country, but would she be content to stay at the estate? Was she still hungry for conquests, or had she at last changed? With his thoughts in a tumult, Rex glanced across the green and saw the very lady in question, walking down the long drive opposite him. He hesitated only for a moment before snapping the reins in an effort to overtake her.

He had to go around the walk, slowing down for other carriages and the increasing number of strollers, but he finally pulled up beside her and called his horses to a halt.

"Good afternoon, my lady."

"Why, Jameson Rex! Good day to you, sir," she said, looking up with a coy smile.

"I trust I find you well?" he asked politely.

She laughed. "Very well, Rex darling. And yourself?"

"Tolerable. But I confess myself happier now, in your company. Would you care to take a drive?"

"But of course," she said.

Rex helped her up into the curricle, then eased the horses into motion again. He took a deep breath and smiled. "And how is it that I find you all alone this fine day?"

"I am well past the age of needing a chaperon, Jameson," she said demurely.

He chuckled. "I was not suggesting the need for a watchful eye, Isabella." He raised one eyebrow at her. "Where are your admirers? You are the last lady I would expect to find alone on this glorious morning."

"Simpering young men bore me, I must confess. I count myself lucky to have been solicited by you and not accosted by one of them."

"I suppose I should be grateful that I am no longer a simpering young man," he replied, a teasing glint in his eye. Lady

Isabella smiled.

"You are still in your prime, Jameson, but you were never like them. You never simpered."

He nodded, but as the silence stretched between them, his demeanor changed. She watched him closely, noting the stiffness of his shoulders and the tense lines around his mouth. She did not like the downturn of his heavy brows, and his shift in mood made her restless. At last she spoke.

"Peter tells me that you are looking for a wife."

If she was hoping for something to signal the direction of his thoughts—a flushed cheek, a raised brow, a sign that he had a favorite pet he was keeping on the side—she was disappointed. He merely nodded.

"Is that not the reason everyone comes to town? To make a match? Is that not the reason *you* are here, Isabella?"

He cast a knowing glance in her direction, and she tossed her head.

"Perhaps," she hedged. "But only if the right man comes along."

She glanced at him through her lashes, an alluring smile upon her blood-red lips. Rex laughed, but his eyes were hardened steel.

"And what qualities would make him the right man, Isabella?" he asked. His voice was flat, his words more like a statement than a question. He went on before she could answer him. "Handsome, titled, *wealthy*," He drew out the word between his teeth, and snapped the reins. The poor horses vaulted into a sprint, and Lady Isabella grabbed the side of the carriage to keep from falling out of it.

"Forgive me," Rex apologized, reining in his horses and his anger. "There is no need to quarrel over the past."

"No," she agreed, "there is not. But there is also no use in pretending that it never happened."

They were silent for a time, and Lady Isabella glanced sideways at Rex's brooding profile, trying to gauge his mood. She must tread carefully if she wished to accomplish her designs.

"I am sorry," she said softly. He stiffened beside her, and she took it as an indication that he heard her. "I know that I apologized ten years ago, when the wound was fresh and raw. The apology was not sincere then. But it is now."

She waited, watching him carefully. Finally he relaxed, and a crooked smile broke across his handsome face.

"It was many years ago, Isabella. Water under the bridge."

He turned to her, and his smile was again sincere. She sighed contentedly, brushing her hand along his arm. Jameson Rex had forgiven her. Though he did not say it in so many words, she felt certain that he would come courting, which was precisely what she wished.

She slipped an arm through his, smiling wickedly to herself. If she played her cards right, this would be even easier than the first time.

Rex was in his study when the butler announced he had a visitor. Peter Mills strolled into the room and took the seat opposite Rex without being asked. He had an amused air about him, and Rex narrowed his eyes when the door was shut.

"Thank you for coming to see me," Rex declared, rising and coming around his desk.

Peter nodded, picking at his cuff.

Rex paced the length of the room, considering his words. Finally he cleared his throat. "Peter, about the wager..."

"Oh yes, the wager," Peter chuckled. "I must say, old boy, I am highly amused by the predicament in which you now find yourself."

Rex stiffened. "What do you mean?"

"Only that you are *supposed* to be making Miss Sarah Mendenhall fall in love with you, are you not? That *was* the idea after all."

Rex narrowed his eyes.

"And yet, here you are: half in love with the little vixen yourself—"

"Peter," Rex said dangerously.

"—and dangling after the fair Lady Isabella as well!"

"I am dangling after no one," Rex snapped. "Now see here, Mills—"

"Oh, come now, Rex, you would be a fool to throw away a chance to marry Lady Isabella," Peter taunted, raising an eyebrow at him.

"I know that," Rex growled. This conversation was not going at all the way he imagined it would. He found himself on the defensive, and the smug look on Peter Mills's primped face made Rex want to strangle him.

Instead, he took a deep breath, returning to his seat behind the desk. "I am well aware that Lady Isabella is just the sort of woman I asked you to help me find. And I am grateful to you for introducing me into her society again."

Peter nodded casually, inspecting his fingernails.

"But there is the matter of the five thousand pounds."

Surprised, Peter looked up. "What of it?"

"I would like to call off the bet."

Peter Mills laughed. "Not a chance. We shook hands on it, Rex. And a gentleman never breaks his word."

His tone was accusing, his eyes mocking. Rex glared at him.

"I have not the money to pay you," he said through clenched teeth.

"You will when you marry Lady Isabella."

"But if I am to court her, I cannot continue to woo Miss Mendenhall."

"Then stop," Peter said lazily. "And when you marry Isabella, you can pay me."

Rex's jaw tightened, and he remained silent. Realization slowly dawned on Peter's face.

"Y o u *are* in love with Miss Mendenhall!" he said incredulously.

Rex would not admit, even to himself, that Peter might be right. "Of course not," he snapped. "But I will not continue to string her along if I decide to court Lady Isabella."

"String her along?" Peter laughed. "What, you think she is falling in love with you, too?"

Rex did not answer. He was no more sure of winning Sarah's affections than he was of his own ability to swallow his pride and ask Lady Isabella for her hand. But Peter did not know that. Rex rubbed his chin, calculating his response.

"She is showing signs in the affirmative," he hedged.

"Which is why I would like to call off the wager—there is no need to hurt her."

"If she is showing signs of losing her heart to you, then you must continue."

"To what end and purpose?"

"Your five thousand pounds, of course. And my further amusement," he added with a wicked glint in his eye.

"And who shall determine when Miss Mendenhall has lost her heart? You?" Rex spat.

"Miss Mendenhall is a unique breed of woman," Peter continued casually. "She is naturally so cheerful and vivacious, that we must use other methods to determine the level of her affection."

"Such as?"

A devilish look shadowed Peter's face. "She must give herself to you."

"That was not in our agreement," Rex burst, standing so abruptly that his chair toppled over.

Peter shrugged, unconcerned. "Then you may propose marriage to her. She has been quite adamant that she will not accept a proposal this season, so if she accepts yours, you will know it is out of love." The last word slid from his lips with a sneer, and it took every ounce of strength Rex possessed not to lay his hands on the arrogant fraud and throw him bodily from the room.

"You know I cannot do that," he said, his voice dangerously low as he fought for control.

"Why not?"

Rex gaped at him. "Propose marriage to a girl with no

intention of honoring my word?"

"Why is that so repugnant to you?" Peter asked. He tilted his head, confusion lacing his words. "You refuse to walk away from an engagement, and yet you have no scruple in fathering an illegitimate child, for whom you are providing!"

Rex trembled with the effort to control himself. What Peter Mills said pierced Rex to the heart, for it brought all of his wrongs and his guilt from past deeds to the forefront of his mind. His beloved Mary had fallen headlong in love, and though Rex had loved her, he had not protected her. He closed his eyes, the guilt washing over him once more. It threatened to consume him body and soul, until suddenly a pinprick of light pierced his consciousness.

Caroline.

He had let Mary down; he would not do the same to Caroline. Caroline needed him. His reputation no longer mattered, for he had accepted his lot long ago. But did Miss Mendenhall's reputation matter? He trembled. *Yes,* he thought. *It does matter. But it cannot matter to* me.

Whatever the cost, whatever he must do, he would do it for Caroline. He had promised Mary as much, and he would not disappoint her again.

Rex opened his eyes, determination etched in every feature. His eyes glinted angrily as he nodded curtly to his guest.

"Very well, the wager is still on: five thousand pounds." He clenched his teeth. "I shall win Miss Mendenhall—on your terms."

Chapter 18

Four months had now passed since Sarah's arrival in London. Four months of parties and balls, the theatre, the opera. Four months of fawning youths whispering sweet nothings in her ear, sending flowers by the dozen, and attempting all sorts of menial feats to impress her. Sarah began to tire of the attention, and it was a relief when her cloud of admirers began to thin.

"I hear that Jeremy Thatcher and Elizabeth Brooks are finally engaged," Lady Rockwell said to her one morning after breakfast.

"And thank heavens for that! I was afraid I might have to bludgeon some sense into him at the last, but fortunately Providence intervened on his behalf."

Lady Rockwell chuckled. "You may yet have to bludgeon some sense into someone. I noticed that Mr. Grimshaw is still sending you flowers and cards nearly every day."

"It *is* every day," Sarah said making a face. "I am rarely out of temper, you know, but that boy is trying my nerves." She sighed, but Lady Rockwell merely shook her head and smiled.

Though several of her admirers' infatuation seemed to have waned, Sarah still held a tight grip on many of the eligible bachelors of the season, and not all of them as hopelessly dull as Freddy Grimshaw. The catty matrons whispered viciously about her behind her back, but Sarah paid them no heed, and they were often silenced by a cold stare from the countess. True to her word, Sarah remained charming, friendly, and agreeable to everyone she met, without any false affection or coy flirtations to sully her good name. To her jealous peers, it appeared she used every artifice imaginable to ensnare the hearts of so many young men, but to her friends and close acquaintances, she was affectionate and sincere; a trifle silly, perhaps, but then, this *was* her first season in London, and she was only just nineteen.

Rosemary and Sarah were out shopping one day near the end of May, enjoying the fine weather and admiring the latest fashions. They were walking arm in arm down Bond Street when Rosemary suddenly stopped. Without warning, she jerked Sarah into a nearby shop, almost causing her to fall on her face in the process.

"Rosemary!" Sarah hissed, catching her balance. "Whatever is the matter with you?"

"Oh, Sarah," Rosemary whispered, her face pale. "I believe he saw us!"

"What on earth are you talking of? Who saw us?" Sarah peered out the window and saw a slight young gentleman walking down the street, his fawn-colored eyes peeking out from under a tall beaver skin hat.

"Why, it is only Thomas Nelson! Why do you wish to avoid him? I thought you liked him!"

"I do like him! But, you see..." Rosemary's face flushed crimson and she shook her head. "I cannot let him see me, I cannot!"

"Well, I think you are a ninny. You will never win his affections hiding in ballroom corners and in shop doorways." Grasping her friend firmly by the wrist, Sarah pulled her out into the sunshine, ignoring her friend's whispered protests and frightened eyes. They emerged from the shop just as Mr. Nelson approached the doorway.

"Why, Mr. Nelson!" Sarah greeted him brightly. "What a pleasant surprise!" She nudged Rosemary with her elbow, who murmured a hello.

"Miss Mendenhall, Miss Reed." The gentleman doffed his hat, a thin smile breaking up his solemn features. "How are you this morning?"

"Very well, thank you," Sarah said demurely, waiting for Rosemary's response. But her friend kept her face down, and was silent.

"I wonder..." the gentleman began. He cleared his throat nervously, circling the hat in his hands. Sarah smiled to herself; he had all the signs of a man in love.

"I wonder if you are planning to attend the Haversham's ball this evening?" He smiled politely at both of them, but his question was directed at Rosemary, who remained stoically silent. Sarah fought the impulse to pinch her friend.

"Yes, I believe we are. Are we not, Miss Reed?"

Rosemary was forced to answer. "Yes, yes, of course. The

Havershams," she stammered, averting her gaze.

Mr. Nelson smiled broadly, and Sarah marveled at the change in his features. His pale brown eyes lit up, and a deep dimple appeared in one cheek. He suddenly looked nothing like the serious young seminary student Sarah was accustomed to seeing, but rather a giddy young schoolboy on the verge of first love.

"I am glad to hear it," he acknowledged, grinning in a manner quite unnatural for a man of the cloth. Sarah beamed.

But Rosemary looked completely miserable. She clasped her hands together, clearly uncomfortable, intent on looking anywhere but at his face. Sarah caught her eye, a questioning look in her glance, but Rosemary shook her head and looked away.

"Well," Mr. Nelson murmured, the light in his eyes fading a bit. He seemed finally aware of Rosemary's indifferent manner, and it caused him to hesitate. He donned his hat with a crestfallen face. "I shall look forward to seeing you this evening."

Sarah cleared her throat, giving Rosemary a sharp look, and Mr. Nelson bobbed his head at her. "Good day, Miss Mendenhall." Then, turning to Rosemary, he nodded. "Good day, Miss Bethany."

Sarah gasped, but Rosemary snatched her elbow and turned her about so quickly that they were ten paces away before Sarah found her voice.

"*Bethany?*" she sputtered. "He thinks you are your *sister?*"

"Now you know why I did not wish to meet him," Rosemary answered sullenly.

"But... I do not understand. How...?"

"It was last month, at the Pearson's dinner party," Rosemary

185

groaned.

Sarah had not been in attendance that evening, so Rosemary was obliged to recount what had happened.

"We had seen each other on several different occasions; at the assembly rooms, at Almack's, at various parties, but we had not been formally introduced. I think everyone assumed that we had been, and since we are both of us so reserved we never pressed for an introduction. Well, last month Bethany had an errand to attend to. She had offered to lend some of her music to Miss Lowell, and I..." Rosemary blushed, "well, I offered to take it to her. I was carrying the books in a small basket, but I was not paying much attention to where I was going."

Sarah hid a smile. The Lowells lived on the same street as Mr. Nelson. No doubt Rosemary offered to play courier in the hopes of catching a glimpse of the young ministry student.

"I tripped on a rock, and though I caught myself before I fell, the books tumbled out of the basket. Just as I was kneeling down to retrieve them, Mr. Nelson came down the walk and stopped to help me."

Rosemary's cheeks were pink with embarrassment, but there was no mistaking the sparkle in her eyes. She turned to Sarah and managed a small smile. "He was so very kind! He helped me to my feet and then retrieved the scattered books. We fell into conversation, and he told me that he had a great love of music; something of which I was unaware. He was turning the pages of one of the books I had dropped, remarking on the songs and asking which were my favorites. At last he took his leave, and I continued on my way.

"It was not until the Pearson's party the following week that I realized the mistake had been made. I was sitting with Mama, and Mr. Nelson approached and began to talk with me. We sat and conversed for half an hour. We found so much to talk of, and he was so very agreeable!" Rosemary sighed, but the smile on her lips faded. "But as he rose to take his leave, he... he took my hand. And he asked if he might come to see me."

"That is wonderful!" Sarah exclaimed, delighted for her friend. But Rosemary shook her head.

"No, it is horrible!" she countered with vehemence. "When I consented to his request, he smiled and said...and said... *'I am glad to have made your acquaintance at last, Miss Bethany.'* "

Rosemary burst into tears, stopping in the middle of the walk. Two women nearby turned their heads and stared at her as they passed. Sarah handed Rosemary a handkerchief, then gently guided her friend out of the way.

"There, there, dear," Sarah soothed, patting her arm affectionately. "It will be all right. But I am afraid I still do not understand—how did he suppose you to be Bethany?"

"It was the music book he looked through," Rosemary explained miserably. "Bethany had written her name inside the cover, and he must have thought it was *my* name!" She blew her nose in a most unladylike fashion.

"Well, I am very sorry for the misunderstanding," Sarah answered politely. "But surely you can tell him—"

"No, it is impossible! How can I embarrass him in such a way? He would be mortified—*I* would be mortified!" Rosemary sniffed forlornly. "There is nothing to be done but end the acquaintance."

"How silly you are! You will do no such thing." Sarah took

her arm and began walking again. They were on the south end of
Bond Street and near to the Burlington Gardens. She directed
their steps towards the green, guiding Rosemary down onto a
bench until she could once again compose herself.

"Now dearest," Sarah began gently, "why should you give
up the acquaintance simply because Mr. Nelson supposes your
name to be Bethany?"

"Because he thinks I am my sister!" Rosemary wailed.

"Nonsense! Has he been talking with your sister? Has he
sought for her favor?"

"No, but—"

"No. He has been enraptured with *you*, my dear friend. Why,
even a blind man could see his regard for you! I saw *that* the
moment he stopped beside us. And he would feel the same
whether your name was Rosemary or Bethany or Mildred or
Fanny," she finished matter-of-factly.

Her friend sniffed. "Do you think so?"

"I know so," Sarah said emphatically. "All we need do is
discover a way to set him right with as little embarrassment to
either of you."

"And how shall we do that?"

"Leave it to me," Sarah said, her eyes twinkling. "I believe I
have an idea."

Chapter 19

"You have been very quiet this afternoon," Lady Rockwell observed as she and Sarah bounced along in the carriage that evening. "I hope you are not hatching another plot like the one you concocted for the masquerade."

"Not at all," Sarah said. "I have not forgotten the scolding I received for that escapade, and I assure you I have no desire to deceive you again."

The countess chuckled. "I am glad to hear it."

They lapsed into silence once more, but after watching her for several minutes, Lady Rockwell narrowed her eyes.

"Out with it, Miss Mendenhall. If not another outrageous adventure, what are you scheming?"

Sarah smiled fondly at the woman across from her. "Dear Lady Rockwell, you may set your mind at ease. I am only forming a plan to help dear Miss Reed out of a very troublesome misunderstanding."

"A misunderstanding, I hope, not born from your own interference?"

"No, indeed!" Sarah refuted with feigned offense.

Lady Rockwell chuckled. The carriage pulled up in front of the Haversham's house, where every window was ablaze. Warm golden light spilled into the cool night air as Sarah and Lady Rockwell made their way up the granite steps to the door, which was held open by a liveried footman.

They were ushered into the ballroom, and Sarah quickly scanned the room, searching for the familiar face of Jameson Rex. She had not seen him as often as she was used to, and she missed seeing the merriment dancing in his eyes and the teasing manner in which they conversed. She frowned. Her idea to help Mr. Nelson extricate himself from the error responsible for Rosemary's misery depended entirely upon Rex's presence at the ball that evening.

Suddenly she spotted him, standing in a corner of the room with Lady Isabella. Though she remained somewhat in awe of the fashionable woman on his arm, Sarah could not wait for another opportunity to present itself. She squared her shoulders and made her way towards them.

Lady Isabella was laughing as she drew near, her hand on Rex's arm, her body nearly touching his. Sarah drew a breath and pasted a smile on her face.

"Miss Mendenhall," Rex greeted her warmly. Lady Isabella looked up to see whom Rex was addressing.

"How do you do, sir?" Sarah curtsied.

"How do you do. Lady Isabella Gray, may I present Miss Sarah Mendenhall." The ladies nodded at each other, and Lady

Isabella smiled at her.

"So you are the young lady who has taken London by storm," she said, an appraising look in her eyes. "I have heard much of you."

"Have you indeed?" Sarah replied, smiling nervously.

"Do not fear, Miss Mendenhall! I have assured Lady Isabella that while you are extremely diverting, you are not as wild as the stories portray you to be." Rex winked at her as Sarah gasped, but it was followed by her sparkling laugh.

"What an abominable tease you are!" she censured, her eyes twinkling.

"Only with you, my dear Miss Mendenhall," he said, bowing slightly.

"I can well believe *that*," Sarah answered, adopting an air of mock severity. "Your atrocious manners would elicit a smart slap across the face from any other female in the room."

Lady Isabella watched the exchange with amazed eyes, her gaze flitting from one to the other. Chuckling, Rex shook his head.

"Come now, Miss Mendenhall, shake hands with me and be friends, before Lady Isabella forms a misguided opinion of either of us."

"Gladly," Sarah said warmly, reaching for his outstretched hand. She clasped it firmly, and he gave her fingers a squeeze.

"Jameson, I wonder if you might fetch me some punch," Lady Isabella asked, intervening.

"It would be my pleasure," he responded. "Miss Mendenhall?"

"No, thank you."

Lady Isabella noticed that Sarah's eyes followed Rex as he strode across the room.

"Are you an admirer of Jameson's?" she asked archly.

Sarah turned back, her face flushing slightly. "No, not at all! We are merely good friends."

"I see." But the calculating look in her eyes made Sarah think otherwise.

"I am afraid you may have mistaken me," Sarah stammered, feeling more flustered by the moment. "But I assure you that you need not be concerned."

"Oh! I am not *concerned*, Miss Mendenhall. Merely curious."

Rex soon returned with a glass for Lady Isabella, and Sarah looked anxiously up at his face.

"I wonder, sir, if I might trouble you for a moment of your time," Sarah asked, casting a tentative glance at the slender woman by his side.

Rex, too, looked down at Lady Isabella, and the black-haired beauty smiled.

"But of course! Take him away, my dear Miss Mendenhall. I can see that the two of you are thick as thieves, and I shall have no part in your plans." When Rex began to protest, she waved him off. "No matter, Jameson dear. I see Peter Mills coming to my rescue." When Sarah turned in the direction she indicated, Lady Isabella leaned in to murmur in Rex's ear. "For you know, I could do with a bit of a *distraction* myself."

Rex turned red at the insinuation, but before he could retort, Lady Isabella sailed away, and he was left standing beside Miss Mendenhall.

"Oh dear, I hope I have not offended her," she murmured, anxiously watching Lady Isabella and Peter Mills retreat. But Rex shook his head, as much to answer her as to clear his senses.

"She seems to think I am one of your admirers," Sarah said doubtfully.

"Are you not?" he asked in mock astonishment.

"Of course not, you wicked man! If anything, *you* are an admirer of mine."

Rex laughed, and nodded in acquiescence. "If that is so, I am not to blame. You are positively the most charming creature I have ever met."

Sarah smiled at the compliment, her teasing eyes intent on Rex's face. "Do not let Lady Isabella hear you say that, for I believe she has claimed you as her own."

"Yes, it seems she is intent on renewing our former agreement."

"Former?"

"Yes. Though we were never formally engaged, there was an understanding between us more than a decade ago."

"Goodness, no wonder she is so possessive! If indeed she has been waiting for your proposal for ten years."

"I do not think she has been *waiting*, since I made it eminently clear I would not be renewing my addresses to her when I first severed our ties."

The minute he spoke it, Rex wished it unsaid. Surprise and then curiosity played across Sarah's features as she waited for him to explain, but Rex was silent. When he offered no explanation, Sarah reached out and gently laid a hand on his arm.

"What made you do so in the first instance, Rex? And why

have you changed your mind now?" she asked softly.

Rex was momentarily stunned. It was the first time she had ever called him Rex—the casual name his close friends and acquaintance called him. Despite their merry friendship, he had always been 'Mr. Rex' to Sarah, and he wondered if she even realized what she had said.

The familiarity of her face, the concern in her features, the sweetness of her voice—all combined to make his long-dormant heart awaken. It beat strangely in his chest, stirring and rousing his senses. The feeling was unnerving. Shaking his head, he changed the subject.

"Never mind. Now, what was it you wished to speak to me about?"

Sarah suddenly recollected her mission with a soft exclamation. "Oh, Mr. Rex, you must help me! It is Miss Reed, you see." Sarah briefly explained the circumstances, her eyes dancing as she recounted the tale Rosemary had told her. It was clear that Rex shared in her amusement.

When she had finished, her clear blue eyes looked up expectantly. "So you see, I *must* help Mr. Nelson to see the error he has made, if Miss Reed is to have any hope of happiness with him."

"Of course."

"So will you help me?"

The crooked grin Sarah knew so well appeared on his face, and her eyes lit up with hope.

"Miss Mendenhall, I am at your disposal. What do you need me to do?"

Rex stood poised a few feet from the entrance of the ballroom, glancing at the faces of those who entered, searching for Mr. Nelson. Sarah had been standing near him only moments ago, but when Rosemary entered the room Sarah quickly intercepted her friend, with a glance at Rex and a smile full of certainty as she departed.

Her confidence in his abilities was flattering, and so necessary to the success of her plan that he dared not voice the concern he felt in even being able to identify Mr. Nelson, let alone in his ability to command his attention for any length of time. He took a deep breath and looked towards the ladies once more. It was fortunate that Rosemary entered the room first, for it meant that Rex would not be required to retain Mr. Nelson for long. Turning back to the entrance, he was just in time to see Thomas Nelson enter the room and blend into the sea of guests milling about.

Quickly Rex followed him, striving to keep him in sight and hoping Sarah still had her eyes trained on him. At last he drew up beside the seminary student, polite recognition dawning in the younger man's face.

"Mr. Rex," he was greeted.

"Good evening, Mr. Nelson," Rex returned. "How do you do?"

"Calm yourself, Rosemary, there is no need for concern."

"Oh Sarah, I wish you would have told me!"

"So that you could have stayed at home, pretending to have a cold, and miss this opportunity? Nonsense."

Rosemary flushed, and Sarah smiled, squeezing her hand. Her eyes darted to where Rex and Mr. Nelson stood across the room, gauging from their body language how the conversation progressed. It seemed to be going well, and she sighed in relief.

"But... but what if Mr. Nelson is so mortified he never wishes to see me again?"

"Just remember what I said, and all will be well," Sarah soothed. Rosemary nodded weakly, and Sarah gave her hand another squeeze. Then, throwing her head back, Sarah let out a loud, bellowing laugh. The sound was so unlike her that Rosemary grasped her arm, alarmed.

"Miss Mendenhall, what on earth—!"

But Sarah ignored her friend and laughed again, turning to catch Rex's eye. He winked at her. That was the signal! Linking her arm in Rosemary's, she turned them both slightly so that they were facing the gentlemen, who nodded politely at them.

"Oh Sarah, I believe I shall faint!" Rosemary moaned.

"If you faint you will never see him again!" Sarah hissed, smiling through her teeth.

A moment passed, and Sarah held her breath. The gentlemen had their heads together and were conversing quickly. Rex seemed quite animated, and soon he clapped Mr. Nelson on the shoulder and the two men came towards them. Sighing in relief, Sarah turned to her friend once more.

"Now, remember," she said to Rosemary, "You are to behave as though you have never been introduced. And for heaven's sake, try not to stammer and blush!"

Mr. Nelson looked up as Sarah's laughter echoed throughout the room. Relief washed over Rex at her signal; he had exhausted nearly every reason he could think of for detaining Mr. Nelson, and he knew he could not continue much longer. Winking discreetly at Sarah, he nudged his comrade.

"Ah, the delightful Miss Mendenhall is in attendance, I see. But there, who is the charming young woman beside her?"

"I believe that is—"

"Is it Mrs. Ashby's niece?" Rex bulled over him.

"No, you are thinking of Miss Mary Anne Woodard."

"Ah, yes! The Titan beauty. I remember her now."

Mr. Nelson cleared his throat. "Miss Mendenhall appears to be in the company of—"

"Miss Grantham? No, my dear fellow, Miss Grantham is quite a bit taller than Miss Mendenhall's present companion."

"Yes, indeed," Mr. Nelson stammered, "but I believe the young lady in question—"

But Rex cut him off again. "Who is she, I wonder? I have not seen her before, for I would remember such a lovely young woman."

"I believe she—"

"We must ask Miss Mendenhall to introduce us. What do you say, Nelson? Would you like to find out who the charming young lady is?"

"Yes, of course. Er, that is—"

"Wonderful! Miss Mendenhall is a friend of mine, and she has seen us. Let us go and ask for an introduction."

Rex dragged Mr. Nelson, still stammering in confusion, across the room. As they drew near, Sarah cried out, "Why, Mr. Nelson! How good to see you. And Mr. Rex, how do you do?"

"I am quite well, my dear Miss Mendenhall, quite well." He looked expectantly from Sarah to Rosemary, and Sarah stifled a giggle. Rosemary looked nervous, Mr. Nelson befuddled, but Rex seemed perfectly at ease.

Sarah smiled warmly at him. "I am glad to hear it. Miss Reed, may I introduce you to Mr. Jameson Rex—I believe you already know Mr. Nelson. Mr. Rex, this is Miss Rosemary Reed."

Mr. Nelson started so suddenly he looked as if he had been slapped. Rosemary let out a soft moan and shot Sarah a withering look.

"Miss Rosemary Reed," Rex repeated, his eyes gleaming. "I am delighted to make your acquaintance." He indicated the open floor beside them and asked, "Do you care for dancing?"

"Well, I do not... that is..." Rosemary cast a desperate glance at Sarah, who could not help but roll her eyes.

Flashing a brilliant smile at both gentlemen, Sarah put her arm through Rosemary's and turned to face her. "My dear Miss Reed, you must not refuse to dance on my account. I am sure that Mr. Nelson will be happy to keep me company while you and Mr. Rex take a turn together." She smiled at her sweetly, prodding her gently.

Rex held out his hand to Rosemary. "May I have the pleasure of this dance?" he asked.

Rosemary nodded woodenly, barely managing to squeak out

198

a timid "yes" before Rex swept her away and into the throngs of the other dancers. Sarah laughed nervously, turning to Mr. Nelson, who wore a bemused expression on his face.

"I believe she is a bit nervous tonight, but Miss Rosemary Reed *is* an excellent dancer," Sarah offered, watching Mr. Nelson anxiously.

"Miss Rosemary Reed," he repeated absently. Sarah could almost see the wheels turning in his head. She watched as comprehension dawned in his solemn brown eyes. Turning towards her, he asked, "Are you well acquainted with Miss... Reed?"

"Oh! Yes, very well acquainted. Miss Reed is my dearest friend in London."

"I see." He was quiet for a moment, watching Rosemary and Rex as they danced. His brows drew together in thought. "Tell me," he began again, "Has she any sisters? I believe I understood..."

"Rosemary is the eldest of four sisters," Sarah broke in. "Her next younger sister, Bethany, is due to come out next season."

"Ah!" A flicker of understanding lit his eyes. "And this sister, Bethany—she is very musical, is she not?"

"Indeed she is, though she is not half so talented as Rosemary. But Miss Reed is very modest; she does not like to be fussed over."

"I should imagine not," he murmured, his eyes trailing her on the dance floor.

Sarah bit her lip, hiding a smile. It was clear that he understood his mistake, and was anxious to reestablish himself in her sight. They stood in companionable silence for the next quarter hour, until the dance concludedand Rosemary and Rex returned to join them.

"Miss Reed, you are an excellent partner," Rex was saying as they walked up.

Rosemary blushed, looking nervously at Sarah for some confirmation that the misunderstanding had been cleared up. Before Sarah could put her friend at ease, however, Mr. Nelson stepped forward.

"Miss Reed, if you are not too tired..." He hesitated. Rosemary smiled shyly up at him, and clearing his throat he asked, "Would you honor me with your hand for the next, Miss Reed?"

Her cheeks turned pink, though she smiled modestly and murmured an ascent. A Viennese waltz was just beginning, and Mr. Nelson led her away while Sarah and Rex looked on. Sarah sighed happily, and the gentleman beside her chuckled.

"Oh, Mr. Rex, you were wonderful!" she cried, smiling up at him. "I knew you would be perfect, and I am *so* glad you were willing to help me."

Her eyes were bright with appreciation, full of gratitude and delight. Rex lifted her hand to his lips and kissed it softly, never taking his eyes from her face.

"It was my pleasure, Miss Mendenhall," he said sincerely.

"How can I ever repay you? Truly, you were magnificent!"

Her tone was earnest, her sparkling blue eyes full of trust. Suddenly Rex remembered what Peter had said regarding their wager: *She must give herself to you.*

His stomach knotted.

Rex rubbed his thumb absently across the back of her hand,

which was still clasped in his own. He heard her breath catch, and he smiled slowly at her.

"I can think of a way..." he said at last, arching an eyebrow at her.

"Oh?" Sarah responded, her smile faltering just a bit.

"Yes." In a flash his other arm shot out, wrapping around her waist. She gasped as his hand pressed against the small of her back, drawing her close.

"Dance with me," he murmured, his lips so close to her ear that it tickled the hairs on her neck.

And he swept her onto the floor.

Chapter 20

"Hold the reins firmly, but not so taut—yes, just so."

Sarah's driving skills had improved immensely over the last several weeks; a testament to Rex's abilities as a teacher. She was perched on the seat of his curricle, wearing a pale pink morning dress and a dove-colored cloak with a matching cap. Her laughing eyes were bright as she glanced at Rex sitting beside her.

"Finnigan seems to have grown accustomed to my touch," she declared, a triumphant note in her voice.

"Of course he has. Your charms are not limited to mankind alone, you know."

Sarah scowled, shaking her head. "Do not speak to me of my charms! I spent all morning attempting to convince Edward Ramsey that I was indeed earnest in my refusal of his hand, but the silly young sop was in complete denial and beyond all persuasion." She gave the reins a vicious flick, and the horses jumped into a faster trot.

"None of that, now!" Rex laughed, reaching for the reins. Sarah relinquished them with a huff, the pouty look on her face forming a dent between her eyebrows almost like a dimple.

"Forgive me," she sighed. "But I was so vexed I could have strangled him."

"I well believe it," Rex replied, amused. "But you must never allow your feelings to alter your hand when you are driving. The horses will feel it, and you do not want to lose control."

"Yes, yes, I know."

He chuckled at her martyred look. "I tried to dissuade you from learning to drive, if you remember. Why should you desire it, when half the young men in the city are still dangling after you? Have you not enough suitors to drive you anywhere you wish to go?"

"Please, Mr. Rex, do not speak to me of suitors!" Sarah said, wringing her hands. Her doleful expression surprised him, and he pulled the horses in, slowing them to a stop.

Turning to her with a look of genuine surprise, he asked, "Why ever not? I thought you enjoyed having so many beaux."

"I do!" she cried, blushing. Taking a breath she added, "That is, I *did*. But that was before they all lost their heads and began to ask for my hand in marriage," she finished in a tumble. "It was a thrill to receive their offers in the beginning, and I confess to have let them go to my head a bit, but there have been so many of late —what with the season winding down and all—that I feel as if I could scream!"

Rex smirked, flicking the horses into a trot once more. "I know more than one lady who would be glad to have your problem."

"That is the worst of it," she lamented. "I know I should feel honored, and at first, it *was* very flattering. But now I hate it."

She turned to face Rex fully, a spark of vehemence flashing in her sapphire eyes. "How can they claim to love and admire me —enough, at least, to ask for my hand in marriage—when they scarcely know me at all? They have seen me at balls and parties, at assemblies and exhibitions, but what is that? How can one become acquainted with another person when their sole interactions are in public society?" She frowned. "They cannot be fortune hunters, for they know I have none. I am beginning to think that men in London have no sense at all."

"Not when a pretty face is before them, at least," Rex added wryly. She shook her head, exasperated, and Rex laughed.

"Try not to be too hard on them," he cajoled. "Not every man is after a fortune, you know."

"Are they not?" she said archly. "I was under the impression that most men of sense seek to improve their fortune by marrying prudently; to a woman of good standing with as many pounds to her name as can be acquired. I had hoped, since I did not fall into that category of blessed female, that *I* at least might be spared the insufferable attentions of such menial beings. But if I am to understand you correctly, sir, a pretty woman—even without a great fortune—is in just as great a danger as an heiress in marrying a conceited, abominable, silly prig!"

Rex shook with suppressed laughter at this diatribe, and though Sarah glared at him, he dared not open his mouth for fear of being overcome. She did not miss the twinkle in his eyes, however, and soon her own mouth twitched. She shook her head, chuckling, which Rex took as permission for releasing his own barely-concealed mirth.

Their laughter rang loud and far, the trilling bell tones of Sarah's laugh blending with the rich baritone notes of Rex's own. When at last they finally ceased, Sarah drew a deep, cleansing breath.

"Ah, Mr. Rex," she said, the quiet comfort of her voice stirring something within him, "you must advise me. What am I to do?"

"There is only one thing you *can* do, I am afraid."

"And what is that?"

"You must accept one of the insufferable prigs, if you are to avoid the proposals of all the rest," he said with a smile.

Sarah laughed and slapped him gently on the arm. "How odious you are! You know I cannot do that."

"Why ever not?"

"First of all, because I gave my word that I would accept no proposal this season. Secondly, because the men who have offered for me have been either abominably conceited or unbearably dull. And thirdly..."

Rex looked over at her as she paused, and was surprised to find that her vivacity on the subject had suddenly been replaced with a quiet melancholy he had never beheld in her before. He peered anxiously at her face, waiting for her to continue. When at last she heaved a sigh and looked up at him, he saw that her usual laughing eyes were dewy with tears.

"I had hoped to be loved by my husband," she said in a small voice. "Not for my beauty or my charms, but for *me*."

Stunned, Rex knew not what to say. Never before had he

beheld such vulnerability, such a sincere admission of her intimate feelings. Gone was the playful, amicable young woman who had won the affections of so many. Sitting beside him was a sensitive, lonely girl who felt deeply and keenly the absence of real love in her life.

It was in that moment, he knew he loved her.

And in the next, he knew that love could ruin him.

The only thing that could have distracted Rex from his ultimate goal was falling in love. He had scorned the idea for years, never believing he would fall victim to its snare. His heart had turned to stone the night Mary died, and only a portion of it had thawed to allow his affection and devotion for Caroline to take hold.

Caroline.

Rex shook his head, suddenly angry with himself. Had he forgotten that her welfare was the sole purpose for his coming to London? His sole reasonfor seeking a wife? It would be foolish, selfish, and absurd to marry a woman so wholly unable to provide the fortune he knew to be absolutely necessary. A tiny part of him argued that more than money, Caroline needed a mother who was generous, kind, and as full of mischief and fun as his golden-haired little girl was, but he thrust the thought angrily aside. He could not, *he would not*, marry Sarah Mendenhall. Any woman who attached herself to him would be censured and despised by polite society, and he did not want that fate to befall her. But neither would he abuse her faith and trust in him by the repulsive suggestions offered to Rex by Peter Mills.

There was only one option open to him now.

He sat stiffly beside her, attempting to sort out the feelings which had so suddenly been thrust upon his mind. He knew what must be done, and though his softening heart cried out at the thought, he was determined to do it. Love was a dangerous game, and he would not allow Caroline to fall victim to it.

While Rex struggled within himself, Sarah had been watching the early summer landscape pass from their view, endeavoring to hold back her tears. Rex guided the horses out of the park and back to Cavendish Square. They were silent during the time it took to return to Lady Rockwell's house—a phenomenon new to their relationship. But it was a comfortable silence, and neither party seemed inclined to break it.

The carriage pulled up in front of the weathered steps, and Rex jumped out to help Sarah down, while his footman went to the horses' heads. Rex took Sarah's hand, and though it may have been his imagination, he thought he felt her press his fingers when she smiled at him.

"Thank you for the drive, Mr. Rex," she said, only a trace of her former melancholy marring her voice. "You are the only man whose company I can keep without falling into dithers afterward."

They both laughed, but it was a forced, unnatural laugh, the likes of which their friendship had never known. The memory of other, merrier laughs that they had shared crept into Rex's mind, and he felt a stab of envy for the lucky man who would eventually win her affections. Sarah Mendenhall was the most darling creature he had ever met. Kind, affectionate, and without greed or guile, she reminded him so much of Mary. But the comparison made him wince. His love for Mary, however deep, had not been enough. She had traded her heart for her body; her purity and innocence for the child she left behind, without even the gift of legitimacy to help her in the world. Guilt and anger mingled in Rex's mind, and he resolved that he would never place another woman he loved in such a position again.

Sarah was watching him curiously, her hand still in his while flickers of emotion flashed across his face. He looked solemnly into her eyes, willing her to see the love in his own that he could never offer her. He lifted her hand and gently brushed his lips along the gloved surface.

"Thank you again, Mr. Rex," she said, smiling sincerely at him. "Good day."

Rex bowed his head slowly, striving to smile around the pain that caught in his chest. "The pleasure was mine, Miss Mendenhall. Goodbye."

It was only three days later, while attending a dinner party at the Carlisle's, that Sarah heard the news.

"Well, Miss Mendenhall, you seem to have lost another admirer," Lady Mills haughtily announced as she and Rosemary approached.

"Thank heavens!" Sarah laughed. "I am glad they are thinning out! For whom, pray tell, may I mourn?" she teased.

"Mr. Jameson Rex."

The impish smile on Sarah's face wavered, and it was Rosemary who gave voice to what her heart had cried out.

"Mr. Jameson Rex! Impossible!" her friend, dumbfounded.

"Not quite," the hawkish woman sniffed. "I heard it from my son, Peter, who heard it from Mr. Rex himself." She smiled in grim satisfaction, watching the color drain from Sarah's face. "He is engaged to Lady Isabella Gray."

Chapter 21

The news traveled quickly. Soon the betrothal of Jameson Rex and Lady Isabella Gray was talked of in every social circle, and their impending nuptials were looked forward to as the crowning event of the season.

To say that Sarah was surprised would not do credit to the shock, and subsequent sadness, that she felt in losing the acquaintance of Jameson Rex. She would not speak of it to Lady Rockwell, or even to Rosemary, for she did not fully understanding her feelings herself. Instead, she poured out her heart in her paintings.

Her hard work paid off, and one morning in mid-June, Sarah succeeded in finishing a piece that not even her exacting tutor Mr. Meijer could find much fault with.

"You have at last managed to correct your proportions," he said after their lesson. "And you have captured the details in the fruit most admirably."

The still life Sarah had painted was a small stack of books with a bowl of fruit on top. She had spent hours perfecting the mottled coloring of the apple skin and the smoothness of the leather tomes. She sighed in relief at her teacher's words, and he smiled at her.

"*Goed gedaan,*" he said. "Well done."

It was these words of praise that completed her formal training. Sarah had at last managed to discipline her hand and harness her natural artistic abilities, and when Lady Rockwell asked if she would like to continue with her lessons, she kindly declined.

"But will you not continue to paint?" the countess asked.

"Oh yes, of course I shall!" Sarah was quick to answer. "But I should like to paint for my own pleasure now, and not to meet the exacting requirements of a tutor."

Lady Rockwell smiled. "I understand completely, *Mein Kind.* When I was a girl, I had the most formidable *maestro.* He was very large, with an equally large voice and a very wet mouth. It was a terrifying combination."

The ladies laughed together, and it was with a great deal of relief the next day that Sarah told Rosemary she had finished her lessons.

"I believe I owe the improvement in my artistic abilities to Jameson Rex," she mused. "The way he taught me to hold the reins is how I at last managed to learn to hold the brush—steady, but not too tightly." She sighed. "While I am glad to give up Mr. Meijer, I wish I did not need to relinquish my driving lessons."

"Why do you not ask one of your other admirers to teach you?" Rosemary asked.

"Because each and every one of them harbors only a superficial regard for me. I would rather have one sincere beau than a dozen silly sopheads." She sighed. "I believe I quite envy you," she said, her eyes full of longing as she looked at her friend.

Rosemary blushed and bent her head to her needlework. Sarah had every right to envy her friend, for the courtship between Rosemary and Mr. Nelson was well under way. The night at the ball had opened the eyes of the young ministry student to his misunderstanding, and after a dignified apology on his part and a rather embarrassed acceptance on hers, they had fallen easily in love with one another.

"If only there was another man to whom I could apply to teach me," Sarah mused, wandering back to the topic at hand. Suddenly she cried out. "Rosemary! What about Mr. Nelson? Do you think *he* would teach me?"

"I am not sure," her friend hesitated. "Mr. Nelson is so proper, you know... I do not think he would wish to be alone in your company, even if it is just to drive in the park."

Sarah laughed. "He would not be alone with me, you ninny, for you shall accompany us, of course!"

"Oh! Well... he might be prevailed upon, in that case," Rosemary stammered, blushing.

"He will definitely do it, you are saying," Sarah quizzed her. "He must be quite madly in love with you, Rosemary! When am I to wish you joy?"

"He has asked to speak to my father already," Rosemary murmured, hiding her flushed cheeks by looking down at her work again.

Sarah gawked at her.

"In truth? Oh dearest, how wonderful!" Sarah cried, clapping her hands in delight.

"Papa will not consent," Rosemary sighed, shaking her head. "I am only nineteen, after all, and Mr. Nelson has not completed his studies. He will need to be ordained and secure a living before we can marry."

"But surely your father will allow your betrothal? Nineteen is a fair bit older than many girls marry, you know."

"Perhaps." Rosemary said, biting her lip. She fell into silence, and Sarah did not press the subject any further. At last Rosemary set aside her needlework and smiled.

"Whether or not my father gives his consent to Mr. Nelson, it need have no bearing on your own felicity. Mr. Nelson is coming for dinner today, and I will ask him if he will take over your driving lessons."

Mr. Nelson agreed to the scheme, and soon the three young people were spending their mornings driving together in Hyde Park. The summer air was warm and the paths of the park bordered with hundreds of flowers. Sarah noticed the blooms as they drove, and a pang of homesickness coursed through her. How she longed for the exotic beauty of the orchids from the Botanical Gardens! How she yearned to see the path strewn with the tiny blossoms of jasmine, their milky whiteness like fallen stars beneath her feet! She sighed and shook her head, chirping to the horses to move along their way.

"I believe you have a natural hand, Miss Mendenhall," Mr.

Nelson remarked one day as their lesson concluded.

"Thank you," Sarah replied, pulling the horses to a stop in front of Lady Rockwell's house. She was quite proficient at driving now, and the praise was well-deserved.

The footman helped her down, and Sarah waved goodbye as Mr. Nelson drove off, with Rosemary beside him. She entered the house and made her way to the sitting room, where Lady Rockwell was waiting for her.

"Home at last, are we?" she asked, an unnatural brusqueness in her voice.

"My apologies, Lady Rockwell, but it was such a glorious morning that I simply could not bear to leave the park." Sarah brushed a kiss along Lady Rockwell's cheek, and the older woman *hmphed* in reply.

"Have you been sitting here alone this morning?" Sarah asked, concern lacing her voice.

"I have been well enough, I daresay. You need not worry yourself with me, Miss Mendenhall." The curtness in her voice persisted, and Sarah hesitated.

"Have I offended you in some way, your ladyship?"

The countess huffed. "No. But you had a visitor while you were out."

"Oh?"

"Yes." Lady Rockwell's eyes narrowed. "Lady Isabella Gray."

"Lady Isabella Gray?" Sarah repeated, her mouth dropping open.

"Yes." Lady Rockwell's piercing gray eyes bored into Sarah's face. "Have you formed an acquaintance with her?"

Sarah shook her head. "I was introduced to her at the Haversham's ball, and of course I know who she is, but I would hardly consider her an acquaintance. And I most certainly did not expect her to wait on me." A light flickered on in Sarah's eyes, and she clapped her hands together. "Oh, Lady Rockwell, was she wearing her jonquil silk gown? I heard it was from a designer in Paris, and I have always wanted—"

"I have not the faintest idea what she was wearing," the countess broke in severely, "for I would not see her. She left her card, and that is all." Lady Rockwell looked stern. "I do not want you to become enamored with her, Miss Mendenhall. She is not respectable society."

Sarah's face fell. "That is what Miss Reed said. But she has been to many of the same parties which we ourselves have attended..." Her voice trailed off when she saw the look on Lady Rockwell's face.

"Miss Mendenhall," she said, her voice kind but firm. "This goes beyond not having a voucher for Almack's. I am certain you have noticed the quality of men with whom she keeps company."

Sarah flushed, and the countess nodded.

"Just be sure to keep your distance," she cautioned.

"But... would it not be a very great insult to ignore her calling card?" Sarah pleaded, clinging to the last thread of hope she saw. She had enough sense not to take Lady Isabella's *conduct* as an example, but Sarah had yet to find her equal in *style.* Her own weakness for fashion made her willing to overlook Lady Isabella's character flaws for a chance to glean any insight into her personal style of elegance.

Lady Rockwell sighed. "You may leave your card for her if

you wish, but I do not want you to visit her." When Sarah protested, she held up her hand, a grave look in her eyes.

"I will not allow you to be drawn in by her, Miss Mendenhall. That is my final word."

Though disappointed in the matter regarding Lady Isabella, Sarah was delighted that the countess allowed her driving lessons to continue. Soon Sarah had mastered the reins, and she began pleading with Lady Rockwell to allow her to drive unaccompanied. It had taken many days and several sulks before Lady Rockwell at last gave permission for Sarah to drive herself around in the countess's phaeton on occasion. It was a bit larger than the type of vehicle Sarah was used to driving, but she assured her ladyship that she was quite capable of handling the reins, and at last the countess relented.

"Be sure that John accompanies you," Lady Rockwell sighed in defeat.

Sarah promised her that she would not venture out without the coachman, and just after breakfast the next morning she asked John to bring the carriage around. The pair of horses chosen for the occasion were jet black, with white stars and stockings, and they contrasted with the pale gray carriage quite nicely.

"Would you like me to drive, miss?" John asked, handing her up into the seat.

"Thank you, John, but I can manage."

The coachman nodded and climbed into the seat beside her. Sarah adjusted her gloves, then snapped the reins across the horses' flanks and they started off.

Sarah had promised Lady Rockwell that she would make only a few morning calls and be back in time for dinner. Her first order of business was to drop a card at the home of Lady Isabella Gray. Sarah had hoped that the countess's stern disapproval of Sarah's wish to further her acquaintance would have softened, but the countess had remained immovable to the last, and Sarah resigned herself to merely leaving her card with the lady's butler.

Lady Isabella's house was one of the large, imposing edifices found in Grosvenor Square, the most fashionable corner of Mayfair. A dozen polished steps led up to the massive front doors, and Sarah eased the horses to a stop at the foot of them. John jumped down from the carriage and went to stand at the horses' heads, while a footman helped Sarah down from her perch on the phaeton. She looked up at the tall, carved doors, feeling suddenly quite small and insignificant. Smooth Roman columns reached clear up to the third story, and dozens of glazed windows stretched across the entire front of the building. Mounting the stairs, Sarah knocked hesitantly with the polished brass knocker. Presently the door was opened by a middle-aged gentleman in an immaculate ebony waistcoat and trousers: clearly the butler.

He bowed her inside, but before Sarah had a chance to leave her card and politely withdraw, Lady Isabella herself emerged from a doorway off the entrance hall.

"Why, Miss Mendenhall!" she cried, a smile gracing her porcelain features. "What a pleasant surprise. I told Winston I would not be at home to visitors this morning, but for *you* I can make an exception."

Sarah's cheeks turned pink with pleasure, and all thought of making a hasty exit flew from her mind. There was a tiny voice in the back of her head that squeaked out in protest, but Sarah rationalized that it would be abominably *more* rude to refuse a direct invitation, and she felt certain that the countess would understand. She followed Lady Isabella upstairs to the drawing room, and was soon seated across from her, sipping tea.

"What beautiful flowers!" Sarah remarked, admiring a large bouquet of cabbage roses on a marble-topped table near the window.

"Jameson sent them over. He knows they are my favorite," Lady Isabella purred.

Sarah smiled. "They are lovely. There are not many roses in India, and seeing so many of them is something I have loved about being here in England."

"Yes, I heard that you are lately arrived from India."

"Indeed. I was born there, and had never been to England before last year."

"Never?" The incredulity in Lady Isabella's voice could scarcely be masked.

Sarah flushed, disconcerted. "Er, no, never. But I do not have any plans to return at present. I should like to make England my home, permanently," she finished in a rush.

"Then you will have to catch a husband," Lady Isabella declared, smiling archly.

Sarah laughed. "That is what everyone keeps telling me."

"They are right." Lady Isabella added a lump of sugar to her cup and stirred it gently. "But since I have managed to capture the affections of Jameson Rex myself, you shall have to content yourself with another gentleman."

The censure of her words were hidden behind the teasing note in her voice, and Sarah smiled.

"I certainly shall. Though I confess I was sorry to lose his services."

Lady Isabella raised her eyebrows at Sarah over her teacup. "Services?"

"Oh! I thought he would have told you. Mr. Rex had taken it upon himself to teach me how to drive," Sarah stammered.

"Hmm," came the murmured response.

They lapsed into an awkward silence. Lady Isabella regarded Sarah shrewdly from her seat opposite. Sarah drank her tea mechanically, searching her mind for something to say.

"Your hat is positively charming, my dear," her hostess suddenly complimented her.

"Do you think so?" Sarah asked, flattered.

"Yes, it reminds me of one I saw in a shop in Paris last year."

"Paris!" Sarah breathed, her face alight.

A slow, calculated smile spread itself across Lady Isabella's face. She arched her delicate eyebrows, and poured herself another cup of tea. "Have you an eye for fashion, Miss Mendenhall?"

"Oh, well..."

"Come, come, my dear," Lady Isabella chuckled. "I can see that you have a passion for it, and I daresay you have a natural eye."

Sarah blushed, smiling modestly.

"I noticed it before I even knew who you were," her companion continued, cocking her head to one side. "Your dresses are perfectly tailored in the most becoming style for your figure, rather than the latest style found in the fashion magazines. That alone bears testimony for your estimable taste.

"And your headpieces," she went on after another sip. "Why, so many ladies wear such ostentatious contraptions on their heads! But you distinguish yourself in a much more elegant manner," she finished, her dark eyes smiling at her guest. "You have exquisite taste, my dear."

"Thank you," Sarah murmured, her eyes alight from Lady Isabella's praise. "I confess that I felt at *such* a disadvantage, being raised in India. The fashion plates from England were always a season or two late, and while I did my best to adhere to the styles at the time, I also tried to predict where the fashions in beauty and clothing were directed, and adjust my dress accordingly."

"Yes, I can see how you have modified the style of your gown slightly," Lady Isabella said, narrowing her eyes and scrutinizing the rose-colored silk Sarah wore. The corner of her mouth drew up in a half-smile, and Sarah visibly relaxed. "It is charming, my dear, as are you."

Sarah was beside herself. Despite her reputation, Lady Isabella was looked to as one of the most fashionable women in town, and here she was, praising Sarah's own taste! Any reservations that Sarah had harbored about her hostess were dispelled; she looked at Isabella with worshipful admiration in her eyes.

Lady Isabella rang a tiny silver bell, and a smartly dressed young maid entered the room to clear away the tea things. Sarah understood the implication and smiled politely.

"Thank you so much for seeing me," she enthused. Lady Isabella nodded, a coy smile on her own lips.

"The pleasure was mine, Miss Mendenhall. I wonder..." She tapped a dainty finger to the side of her mouth, her full lips twisted in thought.

"Yes?" Sarah breathed, anticipation tingling her senses.

Lady Isabella arched her delicate eyebrows. "There is a milliner's on Fleet Street, near Ludgate. Are you familiar with the area?"

Sarah shook her head. A smile lit Lady Isabella's features, and she leaned forward a little, as if imparting a secret.

"Madame Trouillet is a *magnificent* seamstress. When I do not have my gowns sent in from France, she makes them up for me here."

Sarah was hardly breathing, her brilliant blue eyes sparkling expectantly.

"Tell her that I sent you," Lady Isabella declared, sitting back with a satisfied smile. "She will not work for everyone, but your natural taste deserves the best, and Madame Trouillet *is* the best."

"Thank you, Lady Isabella," Sarah said with feeling. Her hostess nodded demurely, and Sarah stood, dropping a curtsy before she turned to quit the room.

"Remember, she is on the east end of Fleet Street," Lady Isabella called out as Sarah reached the door. Sarah smiled again in gratitude, and the door shut behind her.

Lady Isabella stood, her willowy figure gliding noiselessly to the window. She looked down through the gossamer curtains as Sarah climbed into the phaeton and prepared to depart. A cruel

221

smile cut across Lady Isabella's face as she watched the carriage out of sight.

"No more distractions, Jameson," she growled. "You are *mine* now."

Chapter 22

Sarah was in such an ecstasy about her meeting with Lady Isabella she could hardly contain herself. The horses were jumpy under her anxious hand, and John looked warily over at her.

"Easy now, miss," he chided gently.

Sarah took a deep breath, striving to rein in her excitement. "Yes. Thank you, John."

The coachman nodded, still tense, but as the horses settled more easily into a trot he relaxed. Sarah tried to concentrate on what Rex had taught her. *Hold the reins firmly, but not taut. Loosen your shoulders. Give clear pulls on the reins, but not too quickly or the horses will overstep. Try to relax.*

She smiled. It had been easy to relax in Rex's presence. The teasing gleam in his gray-blue eyes, the deep timbre of his laugh, the soothing sound of his velvet voice when he spoke to her... A pang of loneliness washed through Sarah as she thought of her friend. She missed him. She missed the comfortable camaraderie they shared; the hidden merriment she saw reflected in his eyes whenever they were together.

Pulling herself out of her reverie, Sarah turned the carriage onto Camden Place and stopped in front of the Reed's home. She let the memories fade away, her excitement building again as she thought of sharing her news with Rosemary. John helped her down, and Sarah tripped up the steps to the door.

Rosemary met Sarah in the parlor off the entrance hall. "Sarah, whatever is the matter?" she exclaimed, the bright eyes and flushed cheeks of her friend causing undue alarm.

Sarah waved her off impatiently. "Nothing is the matter, but oh, Rosemary! I have had the most delightful visit with Lady Isabella this morning!"

"Lady Isabella Gray?" Rosemary asked with surprise.

"Yes, and she was positively divine! I wish you could have seen her—so polite, so complimentary!" Sarah sighed dreamily, sitting down.

"I did not know you were such intimate acquaintances," Rosemary answered warily.

"Oh, we are not," Sarah laughed. "I was merely returning her visit from last week."

"She called on you last week?"

"Yes, when you and I were out driving with Mr. Nelson." Sarah tapped her chin thoughtfully. "I was very surprised to hear that she had paid me a visit. And in truth, I was not *supposed* to have called upon her today. Lady Rockwell said she was not polite society and that I should not make myself acquainted with her."

"Then why did you go?" her friend asked, shock coloring her

tone.

"I did not mean to! That is, I did call on her this morning, but I only planned to leave my card. Lady Rockwell had agreed that I might at least do that, but Lady Isabella came into the hall just as I entered the house, and I simply could not refuse to see her then, you know. Not when she was so glad to see me, and so hospitable... could I?"

"I suppose not," Rosemary acknowledged after some hesitation.

Sarah let out her breath, a smile lighting her features once more. "I am glad to hear it. For you would have done the same thing, would you not? And if *you* would do it, then I have no reason to be ashamed of my decision. Though Lady Rockwell will not be pleased," she added as an afterthought.

Rosemary was certainly less convinced than her friend, but Sarah went on without seeming to notice.

"And I am glad that I did, for you will not guess what she said to me!" Sarah gushed, leaning forward. "She said I had *exquisite taste.* Me! Can you believe it?"

"Well, that was very—"

"But that is not the best of it," Sarah continued in a rush. "She gave me the name of her *personal* dressmaker, and told me to tell Madame Trouillet that she sent me!" She fell back against the cushions, her dreamy eyes staring up at the coffered ceiling.

"Madame Trouillet?" Rosemary repeated.

"Yes, do you know her?"

"No, I have never heard of her." She frowned at her friend. "Are you sure that was her name? Not Madame Traisseu?"

"No, it was Madame Trouillet, I am sure of it. She is

established on Fleet Street."

"Fleet Street? But that is near the City." Rosemary looked gravely at her friend. "I do not think a reputable dressmaker would be established on Fleet Street."

"Nonsense! She must be reputable, or Lady Isabella would not employ her services," Sarah said. Ignoring the troubled look on Rosemary's face, she smiled. "I am going there now. Would you like to accompany me?"

Rosemary sighed. "I cannot, for Mama and I are going out. She will be down any moment."

Sarah nodded, and the ladies rose and embraced. Concern for her friend once more clouded Rosemary's sweet face. "I wish you would not go," she said emphatically. "I do not think it is safe."

"Thank you for your concern, dearest," Sarah replied, squeezing her friend's hands. "But I am sure that all will be well. You may call on me tomorrow and I will tell you all about it." She tossed a saucy smile at her friend, and Rosemary forced a laugh. Kissing one another gently on each cheek, the friends parted.

John helped Sarah up into the phaeton once more. Adjusting her gloves, Sarah mulled over what Rosemary had said: *I do not think a reputable dressmaker would be established on Fleet Street.*

"Nonsense," she muttered, snapping the reins.

"Beg pardon, miss?" John asked, cocking his head.

"Nothing, John. I am only talking to myself." She flashed

him a smile, and he chuckled, shaking his head.

But Rosemary's words echoed in Sarah's head. What if her friend was right? What if there *was* no dressmaker on Fleet Street? Her brow furrowed. She was not very familiar with London as yet, and what little she did know was confined to the West End.

"John," she asked presently. "Where is Fleet Street?"

"It be east of 'ere, miss. Th' Strand turns 'to Fleet Street down near th' City."

Sarah relaxed. The Strand was a major thoroughfare, and though a bit out of fashion now, it was still frequented by many of London's elite society.

"Thank you, John," she returned, bestowing an angelic smile on the aging coachman.

He nodded, seeming to hesitate. "Beggin' yore pardon, miss, but what be yore business on Fleet Street? 'Tain't no place for a lady, miss."

Sarah pursed her lips. First Rosemary, and now John! She did not think it was any of their concern whether she went to Fleet Street or not, and it vexed her that they insisted on knowing better than she.

"I was merely curious, John," she answered stiffly, her eyes straight ahead as she flicked the horses into a faster trot. The coachman nodded, and though he glanced at her sideways from time to time, he said nothing more.

While John maintained a respectable silence, Sarah did some quick thinking. Of one thing she began to be ever more certain: if she was to visit Madame Trouillet on Fleet Street, she would have to go alone. Based on both Rosemary's and John's reactions to the news, there was no doubt in Sarah's mind that the countess would refuse to let Sarah go, and Sarah could not allow that to happen. She was quiet as they drove along, considering how and when she might be able to slip away to Fleet Street.

Sarah stopped the carriage in Bond Street to make a few purchases, then left her card at the homes of a few friends nearby. She was anxious to go home and think the matter over, and after an hour's worth of errands she turned the horses homeward. Soon they pulled into Cavendish Square, and John hopped down to help Sarah descend.

It was the perfect opportunity.

"On second thought, John, I believe I will take a turn in the park," Sarah remarked, flicking the reins once more and setting the carriage in motion.

"But, miss!" John cried, stumbling after her.

"Do not fret, John! I shall be well!" Sarah called over her shoulder to the dumbfounded coachman.

The sudden thrill of her escape coursed through her veins, and Sarah smiled to herself. What did Rosemary and John know about Madame Trouillet? Or about Lady Isabella? A tiny voice inside of her said that though they may not know her better, they had certainly known her *longer*. Sarah hesitated. She knew that Lady Isabella did not have a very good reputation, but she had been so kind! So sincere! Sarah's insides fluttered as she recalled her conversation with Lady Isabella, and any thought of an ulterior motive on Lady Isabella's part flew from Sarah's mind. *I shall see for myself,* she determined, turning onto Oxford Street.

Though not entirely sure of her destination, Sarah knew she would need to travel south and east to get to the Strand. She continued confidently on her way, smiling and nodding at the drivers she passed, and striving to keep her excitement in check lest the horses get nervous once more.

At last she came to Charing Cross, and she breathed a sigh of relief. The familiar monument was located at the junction of Whitehall and the Strand, and it was onto the latter street that she turned her carriage. She felt easier knowing that her destination was on this road somewhere, even though she knew not how far she must travel before it became Fleet Street. She would simply keep driving until she made the transition, and then, if needed, ask a kindly soul for the direction to Madame Trouillet's.

Humming to herself, Sarah's spirits rose as she passed the busy shops and coffee houses along the way. Before the cream of London's society moved to Mayfair, the homes of the aristocracy were found along the Strand, and though a little out-of-date, Sarah felt quite comfortable with her surroundings. Lady Rockwell would have found nothing to censure about her present location. She chirped to the horses and they quickened their pace, her heart singing with anticipation in time to the *clip-clop, clip-clop* of their hooves along the cobbles.

It was not long, however, before her merry heart began to grow uneasy. The farther she drove from Charing Cross, the less hospitable the shops and storefronts became. The road took a short jog to the north, and she suddenly found herself on the west end of Fleet Street. The buildings crowded together; dirty, dark and forbidding as she drove past. Gripping the reins more tightly, she urged the horses onward, but they whinnied and pulled, kicking at the traces.

"Whoa now, easy there," Sarah soothed, as much to herself

as to the nervous animals. Taking a deep breath, she strove to remember her driving lessons. She let out the reins a bit, relaxing her shoulders and speaking low to the horses. Their ears turned back at the sound of her voice, and soon they were calmer.

Sarah wished she were calm as well. Focusing on the horses had momentarily distracted her from the dismal surroundings in which she found herself. But as she coaxed the horses along the street once more, a nervous knot began to form in the pit of her stomach.

"Perhaps it is a little farther... perhaps the neighborhood becomes more civilized nearer the end," she whispered to herself.

But her hope was in vain. The farther east she drove, the more hostile and dirty the road became. A creeping sense of fear stole over her, sending chills down her spine. She shook it off, striving to maintain her composure.

The horses could feel her anxiety, however, and she struggled to control them in the ever narrowing street. It was now quite clear to her that a gross mistake had been made. But whose mistake was it? That same rational voice within her lectured that the only mistake that had been made was Sarah's, in trusting the flattery of Lady Isabella over the counsel of her own friends. It was a discomforting thought. Had Lady Isabella deceived her? Did she send her here, only to make a mockery of her? The thought stung. But even now, in the middle of a filthy street, with broken windows and darkened alehouses crowding in on her, a glimmer of hope burned within her breast. *Perhaps I have merely taken a wrong turn...*

"Hello there!" she called to an open doorway, stopping the carriage. The horses stamped and snorted, restless and uneasy. A pair of men emerged—unshaven, unkempt, and reeking of whiskey. Sarah's eyes widened, and her heart raced ahead at a thundering pace. Swallowing her fear, she attempted to smile at them.

"Good... good day," she squeaked out. Clearing her throat, she said, "If you please—do you know a Madame Trouillet of Fleet Street? She is a dressmaker."

The men looked her over with glassy eyes, snickering to one another. Sarah clutched the reins, her clammy hands slipping inside of her gloves.

"This be Fleet Street," one of them slurred. "But I ain't never heard 'o no Madam Trooyay. But mebbe we can 'elp yeh?"

His companion cackled as the color drained from Sarah's face. Shaking, she tried to speak past the bile that rose in her throat. She coughed, pulling on the reins.

"Thank you, but I... I..."

Sensing her alarm, the horses were backing up, and the carriage with it. Sarah had no idea how to turn them or guide them in reverse, and she panicked. Pulling up on the reins, she stood, and they stepped faster, angling to the left. Suddenly the back of the carriage collided with the storefront behind her, unhinging a shutter and causing it to fall clattering to the street. Sarah screamed and the horses bolted, pulling the phaeton back the way they had come. She toppled backwards onto the seat, the shouts of the men behind her fading into obscurity as the carriage careened out of control.

Chapter 23

Rosemary was just coming down the steps of the Nelson's home when she saw a familiar figure on horseback riding down the street. She drew in her breath, a sudden impulse gripping her senses.

"One moment, Mama," she breathed, clutching her mother's arm.

"Rosemary!" her mother chided, but Rosemary was already running after the retreating figure.

"Mr. Rex!" she called, "Mr. Rex!"

Rex reined in his horse, turning at the sound of his name. He spotted Rosemary behind him, calling and waving to him as she ran towards him. He turned about, ready to meet her.

"Miss Reed," he greeted her, touching the brim of his hat to the young lady who stood beside his horse. Her chest was heaving with the exertion of her pursuit, and he waited politely for her to catch her breath.

"Mr. Rex," she repeated, gasping for air. "I wonder if... if..." Suddenly she hesitated. Turning back, she saw her mother standing at the bottom of the Nelson's steps, watching them.

Rex was off the saddle in a moment, gently turning Rosemary back to face him. She winced at his touch, and he drew back, not wanting to make her uncomfortable.

"What is it, Miss Reed? Is something wrong?" he asked.

Rosemary refused to look at him, and he cocked his head, striving to see her face. Suddenly he laughed.

"I admit that over the years I have had a fair number of women chasing after me, but I had not thought it of *you*, Miss Reed," he teased.

Rosemary finally lifted her face to him, and the lighthearted banter died on his lips. Her eyes were wide and frightened, and her lip quivered. Something was definitely amiss.

"What is wrong, Miss Reed?" he asked, striving to keep his voice even. "Are you well?"

"Yes, yes, I am well," she said, wringing her hands.

Rex frowned.

"It is Miss Mendenhall!" she suddenly exclaimed, her eyes stricken.

Rex felt as if he had been plunged into a barrel of rainwater. In that moment he knew that despite his attempts to remove Sarah Mendenhall from his life, she had captured his heart, wholly and completely, and there was no escaping *that*. His mind flashed to that terrible night, so many years ago, when he had lost his beloved Mary. The same sickening dread filled his heart once more—would he lose Sarah as well?

"What has happened? Is she safe? Is she well?" he nearly

shouted.

"I do not know," Rosemary confessed. "That is why I called out to you."

Rex tensed. "What do you mean?"

"She came to see me this morning," Rosemary began. "And asked me to go with her to Fleet Street."

"Fleet Street?" Rex repeated, surprise effectively dissolving his alarm. "Why on earth would she wish to go there?"

"She heard that there was a fashionable dressmaker in that part of town, and wished for me to accompany her there."

"There are no dressmakers on Fleet Street," Rex said flatly.

"That is what I tried to tell her, but she would not listen. I... I fear she may have gone there alone."

"Surely not! The countess would never—"

"Sarah was driving the countess's carriage herself this morning," Rosemary broke in softly.

Rex stared at her. If Sarah had driven herself to Fleet Street, there was no time to lose. He seized Rosemary's arm, causing her to jump.

"When did she leave your house?" he demanded.

"Not two hours ago," Rosemary gasped.

Rex released her arm, the color rising in his face. "Forgive me. I did not mean to—"

"It is nothing," she assured him, her own face flushing.

He nodded, then quickly remounted his horse and turned for the main road.

"Will she be alright?" Rosemary cried up to him.

Rex turned, his stormy eyes boring into her own. "I do not know. But I will find out."

He turned, kicking his heels into the horse's flank. It reared a little, then jumped forward and galloped down the street.

"I will send you word!" she heard him shout.

Rex had only moments to decide which to do first: check to see if Miss Mendenhall had returned to Cavendish Square, or head straight for Fleet Street. Following the dread in his heart, he turned his horse south off of Oxford, dodging between the carriages and pedestrians crowding the streets. An angry yell caused him to pause, and as he reined in his horse, he narrowly avoided colliding with a cart. The driver shouted and swore at him, but Rex paid no heed as he pulled his horse around. Plunging down a narrow alley, he whipped his horse into a gallop once more. He emerged onto a slightly wider, less frequented side road. Keeping his horse at a swift pace, he raced on, his keen eyes taking everything in, ready to pull up at a moment's notice.

Soon he arrived at the same monument Sarah had passed at Charing Cross. He spurred his horse onward, flying past the quaint little shops and pleasant homes along the Strand. He knew that in a few hundred feet he would reach the western end of Fleet Street, and he steeled himself for what lay ahead. Slowing down, he strained his eyes and ears for any sign of Sarah. If he could only find her, he might be able to save her.

He would not let Sarah suffer the same fate as Mary.

Sarah screamed again as the phaeton bounced along the cobbled street. She had been standing when the horses bolted, and the force of their flight had thrown her backwards onto the seat, knocking the reins out of her hands. She grasped for the thin leather straps with one hand as she clung to the side of the seat with the other, desperately trying to keep herself from falling off the careening vehicle. Buildings and signs whipped past her in a frightening blur, and she felt sick to her stomach. She finally managed to grab hold of one of the reins, but the other slipped over the side of the carriage and dragged, useless, along the ground.

"Whoa! Whoa!" she cried, trying to force her voice past the lump of fear in her throat. But the horses were beyond control, and her words were carried away unheeded by the wind. Panic filled her breast as she realized the danger of her situation. Drawing upon every ounce of strength she possessed, she managed to pull herself upright onto the seat, feeling dizzy as the shops whirled past her. She looked ahead, trying to anticipate what was coming.

The street was widening, and more traffic meant more obstacles. Shouts and screams from passersby and other coachmen mingled with her own as the horses continued their frantic flight, dragging the carriage bucking and weaving behind them. She was nearing the end of Fleet Street when her attention was suddenly arrested by the sound of someone shouting her name.

"Sarah!"

She turned, and managed a fleeting glimpse of Jameson Rex sitting astride his horse, a look of horror frozen on his handsome face. But just at that moment, the horses encountered the narrow turn where Fleet Street meets the Strand, and they veered to the left. Sarah screamed as the carriage tipped on its side, balancing momentarily on the right two wheels before the traces snapped and the force of the momentum sent the carriage crashing into a nearby building. An eruption of glass and shattering wood split the air. Sarah was thrown from the carriage as the world exploded around her.

Rex was off his horse and running towards the wreckage before the shouts and screams on the street even reached his ears. His heart was pounding as he dug through the carnage, desperately searching for the woman he loved. The owner of the shop was near the back of the store, bending over the remains of a shattered cask.

"Over 'ere!" he shouted.

Rex climbed through the ruins to where the man crouched, and his heart stopped. There, lying on the cold, dirty floor, was Sarah. Her face was smeared with blood and her dress was torn, but even in her hellish surroundings she looked beautiful. Rex knelt on the splintered wood, raising her lifeless hand to his lips, and wept.

Chapter 24

Two weeks later

"How dare you show your face here again?"

Rex met Lady Rockwell's icy stare with calm indifference.

"Your ladyship, my only desire—"

"Is to plague the life out of me?"

A wry smile tugged at the corners of Rex's mouth. "If that is what it takes."

She glared at him. "I have made it eminently clear that you are not welcome in this house. You will not be permitted to see her, neither now, nor ever again." She turned on her heel and stalked away from him, turning back once she reached the drawing room door. "I will not see you again, Mr. Rex. Please do not continue this nonsense."

Rex sighed when the door shut behind the countess. The past fortnight had been one of the most harrowing of his life, and he had haunted Cavendish square daily for news of Sarah's condition. But since the day he had brought her still unconscious form, bruised and bleeding, home from Fleet Street, he had not laid eyes on her. Rex had feared the worst, and had been beside himself with worry for the first several days. Lady Rockwell's constant refusal to give him any news or allow him to see Sarah made things even worse, but after three days he had at last managed to catch Dr. Matthews as he emerged from the countess's home.

"She has a long road ahead of her, but she will live."

The doctor's words were balm to his soul.

Though his gravest fears were eased by the doctor's reassurance, Rex was still anxious to see Sarah for himself. But Lady Rockwell refused. Day after day he knocked on the massive front door, and day after day the countess denied him entry.

Having been dismissed once more, Rex got wearily to his feet and trudged out of the house, the countess's stern command still ringing in his ears. It would not be pleasant to face her again, but he refused to stay away until he had been granted an audience with Miss Mendenhall. His mind and his heart were restless, and he needed answers.

Glancing up at the third story windows and wondering which room was hers, he took the reins from the boy holding his horse and swung himself up into the saddle.

Lady Rockwell watched as the horse carrying Rex cantered away down the street. It was difficult not to admire his persistence, but his constant visits were wearing on her nerves. She sighed.

"What is troubling you so?" Sarah's weak voice called from across the room.

The countess turned and hurried over to her. "*Mein Kind*, you need to rest. Never mind what is troubling me."

Sarah sighed, then winced as the movement sent ripples of pain coursing through her body. She had broken three ribs, and though relieved of her restrictive corset, her torso was wrapped tightly to prohibit movement. In addition, her head was bandaged from a cut she had sustained over her left eye, and her right arm was broken, just above the wrist.

"It was Mr. Rex again, was it not?"

The countess did not answer, but Sarah knew by the set of her jaw and the way her lips pressed into a thin line that it was, and she managed a wan smile.

"I wonder who will relent first—you or he?"

Though she was battered and bruised in body, Sarah's teasing spirit was alive and vibrant, and the countess could not restrain a chuckle.

"If I relent, it will only be because he is more tenacious than I am patient."

Sarah winced through her own laughter, and Lady Rockwell frowned. "I am sorry. I am making you uncomfortable."

"No, no, I am well. It feels good to laugh. But thank you for your concern."

"Of course. Now hush, you must rest yourself."

Making a face, Sarah tried to sit up. "Resting is nearly as dull as sleeping." She summoned Betsy from her seat in the corner to come assist her.

"Miss Mendenhall, stay where you are! You will never heal

properly if you will not stay situated," Lady Rockwell lectured.

"I cannot abide lying down all the time," Sarah grumbled. With Betsy helping, she at last managed to push herself up into a sitting position. Her breath came in shallow gasps, her face lined with pain. Lady Rockwell watched her young charge with anxious concern.

When some color had returned to Sarah's cheeks and her breathing slowed, the countess allowed herself to relax. She had not realized how much Sarah had come to mean to her until she had nearly lost her. The sweet, spirited young lady had captured Lady Rockwell's heart right along with the rest of London's.

With the pillows tucked comfortably around her, Sarah turned her gaze back towards the countess. "Why will you not let him come?"

Lady Rockwell pursed her lips. "Not again, Miss Mendenhall."

"I only wish to understand why you will not let him see me."

"There are many reasons."

"Such as?"

"For one thing, you are not in your stays nor properly dressed to receive visitors."

"There is nothing I can do about my stays at present, but I can dress. Dr. Matthews has given me permission to rise from my bed, after all."

"Miss Mendenhall, you *must* rest if you wish to recover. The exertion of visitors will not be good for you."

"Then why have you allowed Miss Reed to visit me?"

The countess pursed her lips. "Miss Reed is a gentlewoman, and your closest friend. I confess I was more concerned about the fuss you raised over my *not* permitting her to come in to you than I was about the strain her visit might place upon you," she grumbled. "But you could hardly entertain a gentleman in your bedchamber, *Fräulein.*"

"But I no longer receive Miss Reed here; I come out to my little parlor and she sits with me there," Sarah persisted.

Lady Rockwell knew she was losing the argument. "Why are you so anxious to entertain Mr. Rex?" she asked.

The color rose in Sarah's cheeks, and she was silent for a moment. At last she smiled. "I suppose I have a weakness for stubborn, headstrong men."

Lady Rockwell's lips twitched, but she did not smile. "Jameson Rex may very well be the reason you are in bed at this moment."

Sarah shifted uncomfortably against the pillows, and the countess continued. "You would not heed my warning to keep your distance, Miss Mendenhall. Now I shall keep it for you." She turned to quit the room, but stopped just inside the doorway. Sighing heavily, she looked back at Sarah. The bandage on her head, combined with the frown on her face, made her appear like an angry Turkish dictator, and the countess smiled in spite of herself.

Making her way back to Sarah's bedside, she reached out and gently patted her unbandaged arm. "I know you probably think I am a crotchety old woman, and in some ways you may be right. But I hope you understand that I have only your best interests at heart, *Mein Kind.*"

"Yes, I know, Lady Rockwell," Sarah sighed. She smiled softly, and the worried lines around the countess's mouth eased.

"Good."

She rose and made for the door again, but turned when Sarah called out to her.

"Lady Rockwell," Sarah said, her voice calm but her eyes sparkling. "Mr. Rex is not the only one who hopes his tenacity wins out over your patience."

"How is she?"

"She is doing much better than I expected, ma'am. Her health and youth have given her great advantage."

Lady Rockwell exhaled, the anxiety she felt as she waited for Dr. Matthews to emerge from Sarah's room melting away with her breath.

"I cannot tell you what a relief that is to hear."

Dr. Matthews looked sternly over his spectacles at her. "Lady Rockwell, I cautioned you before on the dangers of exerting yourself in nervous energy. Miss Mendenhall will recover, but if you are not careful, you shall find yourself in a sickroom of your own."

"Yes, yes, I know," the countess replied with a sigh. "I have felt as much."

The physician's eyebrows rose. "Have you been unwell?"

"Nothing further than what we have discussed before. I tire quite easily. And my palpitations vex me in the evening, at times."

Dr. Matthews nodded grimly. "Precisely my point, ma'am." He rose to take his leave, looking earnestly down at her. "Take care, your ladyship. And do not hesitate to call on me if you find you need my services before my next visit. I have not been coming for Miss Mendenhall's sake alone, you know."

"Thank you, Doctor," Lady Rockwell responded brusquely. She rose as the gentleman departed, but before she had a chance to sit down again, Lawrence stepped into the room.

"Mr. Jameson Rex is here to see you, ma'am."

She sighed. "I thought he might be. Show him in, please."

The butler bowed as Lady Rockwell returned to her seat, and soon Rex was ushered into the room. The door shut quietly behind him.

"Lady Rockwell," Rex began, "I would like to see Miss Mendenhall, if you please."

His tone was respectful, but there was a stubborn set to his jaw, bordering on defiance. How like Sarah he seemed in that moment! *No wonder she has developed a tendre for him*, the countess thought with a frown. From her position on the settee, Lady Rockwell cleared her throat.

"Come in and sit down," she commanded.

Rex did as he was told, taking a seat on the sofa opposite her. Lady Rockwell stared down her nose at him, her piercing gray eyes searching Rex's own.

"Did I not inform you yesterday that you were not to return to this house?"

"You did," he answered, meeting her gaze.

"And did I not forbid you from harassing me further for permission to see Miss Mendenhall?"

"You did."

"Furthermore, was it not clear to you that you shall not have

244

my permission to see her ever again?"

"It was."

"Then why," she asked, her eyes snapping with suppressed exasperation, "are you here?"

Flashing her a crooked smile, Rex replied, "I must be either wholly indifferent or entirely too stubborn to care, I suppose."

The countess's thin lips twitched at the corners.

"It must be the latter," she finally informed him, a hint of amusement in her eyes. "But not your obstinacy alone—Miss Mendenhall insists on seeing you as well."

"She wishes to see me?" Rex asked incredulously.

"She does. Though why, I have yet to discover." Her voice grew brusque once more. "There is a workroom on the third floor that has been made up into a parlor in which she can receive visitors. Her health is still too delicate for her to move a great deal, and she tires easily.

"You will limit your stay to no more than thirty minutes," she declared, eyeing him severely. "And you will not return again."

Rex was nodding, still reeling from the discovery that Sarah wished to see him. Would she be happy he had come? Was she angry? Did she blame him at all? Rex winced at the thought. He certainly blamed himself for her injuries, and he had been plagued with the thought that she blamed him as well.

The countess rang a bell, and the butler returned to the room.

"Lawrence, please show Mr. Rex into Miss Mendenhall's parlor," she directed. "She is expecting him."

Rex stood, and after bowing to the countess, followed the butler upstairs.

The door shut softly behind Lawrence as Rex stood just inside the makeshift parlor, pain and hesitation warring for dominance in his expression. Sarah was seated on a chaise in the middle of the room. A maid was at her side, adjusting the pillows behind her before retreating to her sewing in a corner of the room. Sarah's bandaged arm lay in clear view, but the wrap on her head had been removed, showing the angry pink skin puckered in a line over her brow. She smiled at him.

"I would stand for you, Mr. Rex, but the good doctor does not advise it."

Her eyes danced merrily, but he could see the undercurrent of pain in her clear blue eyes. She reached her unbandaged hand out to him, and Rex slowly made his way over to her. He bent to kiss her hand.

"Miss Mendenhall, I hardly know how to adequately express to you my deep regret for what has happened. I know that I have no right to come here; no right to beg for your forgiveness, but I do so, with all my heart."

Her eyes softened. "Come now, Mr. Rex, you are my savior! I am so very glad that you were there that day. Had you not been..." Her voice trailed off, and she shook her head. "But you were. Thank you so much for your assistance."

"Do not thank me!" Rex cried, turning away from her. Rubbing his anguished eyes, he tried desperately to erase the image of her fragile figure being flung through the air like a rag doll. "You have nothing to thank me for," he continued in a low voice. "I know perfectly well that I am to blame for your present injuries; do not pretend otherwise!"

"Mr. Rex," Sarah replied rather petulantly. "You are being completely irrational, and unless you begin to speak some sense I will dismiss you at once."

Surprised, Rex turned back to face her. Her normally sweet face was twisted in a scowl, and her sapphire eyes were snapping with anger. His jaw dropped open.

Suddenly her face relaxed, and she giggled. "Oh Mr. Rex, you did not think me serious, did you?" She tried to suppress her mirth, but the laughter bubbled out of her and she grimaced, holding her side.

Rex crossed quickly over to her. "What is the matter? Are you in pain?"

His brow was furrowed in concern, but Sarah shook her head slowly, striving to calm her breathing before she replied.

"I am well. Laughing hurts my side, that is all."

Rex momentarily allowed his eyes to stray to her waist, and for the first time he noticed that her petite figure had a more natural shape to it—it was not confined to the restrictive contours of a corset. His eyes snapped back to her face, shame burning his cheeks as he realized she was watching him.

"Forgive me, I..." He cleared his throat.

"No matter." Sarah's cheeks were tinged pink as well, but she smiled at him. "I have a few broken ribs, that is all."

Rex drew in his breath, eyeing her bandaged hand. "And a broken arm?" he asked through clenched teeth.

"Yes."

His gaze landed on her forehead, then he shook his head, turning away once more. Sarah waited patiently for him to compose himself, but when he did not face her again she called out to him.

"Mr. Rex?"

He slowly turned around, his face grave, his shoulders stiff. "How is it possible," he asked in a low voice, "that you do not hate me? How can you even bear to look at me?"

"Mr. Rex, you are not to blame for my present situation," she said gently, her eyes warm. "You have been a most considerate friend to me, and I am happy to see you again."

"None of this would have happened if I had not taught you to drive."

"Nonsense! You would not have given me lessons had I not teased you into them."

Rex sighed. "That is true, at least."

"Of course it is," Sarah said. She smiled up at him, and though he did not smile back at her, his look softened.

She shifted in her seat. "No one is to blame but myself, and I assure you, I am heartily ashamed of it."

"How is it that you will place the blame entirely on your own shoulders, and yet excuse the actions of others for *their* part in the scheme?"

"Because I have been foolish, and foolishness can never be excused." Her cheeks burned as she looked away.

Rex took the seat beside her. "Everyone is foolish at times," he said gently.

"But I have been foolish in the most *insufferable* way!" she lamented.

"What is so insufferable about visiting a part of town with which you were unfamiliar?"

"I went alone, if you recall," she said wryly.

"Yes, and that *was* quite green of you," he chuckled.

Sarah smiled companionably, but then she sighed. "If it were merely that I went alone into an unfamiliar part of town, I believe I could forgive myself. But that is not the worst of it."

Rex raised an eyebrow at her, and Sarah squirmed uncomfortably under his gaze.

"I allowed myself to be flattered, and my head was turned by the silly compliments paid to me, and I heeded *them* because I wanted to, and ignored the advice of my friends." She sighed mournfully.

"Flattered by whom?" Rex asked, confusion clouding his face. "What have the compliments of others to do with your driving to Fleet Street?"

Sarah realized her mistake too late. "Oh! Nothing, I suppose. Mr. Rex, would you care for some tea?"

He laughed. "No, no, Miss Mendenhall, that will not do. I insist on knowing your meaning. Whose flattery led you into such foolishness?"

Sarah was clearly uncomfortable. "Please, Mr. Rex, you do not know what you are asking."

"Do I not?"

"It will not please you."

"On the contrary, it will please me very much to know whom I might blame for your present situation, since you will not allow me to accept the responsibility myself," he said sarcastically.

"I told you, Mr. Rex—*I* am to blame."

"Just so—but who is the cad that goaded you into it?"

Sarah was quiet for a moment, studying him. One side of his mouth was drawn up in the appearance of a smile, but Sarah knew the dangerous glint in his eye was anything but amused. She blew out her breath.

"Lady Isabella Gray," she confessed at last.

The expression on Rex's face froze. "Lady Isabella Gray sent you to Fleet Street?" he repeated incredulously.

"Yes."

The explanation rushed out of her mouth in a sudden torrent. Sarah told Rex how she had looked up to Lady Isabella; how she had wanted to be noticed and admired by such a fashionable lady. She told of Lady Isabella's calling on her in Cavendish Square, and how Sarah had not *meant* to actually return her visit, but in truth had *wanted* to see her. With bitter tears, Sarah repeated to Rex the words she had spoken.

"I would not have gone to Fleet Street if Lady Isabella had not told me that I had exquisite taste, and that I would do well to employ her personal seamstress Madame Trouillet, who was established there. But I *wanted* to believe her, and so I went. I wanted to believe that I was fashionable and stylish, that I was as elegant and refined as *she* is—that *she* thought I was!" Sarah stared dejectedly at her hands, the wrap of her bandaged arm a vivid reminder of her folly. "But I am not. I was a fool, and I am lucky that my foolishness did not cost me my life."

Rex listened, dumbfounded, as Sarah related her tale. The mounting horror he felt at the realization that Lady Isabella—his betrothed!—had deliberately sent Sarah on a fool's errand to Fleet Street was sickening. The longer he listened, the more angry and disgusted he became. He knew enough of Lady Isabella's character to know that she would never have bothered about Sarah if she had not seen her as a threat. But to descend to such malicious practices! To send an innocent young lady to almost certain doom! His lip curled in revulsion.

And then, when he was sure that his disgust could not grow any greater, he realized that *he* had brought this about. He had sought to protect Sarah—her sweetness, her innocence, her vivacity—by stepping out of her life and attaching himself to another woman. Instead, his impulse had led her to the very brink of disaster. If he had not proposed to Lady Isabella, she would not have thought to defend her territory, and Sarah would never have been in harm's way. The anger churned within him like a vat of boiling tar.

The moment Sarah finished speaking Rex shot to his feet. He paced to the window, fighting for control. After several moments passed in silence, Sarah's voice reached out to him once more.

"I am sorry, Mr. Rex," she said quietly, "if I have caused you pain."

He laughed humorlessly. "You are not the one who is sorry, Miss Mendenhall." He turned to face her, and Sarah gasped at the viciousness burning in his eyes. "And I am not in pain. Not, at least, in the kind of pain you feel you have inflicted."

"But... Lady Isabella! Your betrothed—"

"Yes, my *betrothed.*" He spat the word. "If she were not my betrothed this would never have happened."

Sarah stared at him. "What do you mean, sir?"

"Precisely what I said." He stalked to the door, as if he were going to leave. But he turned about quickly, his words falling in a tumble.

"You will not say it yourself; you are too good and kind to think so ill of her, so I will say it for you: Lady Isabella deliberately deceived you. I am certain she knew *exactly* what she was doing. She knew that some mischief would befall you on Fleet Street, and she knew precisely how to make it happen. Oh, do not look so shocked, Miss Mendenhall! I assure you, her arts and allurements have led more than one innocent into perilous paths."

Sarah's mouth had fallen open, and she shook her head slowly, as if in a daze. "I cannot think so ill of her."

"I can!" Rex shouted, crossing to the window once more.

"But why?" Sarah cried out, striving to understand. "What has she against me?"

"You are a threat, Miss Mendenhall!" he exploded. "She sees my regard for you, and it infuriates her because she knows how I despise *her*! How I have always despised her! Yes, I have sought her hand, but only because no reputable woman would now have me. She knows this, and she hates it. She wishes she could have secured my affections out of her own merit, and seeing my regard for you has cast her own faults into greater relief. You are everything that she is not; everything that she wishes she was so that she might have the same claim on my affections. She sent you to your doom because she is a jealous, spiteful, venomous, woman who could not bear to see that the love I feel for—"

He stopped abruptly. Sarah's face was pale, and her usually cheerful demeanor was buried beneath a stunned realization of what his words meant.

"You..." she began, her voice barely above a whisper.

But Rex would not stay to hear the rest. With his cheeks burning and his anguished eyes defeated, he turned on his heel and strode to the door.

"Goodbye, Miss Mendenhall," he said, grasping the handle.

"Rex!" Sarah cried out.

But he was gone.

Chapter 25

Infuriated with both himself and Lady Isabella, Rex stormed from the house. His angry steps led him halfway to Oxford street before he realized he had left his horse at Lady Rockwell's. Too angry and mortified to turn back for it, he continued on foot to Grosvenor Square.

The meeting with Sarah had not gone well, and that was putting it mildly. He had gone to Cavendish Square, expecting another rebuttal from the countess, and had instead learned of the vicious actions of Lady Isabella. Not that alone, but he had debased himself by declaring his love for Sarah in the most unflattering, humiliating manner! His cheeks burned at the memory, but he found he could not be sorry that she now knew his true feelings. *At least she knows that I love her*, he thought to himself. *Even if that love is in vain.*

Not ten minutes after leaving Cavendish Square, he found himself at his destination, his anger having fueled his speed. Lady

Isabella must be dealt with immediately, and he knew it would not be pleasant. He braced himself for the argument to come.

Rapping sharply on the door, Rex endeavored to compose himself. Being admitted by the butler and assured of his lady's presence at home, he took the stairs two at time and burst into the drawing room, pulling up short at the sight before him.

"Jameson!" Lady Isabella cried in alarm, her hand flying to her breast, "What a fright you have given me!"

She wore a low cut dress of crimson taffeta which exposed her bare shoulders and much of her ample bosom, and her cheeks and lips were daubed with rouge. A guilty look was arrested on her face.

"Hello, Isabella," he returned, his voice hard. "What are you doing here, Mills?"

Peter was seated next to Lady Isabella on the chaise; his cravat rumpled, his hair disheveled, his expression far less ashamed than it ought to have been. "I am merely visiting my old friend."

"The last time I checked, *your* friend was *my* fiancée."

"So she is," Peter retorted, smirking at him.

Sensing the dangerous mood that Rex was in, Lady Isabella turned to Peter. "Peter, perhaps you should go." She glanced at Rex, whose murderous eyes were fixed on her face.

"No," Rex spat. "Let him stay. It will save me a visit later."

"Jameson, what on earth is the matter?" Lady Isabella asked, her face flushing. She clearly wished to shift the focus to something else.

A laugh burst forth from Rex's lips, and he took a few steps towards them. "What is the matter? Why Isabella, I did not think even *you* were that green." His eyes flickered between the two persons before him, then he shook his head in disgust. "But aside from the obvious, can you not guess the reason for my anger? If I told you I have come from Cavendish Square, would you be able to feign ignorance then?"

Her face reddened, and she pursed her lips. "If this is about that young chit Miss Mendenhall, I can assure you—"

"Of what? That your underhanded scheme nearly got her killed?"

"If she was silly enough to go by herself, that is not my concern."

"You purposely gave her a false direction."

"I did." The coldness in Lady Isabella's voice fueled the anger in his own.

"Then you admit that you wished for some evil to befall her?"

"I wished to rid you of your *distraction*, Jameson." She glared at him. "I will not be made a fool."

"So what does that make me?" he snapped. "I have come to confront you about the accusations on this head, and find you alone in a room with a confirmed scoundrel, when our betrothal is not even a month old, Isabella!"

"If I am a scoundrel, then you, sir, must be the devil himself!" Peter declared, rising from his chair.

Rex glared at him. "Stay out of this, Peter."

"I will not," he answered, his gaze and stance defiant. "You have ridden your high horse for too long, Jameson. How can you hold your intended to a standard of purity which you yourself have not kept? You will be taking her home to your mistress's child, for heaven's sake!"

The air whooshed out of Rex in a rush. He felt as if he had been punched.

"You," he choked, "know nothing of my life."

Peter snorted. "I know enough. I know what a hypocrite you are. You have looked down your nose at me for years, preaching about morals and propriety and honor. And all the while you were tasting of a lady's delights yourself! How does it feel, I wonder, to now be sunk so low?" His eyes were mocking, his voice laced with derision. "You are fortunate to have found a lady who does not object to the life you have led, even if she knows the real reason you came crawling back to her."

Lady Isabella glared at him, but Peter ignored her. Rex clenched and unclenched his fists, the anger rolling off him in waves.

"You see? You cannot even deny it. I know how desperately you need funds," Peter continued, his voice menacing. "And by what means you were willing to acquire them."

Rex threw himself at Peter, wrapping his hands around the younger man's throat before he had a chance to protect himself. Lady Isabella screamed.

"You know *nothing* of my life!" Rex repeated, shoving the man away from him.

Peter stumbled to catch himself, gasping for air as the blood rushed to his face.

"Get out of here, both of you," Lady Isabella commanded, her eyes flashing.

"With pleasure," Rex hissed, turning on his heel. "We are through, Isabella. For the last time."

"You owe me money," Peter croaked.

"I owe you nothing," Rex spat. "Your miserable life is not even worth five thousand pounds, but I will grant you clemency in exchange for it. I am a better shot by far, Peter, and you should be grateful that I do not call you out. The last time I checked, meddling with a gentleman's fiancée—however loose her own morals—is a matter of honor."

Lady Isabella gasped in outrage, and Peter sputtered angrily beside her, but Rex strode out the door without another word, slamming it behind him.

Chapter 26

Though Dr. Matthews had given his consent a fortnight ago for Sarah to leave the house, Lady Rockwell had refused to allow Sarah any farther than the back gardens. Sarah would surely have gone mad with boredom had it not been for her countless visitors. Though Rosemary had called nearly every day since the accident, the visit from Jameson Rex had opened the floodgates for her many admirers to grace the home as well. Cards, flowers, and carriages arrived in a constant stream in Cavendish Square, and Sarah had been grateful for the distraction they provided.

Though she welcomed her friends back with open arms, she was wiser now. No longer did she care for amusement for amusement's sake. The season was waning, and with it her popularity. Her circle of associates grew smaller as she gently but firmly refused the attentions of many of her former admirers. She found within her decreasing sphere of influence a more steady set of friends and acquaintances, and of this she was glad.

Sarah and Rosemary sat in the Reed's barouche as the family's coachman turned into Hyde Park. The pungent smell of a city populated with three million people filled the muggy July air, but Sarah breathed it in with gusto. She had been confined to the stuffy rooms and restrictive garden of Lady Rockwell's home for the past six weeks, and even the bitter smells of smoke and excrement were enjoyable simply for the variance they provided.

"Oh, Miss Reed, how good it is to be out!" she sighed.

"I am glad you are feeling well enough to leave the house."

"I have felt well enough for a fortnight at least. And though I was greatly pained to miss so many balls and parties, I could not bear to go against Lady Rockwell's wishes. Not after her kindness and attention."

"Will you be going to Almack's tonight?"

"Of course!" Sarah cried gaily. "I would not miss it for the world."

They spent a pleasant afternoon in the park. The two friends strolled along the path beneath their parasols, admiring the roses and other vegetation.

"I never tire of flowers," Sarah said, burying her nose in a cluster of champagne-colored roses just off the path.

"That is fortunate," her friend said, "since your room is always overflowing with them. How many vases are filled at the moment?"

"I have not the faintest idea."

"Are they from the usual admirers?"

"Most of them," came the indifferent reply.

The truth was, Sarah could not recall which gentleman had sent which flowers. Her heart beat a little faster with the arrival of each bouquet, until she read the enclosed note and realized that it had not been sent from the one person she most wished it to be.

Ever since she had learned of his broken engagement, she had looked for Rex. Every carriage that arrived and every visitor's name announced, she hoped was his. But he stayed away.

And Sarah could not understand why.

She knew that he loved her, though her shock at his almost point-blank declaration had been real. Until that moment, she had never supposed that his teasing compliments and careless flattery hid deeper feelings. When he first began to take notice of her, Sarah had excused his behavior as mere adulation, intended to turn her head and arrest her affections in much the same way that the other young men tried to secure her regard. But it was not long before he began to distinguish himself from the others. She had enjoyed his company and his friendship in a way that she soon became accustomed to, and she missed him dearly.

When Sarah returned to Cavendish Square for dinner, she was not surprised to hear that two more arrangements of flowers had been sent and a handful of calling cards were waiting for her. She hummed happily to herself as she climbed the stairs to her room, removing her gloves and handing them to Betsy as she entered.

"Some new flowers 'ave arrived for you, miss."

"Yes, thank you, Betsy."

Sarah glanced towards her dressing table where the blooms were displayed, and froze. One vase was filled to overflowing with hothouse flowers in every shade and color, but it was not those flowers that arrested her attention. It was the collection of tiny white blossoms clustered upon shrubby branches, carefully arranged in a squat little bowl, that held her speechless.

Drawing a breath, Sarah walked reverently over to admire them. The snowy petals spilled over the edge of the small crystal vase, and she leaned forward, inhaling their heady fragrance. She closed her eyes, smiling.

"Jasmine," she said in awe. "Wherever in the world did he find it?"

"There was no card, miss," Betsy said uneasily. "These other flowr's are from Mr. Grimshaw, but I'm not sure who sent th' pretty white ones."

Sarah was shaking her head, though a smile was on her lips. She did not need a card to tell her from whom the flowers came. There was only one man in London who knew they were her favorite; only one man in London who had become so well acquainted with her.

Jameson Rex.

The ball at Almack's was as delightful as Sarah anticipated. She tired more easily, and she was mindful of the aching feeling in her side whenever she laughed too hard, but otherwise the evening was a wonderful return to society for her. As much as she enjoyed it, however, she was far more interested in the party given by the Brooks the following evening, in honor of their daughter's engagement to Jeremy Thatcher.

Sarah dressed with extra care, smoothing the skirt of her peacock blue gown as Betsy put the finishing touches to her hair. Sarah smiled at her abigail's reflection, and Betsy smiled back.

"You look lovely, miss."

"Thank you, Betsy."

"Would you like me to make a paste to cover your scar, miss?" she asked hesitantly.

But Sarah shook her head emphatically. "No, Betsy, thank you." She gently touched the pink crease over her brow, smiling grimly. "I am glad it is there. It serves as a reminder of my folly, and a warning to keep my vanity in check."

Betsy nodded, but Sarah did not think she really understood. It seemed to Sarah's mind as if she had grown ten years older and wiser over the last several weeks. She had had ample time to reflect on the attitudes and behaviors which led to her accident, and the discoveries had not been pleasant.

When Sarah first arrived in London, she assured Lady Rockwell that she was neither vain nor spoiled, but the weeks of confinement and self-reflection showed otherwise. Sarah found in herself a deplorable amount of vanity, conceit, and tenacity. The discovery caused her much uneasiness, and she was certain that these human frailties had contributed to the accident.

"Lady Rockwell," she asked on one occasion, after a particularly painful session of introspection. "Have I become an insufferable nuisance?"

Lady Rockwell chuckled. "No, my dear, you have not. You have become—shall we say, more *aware* of your charms since your first coming to London, but you are not overly vain, and certainly not insufferable."

"I am glad to hear it," came the meek reply. "But I am sorry that I have allowed what vanity I *do* have to overcome my sensibilities on occasion."

"Yes, that is a great pity."

"It *has* served its purpose, I suppose," the young philosopher mused, "for I have discovered my weakness with time enough to allow for improvement. And I do so wish to improve myself, Lady Rockwell. I do not wish to always be falling into scrapes."

"Yes, you do seem to have a propensity for mischief," the countess declared with a twinkle in her eye. Sarah smiled.

"Well, I shall do my best to rid myself of any such unfavorable tendencies," she resolved. "Though you must admit, life will be far more dull around here when I succeed."

They had laughed together, and Sarah smiled at the memory as she prepared for the evening at the Brooks's. Glancing at herself in the mirror, she leaned in, close enough to count the freckles scattered across her nose.

"You are a silly young girl," she whispered to her reflection. "But I love you all the same. Just be sure to keep your head firmly on your shoulders from now on, and not allow it to be turned so easily by flattery and gossip. Understood?"

She blew a kiss at the glass, then turned and danced happily from the room. Her steps were light as she tripped down the stairs to the waiting carriage, her heart soaring as they pulled away from the house. The ball at Almack's had been lovely, but the person whom Sarah most wished to see had not been in attendance last night. He was not allowed.

But tonight she was sure to see him. The Thatcher's had spared no expense in throwing an elaborate party for their second eldest daughter and her betrothed, and Sarah knew that everyone who was anyone would be there. Her cheeks grew warm as she remembered the last dance she and Rex had shared; how he had swept her into his arms and onto the dance floor in a burst of passion. The tiny flutters in her stomach grew in intensity as she anticipated dancing with him again.

The opportunity never arose, however. Long after the last few guests had straggled in, Sarah watched for his tall form to come striding into the room, his gray-blue eyes searching for her own. But he never came. Whether he had not been invited or simply chose not to attend, Sarah did not know, but the disappointment she felt at his absence was acute.

"Why such a frown, my dear?" the countess asked over supper. "Are you not enjoying yourself?"

"Oh! Indeed, I am," Sarah replied brightly, forcing a smile to her lips. "I suppose I am tired, that is all."

"Then let us go home. I shall send for the carriage directly."

Sarah offered no objection, and after the meal she followed her chaperon meekly to the door. This alarmed Lady Rockwell far more than Sarah realized it would, and as the days continued and Sarah grew more and more melancholy, the countess found herself seriously disturbed. No amount of coaxing, prying, or lecturing seemed able to penetrate the depression that weighed upon her young charge, and she finally called upon Dr. Matthews to examine her.

"She seems in excellent health," he declared to Lady Rockwell, when they were alone after his examination. "Her injuries have healed remarkably, though she may retain a bit of a scar on her forehead."

"But her spirits are so low! Could you not discover any reason for her melancholy?" The countess's voice was heavy with concern, and Dr. Matthews furrowed his brow.

"Is her appetite good?"

"Tolerable."

"Is she getting any exercise?"

"Yes, she walks in the park nearly every day."

"Has she had any visitors? Any friends coming to call?"

"Heavens, yes!" Lady Rockwell declared, throwing her hands up in exasperation. "We are almost overrun with callers, at all hours of the day."

"And how does she receive them?"

"She seems to perk up when she hears the bell, though she often appears even more depressed after they leave."

"Perhaps there is a certain friend she is hoping to see," the doctor suggested.

"I cannot imagine that. Every lady and gentleman she knows has come to see her except—" The countess suddenly snapped her mouth shut, realization dawning on her.

Dr. Matthews nodded at her expression. "That must be it. Has she quarreled with a friend who is normally attentive?"

"Hardly," Lady Rockwell answered stiffly.

"Well, whomever it is, it seems to me that—"

"Dr. Matthews, thank you for coming." Lady Rockwell stood, clearly dismissing the man and whatever he had been about to say. "I appreciate your concern, but I believe I now know the cause of her distress. I shall handle it directly. Thank you."

The good doctor rose from his seat, bowing politely as the butler showed him to the door. Lady Rockwell watched him go with cool indifference, but as the door shut behind him she sank to the sofa, her shoulders slumping.

"Oh, Sarah," she murmured. "What have you done?"

Chapter 27

Breakfast had become a rather dismal occasion in Cavendish Square. Instead of coming to the table with bright eyes and flushed cheeks, Sarah was now quiet and somber over the meal. The light in her eyes and the spring in her step had nearly vanished, and Lady Rockwell now knew the reason why.

They were just finishing another morose meal together when the countess cleared her throat. Sarah was staring languidly out the window, her plate of food barely touched.

"Miss Mendenhall," Lady Rockwell began, her voice a bit gruffer than she intended.

"Hmm?"

"Miss Mendenhall," the countess said more softly. "There is something I wish to tell you. Something you need to know."

Sarah turned, her interest piqued.

Lady Rockwell sighed. "He will not be coming, Miss Mendenhall," she murmured. "Not ever again."

The color drained from Sarah's face. Slowly she lifted a trembling hand to her forehead, tracing the thin pink line across her brow.

"Has... has something happened?" she asked, her voice faint.

"No," the countess responded, rather brusquely. "But I have asked him not to return."

"Why?" The fire was instantly back in Sarah's eyes.

"I warned you, when he first arrived in London, to be cautious," Lady Rockwell explained, her voice gentle but firm. "But you did not heed my warning, and look what has happened!"

"Nothing has happened," Sarah said, turning away.

"Miss Mendenhall, you know perfectly well I am not to be trifled with," the countess declared, her own temper rising. "Nothing has happened? Not only were you injured nigh unto death, but now you will not eat, you hardly sleep, the balls and parties and admirers you once enjoyed seem to hold no amusement any longer... Miss Mendenhall, *you have fallen in love with Jameson Rex!*"

The accusation hung in the air like the tolling of a death bell. A crimson spot burned in each of Sarah's cheeks, and her eyes flashed defiantly as the seconds passed.

But Sarah did not deny the claim.

"Since you did not heed my warning, I have taken it upon myself to protect you from further injury. Mr. Rex has been refused admittance into this home, and you will not see him again."

"You have no right—" Sarah began, her voice shaking.

"I have every right, *Fräulein!* You are a guest in my house, and as such you are under my protection. My *protection*, Miss

Mendenhall." She gazed intently at the young lady across from her, who stared unflinching back. "I allowed your acquaintance with him against my better judgment, but I will no longer allow you to associate with him. He is a scoundrel, Miss Mendenhall! The very worst of libertines! Villainous, treacherous, deceitful—"

"I will not hear any more!" Sarah cried, standing abruptly and running from the room.

"Miss Mendenhall!"

But Sarah's wracking sobs were heard retreating up the stairs, and a slamming door was the only answer to the countess's stern rebuff.

An oppressive pall hung over the household for the remainder of the day. Conversation between Sarah and Lady Rockwell was forced and polite, though no further outbursts were heard from either party. The next morning showed only a marginal improvement, and Lady Rockwell wondered if she and her young charge would be at odds for the remainder of the season.

Three days after their disagreement, Sarah knocked timidly on Lady Rockwell's dressing room door.

"Come in," the countess called.

It was early, and Sarah was surprised to find that Lady Rockwell was already dressed. She entered the room with hesitant steps, but the countess smiled and held an arm out to her.

"*Guten Morgan*, Miss Mendenhall," she said warmly.

"Good morning, Lady Rockwell," Sarah answered, taking

her hand. Lady Rockwell smiled and patted the bench.

"I wanted to apologize," Sarah began when she was seated beside the countess. "I have been sulky and ungrateful, and I am sorry."

"Apology accepted, my dear. Though it was not my intent to upset you, I understand why you reacted as you did."

Sarah swallowed. Squaring her shoulders, she smiled at the countess. "Thank you. But I want you to know that I respect your decision, and I will honor your wishes."

The countess raised her eyebrows.

"But I have a request to make."

Lady Rockwell sighed. "Of course you do."

Sarah smiled faintly. "I should like to send him a letter."

"No."

"Please, Lady Rockwell. I... I should like to see him again."

"Did you not just agree to honor my wishes?"

"Yes, Lady Rockwell, I did. And I fully intend to. I do not wish to invalidate your decree by asking him to see me here, but I would like to ask him to meet me somewhere else. So that I may speak with him."

The countess stared at her. "Are you out of your senses, Miss Mendenhall?"

"Please, Lady Rockwell, if you would but listen—"

"*You* will listen to me, *Fräulein.* Mr. Rex is—"

"I am fully aware of your opinion of Mr. Rex, Lady Rockwell," Sarah interjected vehemently. She took a breath, striving to compose herself. After a moment she continued. "All I ask is that you allow me to inform him of *my* opinion."

The countess regarded her shrewdly.

"This you may accomplish in a letter itself."

Sarah winced. "Lady Rockwell, I will not go against your wishes if you expressly forbid me to see him ever again. But I should at least like to try. Please? May I please write to him and ask if he will see me?"

Her pleading eyes were more than Lady Rockwell could bear. The yearning she saw reflected in them brought painful memories to the surface; memories from her own past that had been hidden for many, many years. The countess sighed, turning away. "Very well. You may write to him and ask if he will receive you. But you must have a chaperon."

"Of course, Lady Rockwell," Sarah agreed, her face shining. "Thank you."

Lady Rockwell was silent as Sarah arose to take her leave. She was nearly to the door, her step lighter than it had been in weeks, when Lady Rockwell called her back.

"Miss Mendenhall?"

"Yes, Lady Rockwell?"

Sarah's hand was on the door, and she was only half-turned back to face the countess. Her blue eyes were sparkling, and the excitement she exuded was nearly tangible. A pang of sadness overcame the countess, and her voice caught.

"Please... promise me that you will not run away. Please, Miss Mendenhall."

A flash of surprise flickered across Sarah's face, and she returned to Lady Rockwell's side. She sat beside the countess and wrapped her arms around the older woman. Lady Rockwell squeezed her arm.

"I promise, Lady Rockwell," Sarah murmured. She felt the

271

countess nod, and Sarah pulled back to look at her, a mischievous grin on her face.

"After all, I did vow *not* to accept a single proposal this season, did I not?"

The conversation with Lady Rockwell had restored Sarah to her usual vivacious self. A brief epistle was dispatched to Rex's residence, asking for an audience, and Sarah hummed about her duties for the next few hours, anxious for a reply. But none came. She sent another letter the next day, and it, too, went unanswered. When several days had passed without a response, she began to worry that he had left town. With the opening of grouse season only a fortnight away, it would not be long until London was a ghost town. The worry that Rex had already gone, or would soon be leaving, gnawed at Sarah.

One morning early in August, Rosemary and her mother called in Cavendish Square. Sarah pounced on her friend as soon as she was in the door, begging her to take a turn about the gardens while the countess and Mrs. Reed visited. Rosemary readily agreed, and the two young ladies took their parasols and went outside.

"Oh Rosemary, I am perfectly delighted to see you!" Sarah cried when they were out-of-doors. "It seems ages since you were here."

"Yes, I am afraid I have been very busy," her friend blushed.

"You mean Mr. Nelson has been keeping you busy," Sarah teased.

The flush on her friend's cheeks deepened, but she smiled. "Partly. But what have you been doing with yourself all this time?"

Sarah laughed. "Pining for you, dearest, more than anything else." She linked her arm in Rosemary's, smiling fondly at her friend. "You know how much I adore you."

The friends meandered the paths in comfortable silence for a time, relaxing in the drowsy summer air. "Rosemary," Sarah said presently, her voice low with hesitation. "I wonder if you could tell me something. Have you... have you seen Mr. Rex anywhere lately?"

Surprised, Rosemary stopped. "Jameson Rex?"

Sarah nodded, not meeting her friend's gaze.

"Yes, I believe I saw him in Bond Street, not two days ago."

"Bond Street!" Sarah repeated, her face lighting up.

"Yes." Rosemary cocked her head. "Is that so surprising? Why do you ask?"

Sarah did not answer, but instead led her friend to a small bench where they could sit. Her brows were drawn together in thought, and Rosemary waited patiently for Sarah to explain.

"If you saw him in Bond Street, then he must certainly still be in town," Sarah said, more to herself than to Rosemary. She looked up at her friend.

"Rosemary, I wonder if you might do something for me."

"Yes?"

"I would like you to send him a letter."

"A letter!"

"Please, Rosemary? I *must* speak with him."

"But why must you send a letter by me?"

273

Sarah smiled sheepishly at her friend. "I will not be sending a letter through you. I need *you* to send him a letter. Signed with your name."

Sarah continued in a rush before Rosemary could refuse. "All I want is to talk to him. But since he will not answer my letters—"

"You have sent him letters?" Rosemary asked, the shock on her face causing Sarah to blush.

"Yes, but he has not answered them. I worried that he had left town." She stared wistfully into space, before heaving a sigh and turning her eyes back to her friend. "Will you help me?"

"What do you need me to do?" Rosemary asked warily.

Sarah smiled. "All you must do is send him a letter. I shall tell you what to write."

Chapter 28

The season was coming to a close, and many of the principal families had already gone to their country estates. Lady Rockwell was impatient to leave the dirty, humid city for the cooler air in Leicestershire, but Sarah insisted they remain, at least until the Reeds departed. Since there were still many preparations to make for Rosemary's forthcoming betrothal, there was no fear that they would make a sudden departure. Though Sarah still worried that Jameson Rex might leave town before she had the opportunity to speak with him, now that Rosemary had agreed to help, her hope was renewed.

Sarah's worry was not in vain, for Rex was indeed making plans to leave. For him, the season had been a dismal disaster, and he would be returning to Summerwood in just a few days, with only minimal funds left with which to provide for himself and Caroline. His steward had written that the northwest corner of the estate had sold shortly after his arrival in London, but the profits were meager and would not last him long. He hoped it would at least be enough money to survive until next season, when he would come to town and try again.

Rex was in his room composing a letter to his steward when there was a knock at the door. His valet entered bearing a silver tray. "This just came for you, sir," he said.

Rex sighed. Would it be another letter from Miss Mendenhall? He hoped and yet dreaded that it was. "Thank you, Walters," he said, taking the card. His servant bowed and left the room as Rex turned the note over in his hands. His name was inscribed on the front, but it did not appear to be written in Sarah's hand. He broke the wafer and unfolded the single sheet of paper Scanning the contents quickly, he frowned. He read the letter again more slowly, his eyes hovering over a few lines of text near the end. He glanced out the window at the bright summer sunlight, then pulled out his pocketwatch to consult the time. Withdrawing a sheet of paper, he scribbled a hasty reply, folding it quickly and addressing the front without bothering to seal it. Striding across the room, he pulled the door open.

"Walters!" he called down the stairs.

His valet appeared at the bottom.

"See that this is delivered immediately, and then have my horse saddled at once—I am going out."

Sarah handed her parcel to the footman, then climbed into the carriage beside Rosemary. Her blue eyes were shining with excitement as she waved a cheery goodbye to the countess.

"Did he reply?" she asked, before they had even left the drive.

"Yes, he did." Rosemary's hands were shaking as she pulled the note from her reticule and handed it to Sarah. "He said he will meet me on the south side of the park near the lake, where the paths separate."

Sarah scanned the note quickly, her smile growing broader. "Thank you, Rosemary. You are the *dearest* friend!"

"Mr. Nelson and I shall be walking the paths of the park nearby. If you have any trouble—"

But Sarah laughed. "My dear Rosemary, how many times must I assure you that I shall be perfectly safe?" Her friend did not look convinced, and Sarah squeezed her hand. "But I thank you. It is a comfort to know that you and your dear Mr. Nelson will be close by should I need any assistance." She smiled warmly at her, and Rosemary seemed to relax a bit.

Mr. Nelson and his sister soon joined their party, and the four of them made their way to St. James Park. It was a beautiful garden at the southern end of Mayfair, with a long, narrow lake at its center and winding paths surrounding it. Though not as grand as Hyde Park to the west, it was a favorite haunt for much of London's society.

"What a beautiful day for an outing!" Mr. Nelson declared as they drove into the north entrance of the park. "I daresay you shall have a very pretty prospect for your painting, Miss Mendenhall."

Sarah was too nervous to reply. Her stomach churned with anxiety as the coachman drove the carriage to a nearby group of trees and parked it under the shade. Mr. Nelson helped the ladies down from the vehicle, took Sarah's artist's valise from the carriage, and the four of them set off for the lake.

Though many of their acquaintance had already left town, there were plenty of people in the park that day. Fleecy clouds provided intermittent relief from the summer sun, and the oblong lake in the middle of the park reflected the brilliant sapphire sky like an enormous looking glass. They wandered the paths, meandering in and out of the trees as they strolled the perimeter of the lake. Sarah's heart beat faster as they passed the west island and turned along the southern walkways.

Near the center of the park on the south side, the path divided. One path led straight ahead, following the edge of the lake, but the other veered off to the right towards the southern entrance. There, another walkway conjoined from the eastern side of the lake, which met with the main path around the lake some distance apart from where it split on the western edge. These three paths formed a large triangular section of lawn, dotted with trees and flowers and smaller side paths. A small bench sat just off the path on the lakeside near the westernmost intersection, where a few tall trees allowed a shady retreat to sit and rest.

The party approached the bench near the fork, and Sarah declared it the perfect location for her landscape. Mr. Nelson erected her easel while Sarah set out her paints. She knew she might not use them, but she had to keep up appearances. When all was in readiness, she sat down on the bench with her sketchpad and pencil, smiling up at Rosemary.

It was the signal the friends had agreed upon beforehand. Taking a shaky breath, Rosemary smiled up at Mr. Nelson and said, "There are some lovely rosebushes near the southern entrance I should like very much to see. Shall we not leave Miss Mendenhall to paint while we explore the park?"

Mr. Nelson was taken aback. "I suppose... if that is agreeable to Miss Mendenhall?"

Sarah laughed lightly. "But of course! Please do not stay on my account."

"Miss Nelson might remain with you, if you wish."

But since the gentleman's younger sister declared that *she* should like to see the rose garden just as well, Sarah declined.

"I prefer to work in solitude as it is. Go and see the garden— I shall sketch the view while I wait for your return."

As the trio departed, Sarah glanced quickly around her. There was no sign of Rex anywhere. Biting her lip, she looked up at the sky. Suppose he did not come? Sarah shook her head, refusing to give up hope. She squared her shoulders and picked up her pencil and paper, thinking that she may as well sketch her prospect from the bench while she waited.

Ten minutes passed, and out of the corner of her eye Sarah detected movement. She turned, and saw a gentleman in a navy blue coat and black top hat approaching from the east end of the lake. He wore tan breeches and polished Hessian boots, and his gait was steady and purposeful. Sarah's heart beat wildly in her chest as she watched his approach. She placed the sketchpad and pencil back in her bag, her hands trembling slightly as she fastened the clasp.

When he was scarcely twenty paces away, Sarah stood. He stopped abruptly, and until that moment Sarah had not considered that he did not recognize her. Rex hesitated only for a moment before continuing in her direction. He was near enough now that

Sarah could make out his features, and though his manner was a bit surprised, he did not seem displeased.

He stopped a few feet away from her, and Sarah found she could hardly breathe as she waited for him to speak. They regarded one another in silence for several moments, but a crooked smile at last split Rex's features.

"I confess I was intrigued when I received Miss Reed's note," he began, his voice light. "I wondered what the 'terrible dilemma' she spoke of was, and what on earth it had to do with me." He chuckled, smiling in earnest. "I might have known that any 'desperate trouble' would come from you."

Sarah laughed lightly. "In that you are right. Dear Miss Reed! I do not think she has ever fallen into a scrape in her life."

"Not, at least, of her own doing," he teased.

His eyes were warm as they rested on her features, but soon his face grew serious. "I thought you would have let matters alone when I did not reply, Miss Mendenhall. You should not have come."

"But how else would I have been able to see you?"

"Precisely my point," he said. "You should have no wish to see me. Furthermore, an unmarried woman should not be sending letters to a man who is not her near kin." He raised an eyebrow at her.

"And unless they are betrothed, an unmarried man should not agree to meet an unmarried woman alone in a park!" she replied with mock severity.

He laughed. *"Touché, mon chérie!"* There was an awkward pause before he nodded at the empty easel standing beside her. "Were you intending to paint?"

Sarah shook her head. "Not particularly. I had hoped to meet with you before I needed my paints, and here you are."

She smiled, and her whole face seemed to light up. The sight filled him with both delight and dread. How he had missed her! His eyes caressed the curve of her chin, the upturn of her nose, the darling little dimple that appeared in one cheek when she smiled. The smattering of freckles on her nose caused him to smile in return, but when his gaze rested on the puckered pink line over her left eye, he sighed heavily, turning away.

"Why did you come, Miss Mendenhall?" he asked, his voice pained. The smile on Sarah's face faded.

"I wanted to see you."

His head whipped around, his words sharp. "Why? What have you to do with me? You should not be here, Miss Mendenhall. I am nothing but trouble."

"I do not believe you are."

She said the words with perfect mildness, her lips softly parted in a gentle smile. He stared at her.

"You do not believe I am dangerous?"

"Not in the sense you mean."

In two steps he was at her side, wrapping his arm around her waist and crushing her to his chest. She gasped, and he reached his other hand up, twisting his fingers into her hair. Tipping her head back, he looked into her eyes. A wicked smile slid across his face, and he bent his head down. She turned her face away.

"Do you still think that now?" he murmured, his breath tickling her ear. She trembled, but did not push him away.

"Mr. Rex, please—you are a gentleman!"

Rex laughed humorlessly. "That is not what I hear." His

nose traced a line along the edge of her jaw, from her chin to her ear. He felt her tense, and he released her immediately, stepping back.

"There!" she cried triumphantly. "You see? Any rake would have taken advantage of my weakness! And yet, *you* released me the moment you felt my fear. You, sir, are no scoundrel."

"Am I not?" he said sullenly, turning away from her again. "You must have forgotten, my dear Miss Mendenhall, what society has been saying of me. What I told you myself."

"No," Sarah replied, lifting her chin defiantly. "I have not. But I am not basing my opinion of you on what society says, or even on what *you* say of yourself."

"Then what is it based upon?"

"Your actions, sir."

"My actions!" Rex laughed darkly, whipping around to face her. "My actions have condemned me! According to my *actions*, I am a confirmed rake. A scoundrel. A cad, a reprobate, a blackguard, a—"

"Enough!" Sarah cried, a troubled look in her eyes. Her voice softened. "I do not allow people to insult my friends, Mr. Rex."

He stared at her, and the look in her eyes deepened. It was sad, almost pained. On anyone else, the expression on her face would have infuriated Rex. He wanted nobody's pity. But on Sarah's cherubic features, her sympathy was almost angelic. He dropped his head, turning away from her again.

"You are none of those things," she continued, her voice soft but resolute. "You are a gentleman. A *gentleman*, Mr. Rex, in every sense of the word."

"You are wrong," he murmured, unable to face her.

"Am I?" Her voice held a challenging note, but he did not respond.

"There is no use continuing the charade any longer, Mr. Rex," she said. "I know you to be a gentleman, because your actions have never shown you to be otherwise.

"When we first met, and in almost every instance since, your eyes have never strayed from my face. You do not look at me—or at any other lady, in my observation—as one would look at a horse: with a calculating gaze to determine whether you wish to ride it or not." She shuddered, thinking of Peter Mills's lazy, wandering eyes. She continued. "You caught me when I fell on Bond Street, but released me to my friend as soon as I was sure of my footing. You called a carriage for myself and Miss Reed when we were caught in the rain. Your sense of decency and propriety is faultless, for even after I put *myself* in a compromising situation by consorting with you to get me to the masquerade, *you* ensured that my honor stayed intact by arranging for a chaperon to escort me to the ball instead of yourself."

Rex was staring at her in disbelief, but her voice carried on. "And during the masquerade itself, when that vile person tried to carry me away, you stepped in to save me. Even during our driving lessons, when it would have been quite easy to get me alone in order to whisk me away from the safety and protection of my friends (as a villainous rake surely would have done), *you* always made sure that the footman accompanied us. In truth, Mr. Rex, as I reflect on our association, I can think of no time whatsoever when you behaved in a less than gentlemanly fashion." He cocked an eyebrow at her, and she laughed. "With the exception of moments ago, but even then you proved yourself to only be playing the *part* of a scoundrel. But I have seen through your disguise, sir, and I will declare it again: you are *not* a scoundrel. Why have you allowed society to think as much?"

She looked up at him expectantly. The slight curve of her mouth and the tiny dimple threatening to peek out of her cheek nearly undid his senses; he wanted to pull her into his embrace and kiss her with all the fervor of his being. Instead, he closed his eyes, shaking his head in wonder at the woman standing before him. She waited patiently, and at last he spoke.

"Mary would have liked you," he said gruffly, the pain in his voice clearly evident.

"Who is Mary?" she asked gently. "Is she..."

"She is Caroline's mother," he answered flatly.

Sarah took a shaky breath. "Caroline is your little girl."

He nodded.

"And was Mary your... your..."

"My mistress?" Rex finished for her, the bitterness like bile in his throat.

Sarah only looked at him.

Rex blew out his breath, taking a step away from Sarah. He turned and gazed out across the lake, allowing the war within him to rage unchecked. For five years he had kept his word. Five lonely, painful years. But must the pain continue? Was there not some other way? Surely Mary had never meant to cause him such grief, not when she had loved him as much as he had loved her. Would she grudge him the chance for relief, the opportunity to rest from the pain and the suffering he had felt since her passing, however unworthy he may be? *No,* he thought. *Mary loved me.*

She would not wish me to suffer; not when I have the chance to be free from the pain.

Sarah watched him closely, seeing him struggle within himself. But at last he turned back to face her, a look of peace on his handsome face. The worried, angry lines on his forehead had been erased, and a sad smile replaced his bitter one. His eyes grew soft, and Sarah drew in her breath. For the first time ever, his mask was lowered, and she saw the vulnerable, broken man who had been hiding behind his careful façade.

"No, Miss Mendenhall," he said quietly, searching her face. "Mary was not my mistress. And Caroline is not my child."

"She... she is not your child?" Sarah whispered, her face pale.

"No. She is my cousin," Rex said, smiling sadly at her. "As was her mother, Mary."

Chapter 29

Sarah sat quietly on the bench as Rex paced in front of her, the untold story pouring from his bitter lips like shards of broken glass.

"My father's brother—my Uncle Wallace—had only one child, and like my mother, his wife died in childbirth. He took her death very hard. He could barely stand the sight of the baby, for she reminded him a great deal of his late wife, and he would not be troubled by her. So Mary was left not only motherless, but practically fatherless as well. She spent nearly all her childhood with me at Summerwood, under the care of her nurse, and she and I grew up as siblings. She was more like a sister than a cousin to me, and we loved each other dearly.

"But without a mother's gentling influence, Mary grew up rather headstrong. She had an adventurous spirit, and a propensity for getting into scrapes." He smiled wryly at Sarah, and was rewarded with a timid smile in return. "I was her hero, for I never failed to find her a way out of them."

Rex grew pensive, and his steps slowed. "But sometimes she would not listen to me. While I was at Oxford, Mary moved to London, and took as her companion and guardian her childhood nurse: a silly, deaf old woman whom Mary had only chosen as a chaperon because she knew that her old nurse would let her have her own way. My uncle was indifferent at her going, and offered little argument. She was one and twenty at the time.

"Free to do as she pleased, Mary lived a life of pleasure. Balls and parties every night, and soon she began to be courted by a Frenchman named Jean Marceau. I did not know him, but she wrote to me of a wonderful, charismatic man who thought she made the sun to rise. Naturally, I was anxious to meet him. I asked my uncle about him, but he felt little concern regarding the matter. To his mind, Mary was of age, and she was free to accept the attentions of and marry whomever she wished. It frustrated and saddened me that he seemed to care so little about his only child.

"So when I returned from Oxford, I made a trip to London to see Mary, and there I met Marceau for the first time." Rex scowled, and took up his pacing once more. "I could see almost immediately what sort of man he was. He wanted my uncle's fortune—Mary's inheritance—and he was feeding her all sorts of falsehoods in order to woo it away from her. She was so starved for love and affection that she believed him. When I told her what I thought, she was furious with me. It was the first real argument we had ever had."

The anger that had flashed across Rex's face was replaced with a look of pain very familiar to Sarah. It was the look on her

287

brother Charles' sface whenever he spoke of their deceased parents.

"Shortly thereafter, my father died," Rex said. "It was not wholly unexpected, as his health had been poor for many years, but all at once I found myself the heir of Summerwood, and responsible for all that my father had. I left London for Surrey almost immediately. Mary and I had not resolved our differences yet; she firmly believed that Marceau loved her and wanted to marry her, and I was adamant that she was being used. Before I left I urged her to send him away, but she refused.

"I returned to Summerwood to meet with my father's steward and discuss the future of the estate. Though I mourned the loss of my father, I felt so uneasy about the situation with Mary that as soon as my business was concluded, I returned with all haste to London, eager to reconcile myself with her. But I was too late."

Sarah could see the fury rising within him again. Rex fought it off; his chest heaving, his fists clenched, his voice strained.

"The day before I returned, she fled with Marceau. She left a note saying that they had run off to be married, and she would send me word soon. I was horrified. Though my uncle cared little for his daughter, he cared a very great deal about appearances and decorum. I knew he would be furious when he heard what she had done, so I decided not to bring it to his attention. At least, not until I had verified proof of their marriage. Mary was of age, and had obviously gone with Marceau of her own free will; there was nothing for me to do but wait.

"I stayed in London for a week, but when I received no further word, I went home to Summerwood. Since he had made no mention of the matter to me, I felt certain that my uncle did not know of her elopement. I was contemplating how to break the news to him, when I received a hastily written letter from Mary, telling me that she was coming to see me. I had no idea what she meant. Was she in trouble? Had she married Marceau? Would they be coming together? I prepared myself as best I could for her arrival, but I did not feel easy about it.

"She came alone. Bitter, broken, and wounded, both in body and spirit. I did my best to console her, but she would not be comforted. 'You were right,' she said to me. 'You were right all along.' "

In anguish, Rex rubbed his hand roughly across his eyes, turning his back to Sarah. His shoulders shook as he struggled to compose himself, and Sarah's heart broke as she watched him relive the pain of those moments years ago. More than anything, she wanted to reach out and comfort him, but something held her back. Instead, she sat quietly on the bench, her hands folded in her lap, and waited. At last Rex continued.

"It was as I suspected," he choked out, his voice rough with emotion. "Marceau only wanted her fortune, and he whisked her away with the promise that they would soon be wed, 'once his affairs were settled.' But the days dragged on. He kept asking her for money, and she kept asking for a wedding. I know how stubborn Mary could be, but apparently he did not. In the end, Marceau left her. But she had already given herself to him, and when she arrived at my home, she was with child."

Sarah drew in a shaky breath, her face reflecting the shock and horror he himself had felt on the occasion. He sank, dejected, onto the seat beside her, dropping his head into his hands with a strangled sob.

Sarah knew not what to do. He sat beside her; a bitter, broken man with a heart so full of guilt she wondered at his ability to feel any love at all. The slump of his shoulders, the shaking of his torso, the curl of his back... she could restrain herself no longer. Tentatively she reached out a hand and laid it lightly on his shoulder. He did not move. She stroked her hand gently across the tautness of his coat, itching to reach up and run her fingers through his thick, black hair. After several moments he stilled beneath her touch, and she quietly withdrew her hand. He lifted his head but did not look at her. Instead, he gazed out over the shimmering water of the lake. When he at last spoke, his voice was calm.

"Marceau had fled to France, so I could not call him out on a matter of honor. I had failed Mary in the worst possible way, and you know not how it has tortured me." He swallowed, determined to finish his tale. "So I hid her there, at Summerwood. We told people that she was gravely ill with consumption, and refused to let anyone see her. My Uncle Wallace was difficult to manage, at first. It seemed that her impending death made him suddenly regret the casual relationship he had always kept with his daughter, and he demanded to see her." Rex shook his head slowly, his face clouded. "For a time, I worried that he would burst in on us, unannounced, and discover the truth. But upon receiving a few letters written in Mary's own hand, he reconciled himself to the situation, and was content to wait until she was well enough to receive him.

"Mary agreed to send the child away after she was delivered, and made me promise never to tell the truth to a living soul, not even my uncle. She was ashamed of her actions, and wished to forget them, and I confess that I wished the same. The guilt I felt for not having done more to protect her was acute. I should never have left her alone in London under the influence of that... that..." He blew out his breath, overcome once more.

"Mr. Rex, surely you do not blame yourself for what happened to your cousin?"

Rex shook his head angrily, standing once more to resume his pacing. "I *was* to blame. Mary had no one else but me. She had no mother, and only an indifferent, unattached father. I was the sole person she loved and trusted in this life, the only one whose opinion she regarded and in whom she confided. I could have prevented her. I should not have left her until I was certain she was safe from that vile man." He looked up, glowering at the trees as he waited for the bitterness to ebb. "But I did not. And because I had failed my cousin so completely in that regard, I agreed to her wishes. I promised never to tell a soul.

"The rest of her confinement passed quickly. But near the end, she became genuinely ill. An infectious fever took hold during her travail. The midwife sent for Dr. Jones, who could see at once that she was in danger. It continued for days, and the sound of her cries..." He shuddered, closing his eyes. "I was sent away to fetch more laudanum, but when I returned," his voice broke, "she was gone."

A silent tear slid down Sarah's cheek for the poor young mother, her mind reeling under the weight of all she had learned. Rex, for once, was still; his arms folded tightly across his chest, gazing stoically out over the water. At last he turned to face her, heaving a sigh.

"So now you know the whole of it," he said softly. "Not only was it Mary's wish that I not share her story, but I myself did not want her reputation sullied the way her body had been. I had not been able to prevent her from being ravaged herself, but at least I have been able to protect her name and her memory."

"But at your own expense," Sarah said softly. "You have raised the girl as your own, taking upon *yourself* the disgrace of an illegitimate child."

His lips pressed into a thin line at her choice of words, but he nodded. Sarah was thoughtful, and soon the familiar dent between her eyebrows appeared, and she looked up at him, frowning.

"Why did you not send the child away, as Mary wished?"

Smiling sadly, Rex shook his head. "I could not send Caroline away. When I arrived home to Summerwood that fateful night, the nurse put the baby into my arms and told me that Mary had named it before she died. I knew that if Mary had given her a name, she would have wanted me to keep the child. I could not deny her that final wish."

They were silent for a time, each lost in their thoughts regarding the poor young mother and her innocent babe. Presently Rex sighed, recalling Sarah's attention.

"So now that you are acquainted with the truth, Miss Mendenhall, you must see the difficulty of my situation. My uncle does not know the entire story. He thought—and I have let him believe—that Mary died of consumption. It was only last year that he learned of Caroline's existence, but since she was calling *me* Papa, the truth never even occurred to him." He smiled darkly at her, and his eyes flickered angrily. "Since he knows I have never been married, it was only natural to assume the worst. His strict propriety and demand for decorum could not be excused, and he has cut me off completely.

"I came to town, desperate to find a lady rich enough to marry me, to save me from my present circumstances. Without my uncle's financial assistance we shall perish," he said, his eyes like steel. "But as you may guess, there are not many heiresses willing to marry a scoundrel such as I."

"But you are *not* a scoundrel!" Sarah said emphatically, no longer able to remain silent. "The injustice of it all is abhorrent! Why, without being privy to such knowledge as I have been, any lady who accepts your hand must herself be—" She stopped abruptly, her color rising.

"Precisely," Rex nodded, a hard glint in his eyes.

Agitated, Sarah stood and paced away from him. She wrung her hands, clearly distraught. Rex watched her warily. Suddenly she stopped, whirling about to face him. "But you broke off your engagement with Lady Isabella," she stated, her piercing blue eyes fixed on his face.

Rex blew out his breath in frustration. "Yes, and a dashed foolish thing it was to do. At least in marrying her, I would have had a fortune at my disposal. Now what am I to do, with the season nearly over? How can I return to Summerwood without *any* prospects, and face my little girl? Who else would marry me with such a reputation?" He shook his head angrily, his dark eyes flashing.

Sarah drew herself up to her full five-foot, three-inch stature.

"I would," she said.

Chapter 30

Rex stared at her, before suddenly throwing his head back and laughing. His entire demeanor changed. One moment, his scowl could have curdled cream, and the next his eyes were twinkling merrily, the smile on his face broad and real. "Oh, Miss Mendenhall," he chuckled. "I should have known that I could count on you to coax me out of a fit of the sullens."

"But I am in earnest," Sarah declared. "I was serious when I said that I will marry you. I do not have a fortune, I must confess —only three thousand pounds. But it will help a little, will it not?"

Rex was speechless. Sarah stood before him, the summer breeze blowing tendrils of her chestnut hair around her face. When he did not speak, she laughed, her cheeks slightly pink.

"Come now, Mr. Rex, why are you so surprised? You are a gentleman, and you deserve a lady for a wife. *Caroline* deserves to have a lady for a mother," she said with feeling.

Rex shook his head, still dazed from the shock of her declaration. He chuckled briefly, but the laughter died on his lips the next moment. "No, Miss Mendenhall. You cannot be party to my shame. I have told you the truth, but it must not be repeated." He looked at her intently, the seriousness in his eyes rendering them a dark, stormy gray. "I will not allow Mary's name to be dragged through the mud. Any woman who unites her name with mine will be brought under condemnation. In marrying me, she, too, will partake of my ruin and disgrace."

Sarah's face softened, and she took a few steps towards him. Reaching out, she placed a hand gently on his arm. "Rex, dear, I know how you feel. Your desire to protect your cousin's memory is admirable, as is your wish to guard my honor. But have you no thought for your own heart? Do you not wish to love and be loved yourself?"

A jolt coursed through him at her words. "Are you saying," he asked slowly, his voice low with disbelief, "that you love me?"

The color on Sarah's cheeks deepened, but her smile grew to fill her entire face. The dimple that Rex found so maddening to his senses appeared in her cheek, and her eyes filled with light, beckoning him into her heart.

"You dear girl!" he murmured, reaching his hands up and cupping her face. She leaned into his touch and sighed, her eyes closed.

Slowly, Rex bent his lips to meet hers. His kiss was gentle, his mouth moving softly against her own. She trembled beneath him, and he smiled crookedly, pulling away.

"Are you certain, absolutely certain, that you wish to be my wife?" he asked, his face anxious.

"Quite certain," she said firmly.

Rex narrowed his eyes, but the corner of his mouth twitched. "And what of your vow? I seem to recall that you pledged *not* to accept a proposal this year."

Her eyes twinkled merrily. "What of it? I have kept my word."

Rex raised an eyebrow at her. Laughing, Sarah grinned at him mischievously. "Can you not see, my love? I have not *accepted* a proposal—I have offered one."

The surprise and shock on his face made Sarah laugh, and soon he was laughing with her. Shaking his head in disbelief, Rex pulled her into his arms once more. The joy that shone from his eyes nearly took her breath away, and Sarah melted into him as their lips met once more.

Mr. Nelson, his sister, and Rosemary found them sitting on the bench, talking and laughing as if they had not a care in the world. The shock Mr. Nelson felt was reflected in his face, his somber brown eyes heavy with regret.

"Forgive me, Miss Mendenhall," he said as they drew near. "We should not have left you alone." His eyes flickered to Rex, who stood cordially as they approached.

"Not at all," Sarah said brightly. "I was only alone for a short time, before I was discovered by Mr. Rex. There is no need to be alarmed, for he has been a perfect gentleman." Her eyes sparkled as she looked at Rex, and he coughed in order to hide the laugh forming in his throat.

Clearly surprised at their informal manner, Mr. Nelson said nothing. But Rosemary stepped forward, smiling timidly at Rex.

"Thank you for keeping her company," she said with feeling.

Rex smiled, his eyes warm with gratitude. "The pleasure was mine, I assure you." He turned back to Sarah. "Now that your friends have arrived to claim your attentions, I shall bid you good day, Miss Mendenhall."

He raised her hand briefly to his lips, his eyes burning with intensity as they gazed into her own. Sarah's heart beat erratically in her chest, and her lips parted in a sigh. Turning to face the others, Rex touched his hat amid the chorus of goodbyes, and strode off. Sarah watched him go with a swelling in her heart she was unaccustomed to feeling. Smiling to herself, she gathered her things and prepared to depart.

The friends returned to their carriage, and were soon on their way home. Mr. Nelson continued to offer his apologies all the way to Cavendish Square, and no amount of assurance on Sarah's part would convince him that all was well.

"But to leave you in the hands of such a cad!" he lamented once more. "I shudder to think what might have happened to you."

Sarah frowned, her patience spent.

"Mr. Nelson, I assure you, nothing untoward happened to me! I was perfectly safe. There were many people in the park today, and had I been in any real danger I am sure someone would have come to my aid."

"And we were only a short distance away, Mr. Nelson," Rosemary added. Sarah threw her a grateful smile.

"I suppose you are right," the gentleman agreed at last.

They left Sarah at the door to Lady Rockwell's home, curiosity burning in Rosemary's eyes as they departed. "I shall send you word directly," Sarah whispered before Mr. Nelson helped her down. This seemed to satisfy her friend, and Sarah waved jovially to them as they drove away. She turned and glanced at the heavy door before her, the magnitude of what she must now tell Lady Rockwell weighing heavily on her heart.

Sarah entered the house and made her way slowly to the drawing room. She had promised Lady Rockwell never to mislead her again, and though in meeting with Rex she had not actually *deceived* the countess, Sarah could not help feeling that Lady Rockwell would be gravely disappointed with her engagement. She wondered if Rex would permit her to relate the truth to Lady Rockwell, but she dismissed the idea almost as soon as she thought it. Rex had entrusted her with his secret, and she would not break faith with him.

There was nothing to be done but tell Lady Rockwell that she was engaged to Jameson Rex, and accept whatever the consequences might be. Taking a deep breath, Sarah squared her shoulders and opened the drawing room door.

She was surprised to find Lady Rockwell asleep in her chair, since it was not a habit of the countess to nap during the day. Her wrinkled chin had dropped against her chest and her hands rested casually on her lap. A light breeze blew through the open window, disturbing a tendril of her silver hair. She stirred, and Sarah tiptoed towards her.

"Lady Rockwell?"

The countess lifted her head slowly, blinking at Sarah, who stood anxiously over her. "Miss Mendenhall?" she croaked, her voice thick with sleep.

"Yes, Lady Rockwell, it is I."

"Sarah," the countess breathed, reaching for her.

Her whispered name brought tears to Sarah's eyes. The warmth in Lady Rockwell's voice was unmistakable. The countess—a model of strict propriety—had broken one of her own cardinal rules. She smiled at Sarah affectionately, and Sarah dropped to her knees, burying her face in the old woman's lap.

She wept, unashamed, for several minutes. The countess's wrinkled hand stroked Sarah's hair gently, her touch as soft as a feather.

"There, there," she crooned.

When at last Sarah lifted her tear-stained face, the countess smiled at her. "Do you feel better, *Mein Kind?*"

Sniffing in a most unladylike fashion, Sarah nodded. Lady Rockwell chuckled.

"I suppose it is too much to expect that you have remembered a handkerchief this morning?"

Laughing, Sarah produced the needed accessory and wiped her face. The countess nodded in approval.

"I am happy to see that you are, at last, beginning to take on the habits of a refined lady." Her eyes sparkled, but Sarah's smile wavered.

"Yes, your ladyship. You have taught me well."

Sarah tried to swallow past the sudden lump in her throat. Breaking the truth to Lady Rockwell seemed almost impossible, but she was determined to do it. She said a silent prayer and cleared her throat.

"Lady Rockwell," she began.

"Do you know," the countess broke in abruptly, turning to look out the window. "I had the queerest feeling when you left this morning. I somehow felt as though I would not see you again."

Sarah smiled at her fondly. "Did I not promise you that I would not run away?"

"Yes," came the murmured reply. "You did."

She was silent for a moment, but slowly she turned her gaze back to Sarah. "You promised that you would not run away with him. But you do intend to marry him, do you not?"

Sarah did not ask how Lady Rockwell knew. She merely nodded, tears forming in her eyes once more.

Lady Rockwell sighed. It was a heavy, grieving sigh, as if some unseen weight was pressing against her chest, forcing the air from her lungs. She closed her eyes, breathing deeply.

"I... I know you must be very disappointed," Sarah began at length, when it appeared that the countess would say nothing else. "But I assure you, I would not consent to marry him if I did not feel him to be the very best of men, regardless of my own feelings."

Slowly, Lady Rockwell opened her eyes. The clouded gray orbs were glassy with unshed tears, but they did not appear to Sarah to be angry. Merely curious, and a trifle sad.

"*Was meinst du?* How can that be possible?" she asked, her voice strained. "When his reputation, and his circumstances, have proven otherwise?"

This time it was Sarah's turn to be silent. She twisted the handkerchief in her hands, contemplating how best to explain the situation to Lady Rockwell without betraying Rex's trust.

"I cannot disclose the whole of his circumstances to you," she began slowly. "But I can assure you, that the man whom society believes Jameson Rex to be is *not* the man I have chosen to marry." She took a breath and continued. "That is all I am at liberty to say on the matter, Lady Rockwell. I am sorry that I cannot explain more to you, but you may be assured that I am fully aware of the circumstances, and have no qualms whatsoever in uniting myself with that gentleman."

The countess grunted, turning away. "Gentleman, indeed," she muttered under her breath.

"Yes," Sarah declared resolutely, her eyes flashing. "A *gentleman.*"

Lady Rockwell studied her face. Sarah's look was earnest, her eyes open and imploring, begging the countess to believe her words and trust her decision. They gazed at one another in weighty silence, the minutes stretching endlessly on as Sarah waited for the rebuttal she felt sure was coming.

"You are nothing like my granddaughter Katherine," the countess said at length. "And though I do not regret my decision to let you stay with me, you have certainly been difficult to manage, *Fräulein.*"

Sarah looked down, clasping her hands in her lap. "I am sorry that I have disappointed you, Lady Rockwell," she said quietly.

"I never said that," came the quick reply. Sarah looked up, confused. A slow, steady smile was spreading itself over Lady Rockwell's face, and with it the repressive mood in the room seemed to lift. "You are nothing like my Katherine," she said again, a twinkle in her eye. "But you certainly remind me of myself when I was younger."

"No indeed! You have mentioned this before, but I cannot believe that *you* were once as stubborn and vain as I have been."

"Oh, but I was, Miss Mendenhall. Obstinate, headstrong, impulsive, tenacious," The countess rattled off Sarah's weaknesses with a practiced air. The shock Sarah felt on hearing herself so censured brought a rise of color to her cheeks, and Lady Rockwell's face softened. "But also generous. Compassionate. Witty, charming, vivacious..." Her voice trailed off, and she smiled warmly at Sarah. "Yes, *Mein Kind.* I was once very much like you."

"But when? What happened?" Sarah blurted, before she could restrain herself. She blushed. "Oh dear, forgive me, Lady Rockwell. I did not mean—"

But the countess was chuckling. "Never mind, Sarah," she said with a smile. "It was many, many years ago. Perhaps I will tell you about it someday... but not now." She sighed. "Come, help me to my room."

"Are you unwell?" Sarah asked, immediately stepping beside the countess and helping her rise from her seat. "You do not usually need assistance."

"No, but today I feel as if I do." She leaned on Sarah's arm, and the two of them walked out of the room together. They slowly made their way to the countess's rooms on the third floor, where Sarah helped Lucy, the countess's abigail, to get Lady Rockwell into her dressing gown and settled into bed.

"You must write to your brother, Charles, and ask for his permission," she said to Sarah when they were alone once more.

Sarah nodded. "I shall write to him tomorrow. But what have

you to say, Lady Rockwell? Do you approve of my choice?"

"Would it make any difference if I said I did not?"

Sarah's lips twitched. "Probably not."

"I thought as much," the countess answered wryly. "But since your brother will likely give his consent, I suppose I must resign myself to the match."

"Thank you, Lady Rockwell," Sarah breathed.

The countess nodded brusquely. "Someday, perhaps, you can explain it all to me. But until then, I must satisfy myself that you know what you are about, and trust your judgment."

Sarah leaned down and kissed her weathered cheek. "Katherine has always adored you," she said softly. "And I do, too."

Lady Rockwell squeezed her hand in reply, and Sarah turned to quit the room. "Would you please tell Mrs. Perkins to have my supper sent up to my room?" the countess asked.

Sarah nodded. "May I join you here for your meal, Lady Rockwell?"

"I should like that very much, my dear."

Sarah smiled affectionately at the countess and shut the door softly behind her.

Chapter 31

Lady Rockwell passed into the next life as quietly as one steps into an adjoining room. She simply did not awake the next morning as usual. Dr. Matthews assured Sarah that her passing was likely painless; merely from the effects of a long life well-lived.

Sarah mourned her death deeply, for once understanding the pain of loss when a loved one passes on. She was barely three years old when her own parents died, and she had no memory of feeling grief on the occasion. The emptiness that remained in her heart from their passing was merely that—emptiness. But Lady Rockwell had filled that portion effortlessly, and now that the hole had been torn open once more, the pain was acute.

Rosemary came to Cavendish Square the moment she heard the news, and Sarah fell into her arms, weeping bitterly. "Lady Rockwell was the closest thing to a mother I have ever known," Sarah cried. "And now she is gone."

"I know, dearest, I know," Rosemary soothed. "But you need not be alone. Indeed, you *should* not be alone in your grief. Come back to Camden Place with me, Sarah. At least until you decide what to do."

"I shall write to my Aunt Ellen," Sarah sniffed. "She resides in Bath when she is in the country, and if she is at home I will go to her."

But Sarah accepted the invitation to stay with Rosemary's family until other arrangements could be made. Rosemary helped Sarah to pack her things, and within two days Sarah was settled in one of the guest rooms of the Reeds' home.

The next few days passed in a blur. Arrangements were made for Lady Rockwell's funeral service, and her barrister was notified. Sarah wrote a letter to Katherine to inform her of her grandmother's passing, but it contained so many ink blots from Sarah's tears, that Rosemary was obliged to rewrite it for her. She also wrote to her aunt in Bath, but was informed that she had not yet returned from India. The housekeeper who had answered Sarah's letter assured her that her aunt was expected in port any day, and promised to send word as soon as she arrived home.

About a fortnight after Lady Rockwell died, Sarah received a letter from Mr. Yates, the late countess's barrister. After reading his note, Sarah drove to his office on Park Street to meet with him in person.

"Miss Mendenhall, thank you for coming to see me. I know this must be a difficult time for you," the gentleman greeted her as they sat down in his office.

"Thank you, Mr. Yates. I confess that I was very surprised to receive your note."

"Were you indeed?" he said politely. "Did you not realize that the countess held you in such high regard?"

"Not high enough to include me in her will," Sarah answered honestly.

Mr. Yates smiled. "I can assure you she did. Lady Rockwell has come to see me several times since her arrival in London, and she always spoke very highly of you."

Sarah nodded, the ache in her chest preventing her from replying. Mr. Yates cleared his throat.

"I understand that you are somewhat related to the late countess?"

"Only distantly. My elder brother, Charles, was lately married to Lady Rockwell's granddaughter, Katherine Greenwood."

"Ah, yes, Miss Greenwood. I have dispatched a notice to her as well." He coughed politely. "Lady Rockwell's estate in Leicestershire was tied up in an entailment, and has been left to a distant cousin—a Mr. Pembrooke, I believe—and the bulk of her private fortune has fallen to Miss Greenwood. Er, Mrs. Mendenhall, I should say," he stammered, consulting the papers before him. "But you have not been forgotten. I suppose you would like to know exactly what has been bequeathed to you in her ladyship's will?"

Sarah nodded.

Turning through the sheaf of papers before him, Mr. Yates's eyes landed on the passage he was searching for. " 'To Miss Sarah Mendenhall,' " he quoted, " 'I bequeath the sum of ten thousand pounds, payable to her in full on the occasion of her marriage, or on her twenty-fifth birthday, whichever blessed circumstance occurs first.' "

Sarah's mouth dropped open. "Ten thousand pounds?" she repeated incredulously.

Mr. Yates smiled at her over his spectacles. "As I said, she always spoke very highly of you."

"But... but that is such an enormous sum!" Sarah exclaimed. "How can I accept such a generous gift?"

"By signing here," Mr. Yates said gently, placing a document before her. Sarah took the pen he handed her mechanically, signing where he indicated as if in a daze. Turning the paper around, Mr. Yates signed as a witness, then looked up into Sarah's face.

"My clerk will send you a copy of the document, and if you will bring it back with your marriage license, I shall see that you are given a draft for the bank where Lady Rockwell's funds are held. If you are as yet unmarried when you reach the age of twenty-five..." He smiled at her, as if the thought of that happening was extremely amusing, "bring that document back and we shall proceed in other ways."

Sarah nodded in mute reply, and stood to take her leave. "Thank you," she stammered, still reeling from the news of her sudden inheritance.

"Good day, Miss Mendenhall," Mr. Yates smiled at her.

The bell above the entrance tinkled softly as Sarah left the building.

"Ten thousand pounds?" Rosemary gawked.

"Yes. I still cannot believe it myself."

Sarah sat limply on a chair in the morning room of the Reed's home. Rosemary sat across from her, the linen she was embroidering left forgotten in her lap.

"I had no idea she held you in such high regard," Rosemary murmured.

Sarah smiled softly. "Nor did I."

"What shall you do with such a sum?" her friend queried, picking up her needlework once more.

"It shall not be mine until I marry," Sarah mused, glancing out the window.

"Oh, well... in a year or two then, when you have found a gentleman whom—"

"I have written to my brother," Sarah broke in, her gaze still on the summer day outside. "I shall be married as soon as he gives his consent."

"Married! To whom!" Rosemary started. "You are certainly not considering Fred Grimshaw, I hope."

"Certainly not," Sarah refuted with a little laugh.

"Then whom?"

Sarah turned to face her friend, her eyes dancing with a hundred different emotions. Joy, grief, delight, pain, mischief, chagrin—Rosemary wondered at her expression until realization began to dawn.

"Not Jameson Rex!" she cried.

Sarah sighed. "Dearest Rosemary, I wish I could explain everything to you. If only *you* were party to the knowledge which I have been privileged to gain."

"But he is a scoundrel, Sarah!"

"He is *not*," Sarah replied, calmly but firmly. "I assure you, Rosemary, that he is nothing of the sort. Do you think I would marry him if he were?"

She frowned at her friend, and Rosemary shook her head slowly, confused.

"No, I do not believe you would. Still..." Her voice trailed off, and she looked apologetically at Sarah, who laughed lightly.

"Come now, Rosemary, this will never do! Truly, he is a gentleman. He is noble, kind, compassionate... one of the best men I have ever known. You must trust my judgment on this matter, dearest. Lady Rockwell did, and I hope you will as well."

"Lady Rockwell knew of your betrothal?" Rosemary asked, surprised once more.

"Yes. And she gave me her blessing," Sarah said softly.

"Then you shall have my blessing as well," Rosemary declared. "If the late countess accepted the match, then it surely cannot be wrong. A more proper, genteel, respectable woman I have never met—excepting Mama, of course," Rosemary added as an afterthought.

Sarah laughed. "I am happy to have your approval, Rosemary." Her eyes sparkled happily at her friend. "Now, what say you to a double wedding?"

The news of Sarah's engagement to Jameson Rex spread like wildfire through the *ton*. At first, Mrs. Reed was appalled to hear of their betrothal, but upon learning that Sarah had been left a generous legacy by the late countess, and that Lady Rockwell herself had sanctioned the match, she was resigned to accept Rex's presence as a regular visitor in Camden Place.

By the end of August London was a ghost town. Most of society had retired to the country, leaving those who remained to enjoy the hot, muggy air in relative peace. Sarah did not suffer in the heat for long, however. A letter had at last arrived from Aunt Ellen, informing her that she was most welcome to come and live with her in Bath. Sarah and Rosemary were thus making the necessary preparations for her departure from town.

"It will probably be several weeks before I see you again," Sarah sighed to Rex one afternoon. They were seated on a bench in Hyde Park, beneath the shade of a magnificent oak tree.

"Surely you do not wish to leave London for *Bath?*" Rex asked in mock disgust.

"What have you against Bath?" Sarah said, laughing.

"Nothing at all, unless you consider the tepid waters, the pressing crowds, the dismal selection of refined entertainment..."

"Enough, enough!" Sarah cried, her eyes alight with laughter. "I perfectly understand your feelings, sir. But would it be so *very* terrible for you to visit, if I were there?"

"*Very*," he teased, taking her into his arms and kissing her forehead. Sarah sighed in contentment, leaning her head on his shoulder.

"I have written to my brother," she said after a moment.

"Then I shall procure a license as soon as he grants his permission," came the reply.

"But it will be *months* before then! How shall I bear it?"

"Quite easily, I am sure," he chuckled. "You shall go to your aunt in Bath, and stir up society there just as much as you have done here, except that you will have the added allurement of being engaged to a wicked scoundrel, and *that* will produce just as many admirers there as you have had here. If not more."

"How abominable you are! Surely my attentions will not be sought when it is understood that I am betrothed to another," she scoffed.

"You are mistaken, my dear. There are a great many gentlemen—noble, principled, and insufferably dull—who shall feel it their solemn duty to rescue you from my clutches, and draw you back into safe, mundane society."

She smiled. "And what shall you be doing with yourself while I am stealing the hearts of the gentlemen of Bath?" Sarah asked, her eyes dancing.

"I shall be in Surrey, preparing my estate for your arrival. With Caroline."

"Caroline," Sarah murmured. Suddenly she sat up, a look of alarm on her face. "Rex! How am *I* to care for a child? I have not the faintest notion what to do! My own mother died when I was very young, and I never had—"

"My dear," Rex cried, laughing. "Do not carry on so! Mrs. Partridge is an excellent nurse. She has taken care of Caroline all her life."

"But a child cannot have a nurse forever. Why, my own *Ayah* was only with me until I was nine. Caroline will need to have a governess, and an art tutor, and—"

"Sarah!" Rex laughed, placing a finger gently on her lips. "All of that can wait. Caroline will have everything she needs, now that she has *you*."

Sarah sighed. "I wonder if she will like me?"

"My darling, she will love you!" Rex said, his gray-blue eyes warm with affection. "Everyone loves you." He brushed a gentle kiss on her upturned lips.

"As long as you love me, I do not care about anyone else."

"Then you have nothing to fear," he said softly, kissing her again.

Epilogue

Nine months later
May 1835
Surrey, England

The wheels of the carriage crunched to a stop on the freshly graveled drive, and a footman stepped forward to open the door. Rex descended the narrow steps, turning back to reach for Sarah's hand. She alighted from the carriage and stood beside him, gazing up at the massive building before them. The gray stone blocks with which the home was constructed were worn with age, pitted and black in some places and encrusted with gold-green lichens in others. But it was still a magnificent house. Wide stone steps led up to the massive front doors, which were centered on the large, rectangular building. Two identical wings jutted out on each side, and more than a dozen glazed windows reflected the late spring sunshine.

"Welcome to Summerwood, Mrs. Rex," Rex murmured in Sarah's ear.

She smiled up at him, and took his arm as they turned to enter the house. Suddenly the doors were flung open and a slim, golden-haired little girl stood in the doorway.

"Papa!" she cried, rushing down the stairs.

Caroline was seven now, and though not as wildly affectionate as she had been at the age of five, it was clear that she loved and missed her adopted father. Rex took a step away from Sarah and opened his arms, and Caroline ran into his embrace. She buried her face in his waistcoat while Rex laughed, wrapping his arms around her.

"My darling girl, how I have missed you!" he said, bending down to kiss the top of her head. "But here now, what is this? Surely you have developed better manners than to ignore your new mama?"

Caroline turned her head and peeked shyly at Sarah. "I am pleased to meet you, ma'am," she recited, her fairy-like voice bright in the warm air.

"Try again, you little imp," Rex laughed, nudging her away from him and stepping back to stand beside his bride.

Caroline's rosy cheeks flushed, but she smiled at Sarah and dropped a pretty curtsy. "How do you do?"

"I am very well, thank you, and very happy to make your acquaintance, Caroline," Sarah replied, smiling broadly at the nymph-like girl before her. She held out a gloved hand, and Caroline took it timidly. They shook hands, and Sarah laughed.

"There!" she said to Rex. "Now that I have met the lady of the house, perhaps you will show me inside?"

Caroline flashed a brilliant smile. "I can show you! Mrs. Jenkins will want to take you over all the principal rooms, and explain to you when the renovations were made and how much the redecorating cost, but *I* can show you where the hidden door is to Papa's study, and teach you the best way to nip buns from the kitchen without getting caught."

Sarah laughed at her youthful exuberance, her own eyes sparkling. "Lead on then, my sprite! I am yours to command."

Caroline took her hand, and the two ladies skipped up the steps and through the open front doors. Rex watched them go, his beautiful young bride with mischievous blue eyes, and his impish little girl with her bouncing, golden curls.

He took a deep, cleansing breath, feeling a warmth in his heart he had not felt for many, many years. He now had a wife, and Caroline had a mother. There was money in the bank to provide for their fledgling family, and Mary's reputation was safely intact; her secret protected in the hearts of both he and Sarah. Someday, he knew, he must tell Caroline the truth. And his uncle as well. But not today. Today, he could be well and whole. Today he could be happy. Here, at Summerwood, he could cast off his disguise, knowing those whom he loved best were not ashamed of what he was.

Today, there was peace in his soul.

*Turn the page for a sneak peek at
Shaela Kay's next book*

THE Rodenburg GIRL

JOURNEYS OF THE HEART BOOK 3

Chapter 1

Strausberg, Prussia 1780

There is something delicate and soothing in the sound of the harp. When the thick, tight strings are plucked in just the right order, a beautiful symphony of sound pours forth that calms and quiets even the most nervous of minds.

Which is precisely why Greta preferred the pianoforte.

She knew how to play the harp, of course. Music was like air to Greta. She had never known a time in her life before music, and she could not imagine living a single day without it. But unlike the harp (which her mother preferred), or the dulcimer (which her sister preferred), when Greta placed her hands on the smooth white keys of the pianoforte, the music came alive. What was written on the page before her did not matter. Whatever notes she played, whatever song she practiced, she infused the melody with the feelings of her sixteen-year-old heart. The music became a living, breathing extension of Greta herself.

The third movement of Johann Sebastian Bach's *Concerto No. 1 in D minor* was a passionate piece, and it suited Greta's mood perfectly. Her fingers were a blur as they flew over the keyboard, striking the notes with forceful precision. The pins in her carefully coiffed tresses slipped with every shake of her head, until an errant lock of honey-blonde hair came loose and bounced erratically around her face. She ignored it. The music increased in tempo, coming to a crescendo as she pounded out the last few measures.

The final notes hung in the air like rich perfume, fading softly as the seconds ticked by. Taking a breath, Greta allowed herself a smile, and reached up to brush the unruly curl away from her face. It bounced back with frizzy determination.

"Our mother would like to see you, Margareta."

Greta looked up at the sound of her younger sister's voice. Katarina's face was pinched in a frown, which could only mean that their mother was in a good humor. Usually when Greta was summoned to her mother's bedchamber it meant that she was in trouble, which would have been cause for Trina to gloat.

"I shall be right there."

Katarina turned on her heel and flounced away. Smiling ruefully, Greta stood from her seat and carefully arranged her skirts, ensuring that her panniers were straight and her petticoats were smooth. She swept through the marbled hall and ascended the grand staircase, stopping in the corridor outside her mother's chambers to check her appearance in a mirror. Her eyes narrowed as she scrutinized the prodigal curl, which her mother would surely notice. Sighing, she tucked it behind her ear until she could properly pin it back.

Turning from her reflection, Greta knocked quietly on the door of her mother's room.

"Come in."

Dorothea Rodenburg was sitting at her dressing table, in an evening gown of midnight blue taffeta. She looked every bit the

Prussian princess—a title which she clung to, despite its relative worthlessnes s . The wars that had plagued the Holy Roman Empire for the last century had resulted in an overabundance of new city states, and an overzealous appointment of Prince Regents to rule over them. So while Heinrich Rodenburg's wife *was* a Prussian princess, she was only a third daughter, and a penniless one at that. It was to her very great advantage that she was a remarkable beauty, or else she might never have married at all. As it was, Heinrich Rodenburg—wealthy, if not handsome— had taken a fancy to her, and she consented to marry him after knowing him only a few short weeks. Having attained what she had been raised to do, her purpose in life shifted. She was a pretty wife with pretty manners who played her role well, intent on teaching her daughters the same principles, and, for the most part, she was happy with her success.

Except that Greta refused to be taught.

Frau Rodenburg's maid was combing and looping her mistress's hair into an elaborate *tête de mouton*, with short curls on the sides of her head and the nape of her neck, and the rest smoothed into an elegant bouffant on top. Greta was always amazed at the amount of work it took to tame her mother's hair, which was as curly as her own. But curls were only fashionable in certain instances, and Frau Rodenburg was determined to beat her unruly mane into submission.

Frau Rodenburg looked at her daughter's reflection in the glass. "Margareta, we have a guest joining us for supper today, and I want you to take exceptional care with your appearance. Your maid has been instructed as to your attire, and Trueden will be doing your hair."

Her gaze slid back to view her own reflection once more, leaving Greta standing shocked and speechless by the bedroom door. When her eldest daughter made no move to withdraw, Frau Rodenburg turned and spoke sharply.

"Really, Margareta, do not stand there like a goat with your mouth open. Did you not hear what I said?"

"Yes, Mama," Greta stammered. "But who is coming to dine? You look as if you are dressed for court."

"Don't be impertinent."

"Forgive me, Mama."

Her mother resumed gazing at herself in the glass. "An English ambassador, the Viscount Ellsworth, has been invited to stay with us, by your father."

"An Englishman?"

"Yes. He is a man of influence with considerable property, and I wish you to be on your best behavior." She looked at Greta's reflection, which was a miniature of her own, and raised her eyebrows. Greta nodded slowly, and her mother appeared satisfied.

"That is all. You may go now. I will send Trueden to your room shortly."

Greta's head was reeling as she returned to the staircase and descended to the second floor. What was an Englishman doing in Strausberg? And what business did her father have with him? Greta chewed on her bottom lip as she entered her chambers, throwing herself backwards onto the bed.

"Lisbet," she called to her maid, who was busy in the adjoining dressing room. "Do you know anything about the visiting ambassador? Have you heard anything below stairs?"

"Only that your mother wishes to make a good impression, Fräulein."

Greta rolled over and propped herself up on her elbows as Lisbet walked in, carrying a larger set of panniers. She placed them on the floor next to Greta's bed.

"I wonder what he is doing here," Greta murmured, eyeing the contraption beside her with loathing. "Mama said he has influence and is very rich—which explains why she wishes to make a good impression," she added, rolling her eyes. "I wonder how much he is worth?"

The matronly servant smiled affectionately at her mistress. "Perhaps you should ask him at dinner," she teased.

"Mama would be furious," Greta mused. Suddenly a wicked smile flashed across her face. "But what a marvelous idea, Lisbet! I believe I shall."

"Fräulein, you mustn't!" Lisbet cried in alarm. Greta laughed at her maid and rolled onto her back once more. Lisbet clucked her tongue.

"Your mother had a new gown sent up for you, special for the occasion. But I have half a mind to keep it from you now, after your teasing."

Greta shot up from the bed. "A new gown? *Zeig es mir!*"

Lisbet chuckled, retrieving a flowing garment of lavender silk from the dressing room. Greta cried out in delight, hugging her maid and crushing the new gown between them.

"Fräulein, the dress!" Lisbet cried.

"Oh, Lisbet, is it not beautiful?" Greta took the garment from her maid and held it to her figure, twirling in a circle. "Wait till Hans sees me in this," she breathed, admiring herself in the glass.

"No one will see you in it until you put it on," Lisbet said, all business once more. "Come now, let us get you dressed. Trueden will be here any minute to do your hair, and your mother will want to see you in the gown before you go down. It will not do to keep her waiting."

Frederick Greenwood, the Viscount Ellsworth, stole yet another glance at the young lady seated beside him. There had only been time enough for a brief introduction in the drawing room before supper, but even those few minutes had piqued his interest in Herr Rodenburg's eldest daughter. He knew that his host had three children, but he was not expecting any of them to be as charming—nor as beautiful—as Greta.

Greta reached for her glass and glanced up at him. Frederick smiled and quickly looked away, only to find his eyes drawn to her a moment later. She was still looking at him.

"I hope you had a pleasant journey, Your Excellency?"

Lord Ellsworth was pulled from his thoughts by Frau Rodenburg's voice.

"I did, thank you," he replied.

"Do you come to Prussia often?"

"Not often, though I have been before."

"And have you been to Brandenburg?"

"No, Your Highness." His eyes flickered in Greta's direction as she coughed, hiding a laugh. His brow furrowed—what had he said?—but he looked back at Frau Rodenburg. "This is my first time in this part of the country."

"And what is your opinion of it thus far?" Herr Rodenburg asked, taking a sip from his glass.

Frederick turned to the man on his other side. "Brandenburg is beautiful. It reminds me very much of home, though perhaps a bit drier."

"Ah, yes," Herr Rodenburg chuckled. "You English are forever drowning in rain and mist over there."

Frederick inclined his head.

"Does it rain *all* the time?" Greta asked. It was the first time she had addressed him directly since the meal began.

"No," he said, pleased with her attention. "But it rains a fair amount of the time. It is very green."

Her head tilted ever so slightly to the right—just enough to dislodge a lock of golden hair, which curled across her brow with maddening charm. He watched, waiting for her to reach a hand up and brush it back into place, but she did not. His lips quirked up in a smile.

"I understand you hail from Kent, Your Excellency," Frau Rodenburg said, breaking into his thoughts once more.

"The earldom is located in Kent, but I hold an estate of my own in Leicestershire."

Greta paused with her soup spoon halfway to her mouth. "The earldom? I thought you were a viscount."

Frau Rodenburg cleared her throat, shooting her daughter a look.

Frederick inclined his head. "Indeed, Fräulein. But my father is the Earl of Rockwell."

"Oh." The renegade curl fell into her eyes, and she brushed at it carelessly.

A bell rang, indicating the end of the first course, and Frederick dragged his eyes away from her face. *Pull yourself together, man. She is naught but a child! And you are here on the king's errand.* He turned himself deliberately to face his host as the dishes were removed, the table linens replaced, and new dishes brought forward. Frederick made light conversation with Herr Rodenburg while they waited, but when he turned back to his plate, he noticed Greta watching him. Her expression was open, curious even, and her full lips were parted slightly, as if on the verge of a smile.

"Fräulein," Frederick said, raising his brow expectantly.

"Lord Ellsworth," she said, "I have a question for you which you may find impertinent. But I cannot help but ask it."

His surprise nearly caused him to laugh, but he checked himself when he caught Frau Rodenburg's poisonous look. It was aimed not at him, but at her daughter, who could not see her mother's face.

"I doubt there is anything you could say that I would find to be improper, Fräulein."

Her eyes brightened. "Shall I take that as permission to speak freely, my lord?" He nodded, and her look grew more earnest. "Have you always lived in England?"

Her question surprised him. "Yes, all my life."

"*You have never lived on the continent?*" she asked, slipping into French.

He grinned. "No. Though I have spent considerable time in various countries, my home has always been in England."

"And your parents—they are both English?"

"Decidedly so."

She narrowed her eyes, but said no more as she turned back to her meal. Frederick's own curiosity was piqued, and after a moment of silence he asked, *"Puis-je demander pourquoi vous voudriez savoir?"*

Greta looked up at him. "I ask because you barely have a discernible accent. Your German is near perfect."

His startled eyes crinkled when he smiled at her. "Thank you, Fräulein. That is a great compliment, coming from one such as yourself."

She laughed—a warm, rich sound, like melted chocolate. "From me? Oh, but I am no one, *Your Excellency*," she said, her eyes dancing.

Before Frederick could ascertain whether she was teasing him or laughing at him, her mother spoke.

"No one!" Frau Rodenburg exclaimed. "Margareta, do not discredit your heritage, nor your own accomplishments. You are a Rodenburg, and your mother is a Keyser. You are most certainly someone."

"Yes, Mama." Greta pinched her lips together, reaching up to tuck the curl behind her ear.

"Not only do you come from such impressive lineage, but your own accomplishments add to your merit. Lord Ellsworth, were you able to hear her from the study this afternoon? She is quite a remarkable musician."

The viscount nodded to the woman smiling tightly at the end of the table. "Yes, I was fortunate enough to have had the pleasure."

"Greta surpasses even her lovely mother in her musical abilities," Herr Rodenburg added. "Now, if only she applied herself as willingly to her other studies, eh?"

Greta grinned at her father, who smiled indulgently at her.

Frau Rodenburg sniffed. "In my opinion, a young lady has no need to be filling her head with numbers and figures and foreign languages. She would be far better served learning the lessons of obedience and docility."

"Yes, because needlepoint is so very important," Greta mumbled.

"Margareta." Frau Rodenburg's voice cut through the air like a dart.

Greta snapped her mouth shut and dropped her eyes. Frederick observed the tightness of her jaw as she reached for her knife and fork. Her knuckles were white as she gripped her utensils.

Herr Rodenburg cleared his throat. "Obedience is certainly a very great virtue," he said, addressing his wife. "But I must disagree with you, my dear, on what you feel to be impractical numbers and useless learning. There is a great deal of usefulness in what Greta is being taught."

Frau Rodenburg pressed her lips into a crimson line. "Just as you please. I am sure you know best how to raise our daughter."

"Dorothea—"

"Forgive me," Frau Rodenburg simpered, rising gracefully from the table. Frederick nearly knocked over his chair in his haste to rise as well. "Your Excellency, please excuse me. I must see to my younger children at present."

She smiled sweetly at the viscount before leaving the room, sparing not a glance for either her husband or her daughter. When she had gone, Herr Rodenburg sat down with a huff.

"My apologies, Lord Ellsworth," he said, raising his glass to a footman to be refilled, "but as you can see, my wife does not always share my views on what constitutes a proper education for young ladies."

"She is not alone in her feelings, I am afraid. Many English women feel the same," Frederick said, taking his seat again.

"Is that so?"

The viscount nodded.

"Hm." Herr Rodenburg swirled his drink, watching his guest over the rim of his glass. Frederick cleared his throat and glanced at Greta, but she was looking at him with the same intense, gray eyes as her father. He flushed.

"What do *you* think about the education of women, Lord Ellsworth?" Greta asked.

Her father laughed. "*Schatz*, do you wish to frighten away our guest with a heated argument on his first day here? Should you not inquire after the weather or the state of the roads?"

Greta's eyes shone with impish delight. "My dear Papa, you cannot possibly think that His Excellency, the Viscount Ellsworth, would be remotely interested in such mundane topics as the weather and transportation." She shot him a look. "Are you?"

Frederick looked between the two expectant faces—the father's, full of gentle humor, and the daughter's, brimming with mischief—before laughing nervously. "I find that such conversations depend entirely upon the person with whom I am speaking, Fräulein."

Greta sat back, disappointed, but Herr Rodenburg chuckled. "A diplomatic answer if ever I heard one," he said, raising his glass.

Frederick inclined his head, willing himself not to glance beside him for the hundredth time that evening. But he could feel Greta's piercing gaze on his face, and at last he turned to meet her eyes.

She did not look away.

Acknowledgments

I will be forever grateful to my Heavenly Father for the blessing and privilege that is mine to be an author. "Unto God our Father be glory for ever and ever. Amen." (Phillipians 4:20)

For my amazing husband and wonderful children: thank you for your love, support, encouragement, and patience throughout this project. I love you so, so, much.

For the countless friends, family members, and fellow writers who helped, encouraged, and critiqued, "I can no other answer make, but thanks, and thanks, and ever thanks." (William Shakespeare)

About the Author

Shaela Kay was born and raised near Seattle, Washington. She studied Theatre and English at Brigham Young University-Idaho, but left her studies in order to be a wife and a mother. When she isn't writing, you can find her quilting, crafting, or homeschooling her four children. She and her husband John live with their family in a little house along the banks of the mighty Columbia River. Visit her online at www.shaelakay.com

www.ingramcontent.com/pod-product-compliance
Lightning Source LLC
Chambersburg PA
CBHW070643180626
46817CB00006B/2222